PRAISE FOR
EVERYBODY KNOWS YOUR NAME

"This book is like your favorite reality show come to life on the page. Andrea Seigel brings her patented wounded angel *noir* vibe and fuses it with Brent Bradshaw's blunt pathos. Together their voices pack a pretty punch. It's a sexy, funny, and poetic book about reconciling your dreams of the future with the drama of your past. I loved it."

—Kirsten "Kiwi" Smith, co-screenwriter of *Legally Blonde* and *10 Things I Hate About You*

"Funny, entertaining, and above all, honest, *Everybody Knows Your Name* examines the trials and tribulations of 'reality' TV, instant fame, first love, and finding out who you are . . . especially when the cameras stop rolling."

—Elizabeth Eulberg, author of *The Lonely Hearts Club*

"A fun and fast-paced novel for music fans or readers looking for a rock and roll reality romance."

—Dana Reinhardt, author of *We Are the Goldens*

"You'll fall hard for these characters. If you're looking for the humor, wit, and heart behind 'reality' TV, it's here in this book." —Melissa Walker, author of *Unbreak My Heart*

"The best voice I've read in years. This is a razor-sharp, hilarious, and surprisingly sexy tale of life in front of the L.A. lens. Read it immediately."

—Rebecca Serle, author of *Famous in Love*

everybody
knows
YOUR
NAME

everybody knows YOUR NAME

ANDREA SEIGEL & BRENT BRADSHAW

VIKING
An Imprint of Penguin Group (USA)

VIKING
Published by the Penguin Group
Penguin Group (USA) LLC
375 Hudson Street
New York, New York 10014

USA * Canada * UK * Ireland * Australia
New Zealand * India * South Africa * China

penguin.com
A Penguin Random House Company

First published in the United States of America by Viking,
an imprint of Penguin Group (USA) LLC, 2015

LIBRARY OF CONGRESS CATALOGING-IN-PUBLICATION DATA
Seigel, Andrea.
Everybody knows your name / by Andrea Seigel and Brent Bradshaw.
pages cm
Summary: "Teenagers Magnolia and Ford unexpectedly fall in love as they share a mansion in
the Hollywood Hills and compete on a reality TV singing competition"—Provided by publisher.
ISBN 978-0-670-01562-7 (hardback)
[1. Reality television programs—Fiction. 2. Singing—Fiction. 3. Love—Fiction. 4. Family
problems—Fiction. 5. Hollywood (Los Angeles, Calif.)—Fiction.] I. Bradshaw, Brent. II. Title.
PZ7.S4562Eve 2015   [Fic]—dc23   2014024548

Printed in U.S.A.

1 3 5 7 9 10 8 6 4 2

Designed by Kate Renner
Set in Gotham Rounded, ITC Espirit, and ConduitITCStd

Dedicated to

everybody knows YOUR NAME

Magnolia

1

When you're a teenager, everybody tells you you're going to change. They say, *Oh, sure, maybe you like that stupid singer and that stupid outfit right now, but someday you're going to look back and think, "What?"*

But then, when you get older, it seems like everybody says you *can't* change, like you've gotten stuck. It becomes too late. Your personality has run into a wall or something. And that's why there are so many divorces.

Anyway, I don't know at what age you can't change anymore, but I'm only seventeen, so I want to believe it's possible that I could turn into someone who's going to be good on this show.

We're supposed to be staying in a mansion in the valley, but last night LA had a freak rainstorm, and all the mansion's skylights leaked. The producers called us this morning to say, "The carpets are soaked, so we're going to put the contestants up in a hotel until we get this sorted out," and my mom said to them, "Really, there's carpet? In the mansion?" She was expecting white marble floors or something. I told her that I was sure the carpet would be nice and fine once it was dry, just to get her off the phone—she loves talking to the producers.

Even though it's still sprinkling, it only took us an hour to get to the hotel, because we live in Orange County and we left after the traffic. Lights are on in every few rooms of a modern gray rectangle on a corner downtown. They make the hotel look like it's trying to send out some secret code. We drive up to the valet, whose blond ponytail is as high and tight as my mom's, and for a second it almost seems like the two of them are eyeing each other competitively. She hands him the keys.

"It's supposed to be sunny tomorrow," he says.

"That's a relief," she tells him, and puts up her umbrella for both of us to get under.

Inside the lobby there's a DJ with his eyes shut standing behind a huge turntable, playing some pretty loud music for girls who are sitting on the dark pink lounge chairs. It's Monday night around eight, so he doesn't have much of an audience. The song he's got on sounds like what would come out of fish if you could capture the sounds of their mouths opening and shutting underwater.

I watch my mom taking in the lobby, and you can see all over her face how happy she is to be there. Some things about her make her seem younger than forty, like the trendy jumpsuit she's wearing and the twenty thin rings stacked on her fingers and that ponytail and the excitement in her eyes.

But then the weird thing is that the exact same things can make her seem older than forty when you take them all in together.

At the reservation desk she says, "I think it should be under her name: Magnolia Anderson? I'm the mom." She leans forward a little. "We're with *Spotlight*."

The clerk looks from his computer screen to me, and smiles

for the first time. "Our manager briefed everyone on the cast visit. Congratulations. You must be excited."

"Can't wait to get started," I say. My mom believes in the Secret, that you can manifest things just by saying them about yourself. I think that's beyond cuckoo. For me, it's like *cooooooooo-kooooooo*. But I am eager to get started so I don't have to wait anymore to find out if I'm going to change.

"Just don't show your nerves," he says. "People get very uncomfortable watching people who can't handle themselves. If you get distractingly nervous, just imagine everyone naked."

The show is going to be on TV, so that's a lot of people. "Everyone in America?"

He makes a face. "Well, let's not torture ourselves. Maybe only the thin, good-looking ones."

I've heard this naked idea before in my life, but I've never seriously had to consider it.

"But you don't think it's even more nerve-wracking to make yourself imagine that the whole country has suddenly turned into a nudist colony?" I wonder out loud. "Isn't that kind of a threatening mental image? To think that everyone isn't just staring at you, but they've also got out their—"

"Okay," my mom interrupts, smiling at the clerk. "Let's not overthink it, my love."

"Maybe you should just get her some Xanax, Mom," the clerk jokes as he goes back to encoding our room key cards. He asks me, "How old are you?"

"Seventeen."

"Seventeen, oh yeah. Now's the time you want to learn how to go through life without being so neurotic, or it will catch up with you. I have friends who are so, so neurotic. They're messes."

"You think I'm neurotic?" I ask.

"When Magnolia sings," my mom butts in again so that this guy doesn't have to answer my question, "she completely gets out of her own head. It's pure. You're going to be so moved that you won't be able to stop yourself from picking up the phone to vote for her."

"I have a TV, but I only watch films on it," the clerk says, handing over our key cards. "But I'm sure that's true."

2

The clerk has put us on one of the top floors. When the elevator door opens, there's a woman backed into the far corner wearing a tight gold minidress. The straps have fallen off her shoulders, and she's got her face toward the elevator wall, so all I can really see of her is her long red hair.

"Are you getting out?" my mom asks, and the woman just says, "Mmm," which makes it pretty impossible to decide if that's a yes or a no. So my mom and I look at each other and then at the woman, who isn't budging, and then we get in, figuring she's at least willing to go on another ride.

The elevator starts with more of a jolt than I was expecting. I lose my balance, and tip over onto the panel with the buttons, which means that my shoulder lights up a bunch of floors we don't need. My mom laughs at me and raps, "Errrrybody in the elevator gettin' tipsy."

At this, the woman in the gold dress rolls along the wall so she's facing us. She's somewhere around thirty, and if I wasn't sure before, now I can tell she's completely wasted.

"You shouldn't play around in an elevator," she slurs. She stabilizes her head and eyes enough to shoot us an amazingly exasperated look that says we should know better. "Can't be doing that, thinking the 'vator is your own house, you know, *jeez*." She huffs out that last word like she's proud of the points she just made. The elevator door chimes and opens on the third floor, courtesy of my shoulder.

"Are you—" my mom says, and I think she's going to finish with something like, *in need of a stomach pumping?* But before she can get out the rest of the question, the woman in the gold dress lifts her head higher and asks, "Dooya recognize me?"

The elevator starts again. My mom takes a step forward like she does whenever she's charged with excitement and can't help herself.

"You are! I loved you in that movie where you play the girl who's torn between the guy you think is trying to kill you and the policeman who's been protecting you. Whenever it comes on cable, I'm going to watch it and I don't care if it's three in the morning!"

"That one," says the woman, chuckling and tucking her hair behind an ear. "A good one, that one. He was always saying, let's go on vacation, come on, let's go see palm trees. I can't get enough of you in a bikini. Listen, I want you. In a bikini. On the inside of my eyelids."

Listening to her, I wonder if I should picture everyone in America in bikinis instead while I'm singing. They could be tossing each other beach balls, riding boogie boards, things like that. Boogie boards are automatically stupid things to think about.

"Which costar?" my mom asks. "The killer or the policeman?"

"Wasn't a killer in real life, ya know."

The elevator opens to no one on the fifth floor.

"Obviously. But he was so good in the movie." My mom nods thoughtfully. "The two of you together, it makes complete sense."

"It sure did. Only once, though, way back then," says the actress. "It only made sense *once.*"

By the time the elevator gets to our floor, the actress isn't the same person who was scolding us for messing around. She's eager to tell my mom trivia from the set, but the information's like a puzzle you can only finish partway because some of the pieces are lost in another box. Either it was the director who wore a wig or else it was the guy who made her wigs for the movie who fought the director. I don't know. It doesn't seem to matter to my mom, whatever the story.

"Were you outgoing when you were a kid?" I suddenly ask the actress. I'm wondering if she always wanted to get out there and perform for others, or if it was something that snuck up and surprised her.

She looks at me like I've startled her. She says, "Areyoo asking if I was a slut?"

In this situation, I think most moms would probably warn the drunk actress to cool it toward their daughters. But my mom says to her, "Obviously you weren't."

The elevator doors open on eleven. "This is us," I say to the actress. "Do you want me to push a button for you?"

She points upward. She's forgiven me. "Going to the roof. There's a pool. There's stars."

I push that button for her, and we say bye, getting out. The actress is saying something about how people should never horse around in the pool—never—as the doors shut on her again.

"She was pretty cool, even if she was sort of out of it," my mom says as we walk down the hallway. "Maybe she's staying here and we'll run into her again. Because I don't know if it counts as meeting someone if they don't remember you."

"You still got to talk to her."

"Technically. But I feel like it doesn't matter unless you actually made an impression. People must come up and talk to her all the time."

"Maybe they don't, especially when she's like that."

My mom still seems disturbed by the way she left things with the actress, so I ask, "Do you want to go up to the pool and try to have a longer conversation? I'm fine by myself for a while." I want this experience to be everything my mom needs from it. If it's too late in life for her to really change, then at least I don't want her collecting regrets.

She shakes her head. I think it's more to shake herself out of the idea of going up there than for my benefit. "No, stop it, I'm fine. Here we are."

She pushes the key card into the reader, and we enter the room we'll be sharing for the next couple of nights, or however long it takes to seal skylights. The two beds are on low gray platforms with lampshades attached to the wall behind them. Then there's one more floor lamp that's just a glowing white tube.

The room feels like it's futuristic and old-fashioned at the same time, like it's a bedroom on a private airplane, but an airplane from a few decades before I was born. The airplane of a swinger. I don't actually know what a swinger likes in terms of decoration, but from the ideas I have about swinging, this seems pretty right.

The weirdest part is that there's a glass wall in between the bedroom and the bathroom, so you can watch someone washing their face. Or even worse, if you're staying with your mom, you can watch someone shower. But thankfully, there's also a white curtain you can pull shut.

My mom says, "Look, Mag, flowers and a note." Over on the built-in desk that runs along the window there's an arrangement. It's very tropical-looking with green and yellow orchids in a tall bamboo vase.

The only other time in my life I remember getting flowers was when I was little and my dad gave me a bouquet of carnations after my dance recital. He told me that you give roses to women and carnations to girls, and that's why he loved carnations. Because he thought they were happier flowers in that way.

"Thoughtful," I say.

My mom takes the note out of the envelope and reads, "'Welcome, Magnolia and Diana.' I'll have to let them know that I go by Di. 'We hope you'll find your room comfortable until we can get you into the mansion—sorry about the last-minute change of plans. Please feel free to order room service on our account. A producer will be calling tonight to make sure that you have everything you need and to go over the schedule for tomorrow.'"

She touches one of the orchid's petals like she's making sure it's real. "Okay, then I'm going to hop in the shower before they call." She starts taking off her rings and putting them next to the vase. Then she goes into the bathroom and checks out the minisoaps and mini-shampoos before calling out, "Mag?"

"Yeah, Mom?"

"What if this is the beginning of a whole new existence?"

"I know," I say.

She pulls the white curtain shut, and I hear the shower come on a few seconds later. I go over to the window and open the long striped curtain that runs the whole width of the room.

The other side of the glass is dotted with raindrops. The view looks out over the freeway and wavering city lights. The hills are in the distance. The streets underneath me shine from the drizzle floating on top of car oil.

I think I'm probably young enough to pull off a whole new existence. I really boxed myself into my old one.

3

Back in elementary school, I used to have a group of five friends. It was easier then. We ate lunch together and hit up the book fair at recess together, but maybe that's just it—everything we did was over at 2:51 p.m. Then we could go our separate ways because we were too young to have social lives and not in charge enough to have to make plans.

Then we got to middle school, which was bigger. And our group of five was automatically expected to join up with other groups that were coming from other elementary schools. So then we were eating lunch in a circle of fifteen, just like that. I was buying fourteen identical gifts at the holidays. Roller-skating in a long chain. Sitting in parks at night and needing multiple tables. The phone was ringing all the time. And by high school it became a group of at least thirty, give or take whoever was mad at whomever or liked whomever on any given day, and it was so many personalities and so many plans (and parties added onto that now too) and just so much talking that I cracked.

One day I broke off and started eating lunch alone in a corner by the history building. I got the nickname Dark Star. A lot of people thought I was depressed or angry or your standard kind of asshole who thinks she's too good for everybody else.

On the third anniversary of my dad's death, I was having a really bad day. It was worse than the second anniversary, but I still couldn't tell you why. I just knew I was going to burst into tears if I walked into fifth-period math.

So I went to collect myself behind the auto shop building, since they only teach those classes in the morning; it's a ghost town after lunch. I lay down on the concrete, and maybe a minute later this long-haired upperclassman guy came around the corner and almost kicked my head with his Vans. He was hiding from a campus security guy, who'd spotted him trying to take off early. The way he put it was, "I was gonna pack it up for the day."

You know how in movies they have those things called meet-cutes? Like when two people knock heads while going for the same frozen yogurt topping. This was more like a meet-sad. The guy asked if I minded if he stayed for a minute, until the narc was gone, and just as I'd suspected, anyone saying anything to me made tears come. They started rolling down my face just because of a nothing question.

People who have seen me cry are confused sometimes because I don't hiccup or sob. I just get a very wet face, very fast. I'm like one of those fountain walls at a restaurant.

"Whoa," the guy said, and there was the first moment between Scott and me.

I know that girls throwing over their girlfriends for a guy is a thing, but in my defense, I had already thrown over my friends for myself. We have a sophomore English teacher, Mrs. Corinthos, who's more worried about female students getting too into their boyfriends than she is about teaching how to write a coherent essay. She's known to call conferences with girls she's seen draped over their boyfriends, even ones who aren't in her class, to tell them that their romance might seem incredibly important right now, but they can't let it take over their lives or they'll be sorry later. Which now that I'm thinking about it, is just another way of trying to convince them that they're going to change.

I had Mrs. Corinthos's class. After she saw Scott jokingly press his lips and then his bare chest to her window to cheer me up on the fourth anniversary of my dad's death, she called me in for an after-school conference.

"So was that your boyfriend who came to show you his nipple?" she asked.

"Yes," I said.

She sighed like she had to break really bad news to me. "Listen, I know he seems like your world right now, but I just want you to remember that you've got to keep up other parts of your life. And I'm not just talking about school. Keep up with your friends. Keep up with your hobbies. What do you like to do?"

Being my English teacher, she of all people should have noticed that I liked writing. That instead of using the week's vocab words in unrelated sentences, I'd been keeping a running plot of an imaginary TV show going for both of our entertainment. I called it *Ships in the Night* (because it was set in a small seaside town and was about people who constantly misunderstood each other's needs). I had two families who hated each other. I had "covert" (vocab) make-out sessions and an unsolved murder. And I turned every vocab assignment into another episode.

I'd gotten less interested in solving the murder than just

updating Mrs. Corinthos on whatever issues the characters were working through. Like Warren Gettysburg, teenage son of the richest couple in town, who had become incredibly "capricious" (vocab) after he realized all the bad things his parents were up to. He couldn't help but start to see his whole existence as this hollow thing.

Anyway, what I said to Mrs. Corinthos was, "I like to make out."

I didn't mean it as disrespectfully as it sounds. I wasn't trying to throw her concern about me back in her face. I was just sticking up for myself.

Because even though I was one of those girls always with her boyfriend, I didn't believe that everything had to come down to me being young and dumb. I was a person who'd gotten seriously stressed out by being a part of a group. And when I met Scott, I was able to combine a friend and a guy I wanted to make out with into one person.

One person!

It was the perfect situation for someone like me.

So what if making out instantly became one of my favorite hobbies? Maybe from the outside it was, *Oh, there's another one of those girls*, but from the inside, I still don't understand why a romance can't matter until you're old enough to say you're going to stay together forever and no one laughs.

Mrs. Corinthos looked so bummed out for me. So I threw her a bone and said, "I also like singing in my room, and in the car too."

"That's it," she said, staring me at me intensely with an important message. *"Get into singing."*

If only Mrs. Corinthos could have seen a semester into the future, then she would have been happy to find out not only that I'd been released from the terrible easygoing influence of my boyfriend but also that I was as serious as ever about singing in the car, and it would lead me to where I'm standing right now.

Scott and I broke up at the beginning of this summer. He was supposed to go away to do environmental studies at Reed, moving to Oregon at the end of June, and I was only going into my junior year.

But then he put off leaving, saying that there were things he still needed to take care of. Those things turned out to be lots of surfing and sleeping on people's couches but didn't have much to do with me. We never talked about why we'd actually broken up if Scott wasn't going anywhere. We just stopped hanging out. But in July he started a habit of calling every few days to pretend like we're actual friends.

So my phone will ring at two in the morning, and Scott will be there, asking, "Did I wake you up, Tiny?" That's what he calls me, even though I'm not ridiculously small or anything.

"What's going on?" I'll say, but I'll wish I could just hang up because I quickly learned that every one of our surface conversations (usual topics: weird things neighbors are up to; pollution at the beach; the theory of the universe as a hologram and how much it stresses me out; secret cures for surf rash) leaves me feeling more hollow than when I picked up.

Why don't I hang up on Scott? Well, here's exactly what I've been getting toward—and I understand this sounds really, incredibly simple—but it is *so hard to change how you act*.

Like at school, I know that there's this idea of me, and all

I'd have to do to shake it up is do something surprising. Smile for a whole day. Invite someone new to have lunch. Join a committee. Wear a conversation piece sweatshirt. I don't know. Same deal when it comes to Scott. Instead of being a person he can still call, all I have to do is not pick up the phone. I think the real obstacle to changing is that once people decide on an idea of you, it's so hard to ditch it yourself that it basically feels impossible.

Which is why I'm here.

4

A few months ago my mom and I were driving to the beach and she had her phone's camera on record, which I didn't know. So I had my head tipped against the window and I was belting out Beyoncé's song "Halo," because my mom always has the radio on a top 40 station and that's what was on. She says it keeps her current, in this way that makes it sound like the Black Eyed Peas deliver her the world news.

She'd already been trying to get on *The Real Housewives of Orange County* for a few years. The producers had brought her in for three different interviews, and they'd even come by to see our house. My mom showed them what she looked like coming down what she called our "grand staircase." But the interest never turned into anything.

When my mom realized she hadn't gotten on the show, first she said that she knew it was because she was too stable. "It's hard to make me cry," she told me, "and people can tell that about a person."

Then she got more depressed about how close she'd come, and she started saying that it was because she didn't have a husband or at least a steady boyfriend.

"But you had Dad," I said, and she shot me a look like I'd gone crazy. Dad died when I was eleven, but he'd left her when I was ten, and so she liked to act like he'd never mattered.

Next thing you know, she was secretly taping me. Then a few weeks ago she was jumping up and down in the kitchen after our phone rang.

"You're on the cast!" she shouted, and I said, "Of what?" and she just said, "Oh my God, you're one of the ten!" and I said, "Ten who?" and we went back and forth like that for at least a couple of minutes before she finally calmed down enough to explain to me what she'd done.

"You're going to be famous," was the last thing she said to me before I went to bed that night. "Even if it's just for a minute."

But being famous is not really what I'm concerned about. What I want is to get out from under the weight of my current existence. It's not that my life is so terrible beyond certain sadnesses. My dad being gone. Scott at a distance. The loneliness I feel, especially in the presence of other people.

It's not that stuff. It's me. I'm sick of myself. I'm sick of looking out from this head. Sometimes I imagine it like my own perspective is a concrete slab that flattened me down. I mean, it didn't just pin me like a bug—it trampled me: *That's who you are. Don't move.* I did it to myself, and my understanding just adds that much more heaviness. I cemented myself somehow, and now I can't see myself any differently.

But I had the realization that going on a TV show could be so disorienting that I'd forget what (I've come to believe) I'm incapable of. Police officers had an assembly at our school last year to talk about teenagers on drugs. One officer said that he'd seen a kid on PCP land a four-story jump like a cat. This kid just thought he could do it. And it worked for him! Not that I'm looking to acquire a drug problem, but I think this show could take my head between its hands and shake it up. I want to be a little dizzy. I want to give up my old securities.

I pick up the phone on the desk and dial Scott's cell number. I have done this way too much.

"Hello?" he answers, sounding groggy. I can practically hear him wrinkling his eyebrows together.

"Hey," I say.

"Where are you, Tiny? What number is this?" he asks.

"In a hotel room in downtown LA. Don't ask." I stare at a drop of water on the other side of the window. "Where are you?"

"At this guy's house in Malibu, in a sleeping bag on his living room floor. We're getting up early to hit the water. You and me aren't that far away right now."

I'm going to be outgoing. I'm going to have energy. I'm going to entertain. I'm going to picture all those people out there boogie boarding naked, even picture their genitals chafing against the plastic foam, and I'm going to be something new to them. And then maybe I can be new again to myself too.

I say, "I called to ask you to stop calling me."

"Whoa," Scott says. "What?"

My mom opens the curtain with a luxurious robe on and her hair wrapped in a big towel. "Is that the producers?" she asks breathlessly, like she's just gone for a swim instead of a shower. "Have they been waiting a long time?"

"What?" Scott is saying.

"So, no more calls. I'm serious. I've got to go," I tell him, and then I hang up the phone.

FORD

5

I'd never seen a desert before yesterday, and now it feels like I'll never see the end of this one. My old Triumph motorcycle has already made it a thousand miles farther than I thought it would. If I break down out here in this wasteland, I'm picturing my road trip turning into an episode of *I Shouldn't Be Alive*, me drinking water out of cactuses, eating scorpions like they're corn chips. Still, there's one thing I definitely like about the desert: it's a *long* way from home.

Home is Calumet, Arkansas. My tiny white three-room shack (I could call it a house, but I'd be lying) so close to the railroad tracks that it sounds like the train rolls straight through my bedroom at night. I never minded that so much, though, because at least I had the place to myself. Compared to the mayhem I dealt with when I still lived with my family, a rumbling train sounded like a lullaby. Getting out of their house was the second best thing that's ever happened to me.

The best? When the producers from *Spotlight* called at the music store a few weeks ago to tell me they wanted me on the show.

I hadn't told anyone that I was going for it. I just borrowed a video camera and recorded myself singing "The Weight" by the Band out on the back porch, only because that's a song I've been singing since I can first remember. When I sent that entry, it seemed like I might as well be throwing my audition into a black hole. But somehow a few months later there was this lady on the other end of the line saying, "We love your voice . . . totally genuine . . . That's what America's about."

After I left work, I walked in a daze until I looked up to find myself at the highway on the edge of town. The sun was going down. The cicadas chirping in the trees, the smell of someone barbequing dinner, the sunset reflecting off the metal grain silos—everything was so clear and bright and loud. Same old town, nothing had changed, but everything felt different.

I'd always wanted to figure a way out of this town, but I never thought today would be the day. Some strange voice on the end of the phone wasn't enough to make it seem real. Music is all I'm really good at, so I daydreamed I could play my way out. But I'd never got any further than playing for six drunks at a West Memphis bar. There isn't exactly a thriving music scene down here.

And before that, as a kid, I even dreamed that I might grow up to try out for a TV singing competition, but when I did get older, I never could afford to travel to a major city for the auditions. Then the last few years that whole *American Idol* thing started to seem on its way down. I read that all those shows' ratings were dropping. It truly seemed like I'd missed my chance, since I had no idea how an ordinary person gets his foot in the door.

Then I saw the ads for *Spotlight*, a new show coming in the fall and looking for talent. All you had to do was send in a video.

I figured, what did I have to lose?

6

I've got only two hundred miles to go, when a blast of desert wind slams into my motorcycle, taking control away from me. I feel my stomach drop as adrenaline shoots through my bloodstream. I'm almost off the road before I push hard on my left handlebar to swerve, straightening out. Breathing again, I tell myself, *Okay, you're still upright.* Fifteen hundred miles is a long way on a motorcycle.

It would have been easier to fly, but my free flight to Los Angeles left without me two nights ago. When the producers sent me the ticket, there was nothing in the world that would have stopped me from getting on that flight . . . well, nothing except being handcuffed in the backseat of a police car while my plane was taking off.

I'd made a bad mistake: I'd gone by my parents' house to try to get my grandfather's guitar, the Telecaster he'd left to me that had magically disappeared the day I moved out.

See, my family has always had a real close relationship with local law enforcement. The county jail has basically been our vacation home over the years; someone or another was always "away" for a stretch. The best way you can understand my family is to think of one of those flash floods that come in the summer, sweeping up everything they touch and leaving a ton of debris behind.

When I got to my family's house and saw they were having a party, I should have just turned right around. Out front, beat-up cars were parked all over the lawn. Drunk guys were shouting and shoving each other around. Couples were making out in the shadows. Once I got inside, I found the living room full of people drinking and dancing to Jay-Z. You'd be surprised how much rednecks like hip-hop.

I spotted my dad on the couch, smoking weed out of a beer can with a hole cut in it. I know it ain't normal, but my family parties together, old and young.

"Hey, John," I said. My dad barely looked at me. We hadn't spoken since I'd gotten that judge to emancipate me six months earlier. John had signed off on it, but he'd taken the whole thing as a personal insult that he wasn't interested in letting go.

"What do you want?" He passed the beer-can pipe to a blonde girl in a black sleeveless T-shirt sitting next to him. She gave me a glassed-over look from behind a piece of greasy hair. I think she was a friend of my cousin.

"Where is everybody?"

"Your mom's at the casino. Your brother's in the kitchen."

"You know where the Telecaster is?"

John just shrugged. "You should ask your brother about that."

I pushed my way through and found my older brother, Cody, trying to light pure grain alcohol on fire while blowing it out of his mouth like a dragon. An alcoholic dragon.

"Well, hell, look who it is," he slurred, punching me in the arm. "The prodigal son or long-lost brother. Or whatever." Then he gave me a half hug, half headlock. "We're still brothers right? What did the judge say on that subject?"

"We're still brothers. Nothing I can do about that," I said.

I didn't know how Cody was going to feel about this TV thing. People would have told you he was the musician in the family since he'd been playing in bands on and off for years. His band even opened for Lynyrd Skynyrd once, like, three years ago when they played in Little Rock. Sometimes we used to play together at bars—called ourselves the Buckley Brothers. But all that ended when I moved out.

Some sketchy guy stepped in between us then and pushed a twenty-dollar bill at Cody, who pulled a couple of pills out of his front shirt pocket and dropped them into the guy's hand.

You know how some people have a family business that everyone is supposed to pitch in and help out with? Well, this is ours. Cops in Calumet claim if they could get rid of all the Buckleys, the crime rate would drop at least 80 percent overnight.

"I'm thinking about kicking you out of the band," my brother said, eyeing me to see if I was going to argue that there wasn't a band to be kicked out of anymore. "You haven't been to practice in months. You too good for your family now?" As the music in the living room switched from hip-hop to country, my sister, Sissy, bounced in through the kitchen door.

"Baby Ford," she said, hugging me. She calls me Baby even though she's only twenty-one. Sissy's good-looking, and that fools people because if you cross her, she'll put a screwdriver in your leg. Ask my uncle James about that—he's still got a limp.

"Dad said you were here. What are you doing, huh?" she asked, looking curious. "You didn't come to party."

"Ford's decided to crawl back and beg for our forgiveness for disowning us," Cody said.

"Not exactly," I said. And then, suddenly feeling embarrassed, I just went ahead and came out with it. "I'm gonna be on this show called *Spotlight*."

"What are you talking about?" Sissy asked.

"You heard me. They liked my singing."

"You're gonna be on TV?" Sissy asked, really not absorbing this information.

"I'm flying out tonight."

"Well, shit, why didn't you tell me?" Cody wanted to know, a nerve-wracking smile coming across his face. "Let me get my stuff and let's go, man."

I made sure I caught his eye because sometimes Cody will dodge you and pretend he doesn't understand your meaning. "Just me, Cody. It's not like a band thing."

"How you supposed to do this without me? I taught you everything you know about music."

"I'm just gonna do my best, I guess," I told him. "Anyway I gotta go. I came by to get my Telecaster."

I could practically hear Cody's bad side clicking on in his brain. "Well, that's gonna be difficult. I sold that old guitar to Marcus at the pawn shop."

I stopped and looked at him. "You sold it? That's my guitar, Cody."

"Family guitar, really. And you left the family, if I remember."

"Grampa left it to me, and I want it back." I ordered myself not to let my hands curl into fists. Because that's what Cody wanted. Because it would mean I was still like them.

"Yeah. And, well, I want to hook up with Taylor Swift, but you don't always get what you want, do you?"

We glared at each other for a minute. His eyes had that look they got when he was making someone miserable—he was enjoying himself. He likes to poke at people, find their weak spots. What I wanted to do was leave. I swear that's what I was hoping for myself. But what I did instead was hit him.

He put me on the floor, fast as lightning. Pinned me down and sat on top of me. Then he hit me on the side of the head with his open hand.

"When are you gonna learn you'll never whip your big brother?"

Sissy was pulling him off me when some tattooed dude appeared in the doorway and yelled, "Cops!"

"Shit!" Cody jumped up and pulled a paper bag full of pills out from its hiding place under the kitchen sink. He seemed like he was going to bolt right that second, but then he reached down and pulled me up. "Don't you have a plane to catch?" he asked, finally looking at me straight on.

We ran out the back door. People were scattering out every exit like cockroaches when you turn on the light. Cockroaches wearing a whole lot of denim.

Out in the backyard you could see the blue lights flashing and the dark shapes of people making for the woods. Rounding the corner of the house, wouldn't you know? I ran right into the outstretched arm of a cop. My back hit the ground first, knocking the breath out of me.

A half hour later I was still in the back of the cop car, wrists throbbing from the handcuffs digging into them. The door opened. "Hop on in there," ordered the cop who'd clotheslined me. I recognized him from a few years ahead of Cody in school—a short, bulky guy named Steve Greggs. He had Cody in handcuffs.

"Oh, hell no," Cody said when he saw me in the car. He twisted to talk to Steve. "Damn it, Greggs, you let my brother go. He don't even live here." Steve tried to put Cody in the car, but Cody definitely wasn't making it easy.

"He's got a plane to catch, you idiot! To Hollywood, you hear? He's gonna sing on TV. If you mess this up for him, I swear, I'll take it out on your ass, Greggs. You were an asshole in high school, and you're still an asshole. Maybe this is your chance to turn that around."

"Shut up, Cody," said Greggs, pushing my brother in next to me. "Things have changed a little since high school."

"Yeah, now you've got a gun instead of a baseball bat."

"Forget it, man. I think you helped me enough tonight already," I told Cody. His ranting was only making things worse.

Greggs slammed the door on us, then slid into the front seat, taking his time with checking out his mustache stubble in the mirror, just to piss off my brother.

"Listen, you dumb redneck! My brother has places to be!" Cody yelled through the metal grate.

"Bullshit," Greggs said. "You Buckleys are trash, always have been. Only places y'all are going are to the state pen in Jacksonville or into the ground."

My brother kept trying to make eye contact with me on the way to the jail, but I didn't want to look at him. I felt hot angry tears behind my eyes, and a terrible frustration. I couldn't believe that I'd blown this chance. It seemed to me that Greggs must be right: failure was in my genes.

It was just before dawn when I was bailed out by Leander, who was waiting for me when I stepped outside. In the end I was only charged with disturbing the peace. I guess my brother had managed to hide the evidence before they caught him, but making me miss the flight—they couldn't have punished me any worse.

During the night, part of me had almost felt relieved that the whole TV thing was over with. I told myself I'd probably just have made a fool of myself anyway. But when I saw Leander, the relief went away and then the guilt rushed in. Leander was the only person who'd ever really seen anything in me. He'd given me my job, he'd rented me my house for almost nothing, and he'd taught me a lot about music.

"I missed my flight," I said.

Leander nodded. He's a guy who looks like he should have a beard. It's confusing that he doesn't. "I noticed."

"Thanks for bailing me out."

It felt bad to have him pick me up at jail. A few years before, Leander had caught me breaking into his store, but he'd ended up dropping the charges on the condition that I work for him to pay for the damage. Eventually it turned into a full-time job, helping around the store and teaching guitar lessons.

I don't know what he saw in me that no one else did. I mean, my teachers used to tell me I was smart and they'd point to my good scores when I happened to be in school on the day of one of those state aptitude tests, but they also said I didn't apply myself. I did apply myself, but it was to screwing up. And trying to fit in at home. None of that mixed well with school, and I finally just dropped out sophomore year. That didn't seem to matter much to anybody.

Anyway, Leander sort of started looking out for me. He was more like a parent than my own parents ever were. He'd buy me meals at the diner, his way of making sure I was eating real food and not just living on cold Pop-Tarts and SpaghettiOs. He talked me into working toward getting my GED. It was when I started going to his AA meetings with him, when I first heard him talk about his family—how his kids don't speak to him anymore—that I started thinking he was trying to make up for past mistakes by helping me out. At first I went to the meetings for the free doughnuts, but then because the people there knew where I was coming from. Most of them had things much worse.

My family found my sobriety really irritating. They all thought I was judging them or something. I found out that if you're going to be around tweakers all the time, you kind of need to be drunk. And I also found out that I really didn't have much of a desire to get loaded once I broke off from the crowd. I stopped needing the meetings. But I just kept to myself more, kept my door closed during parties, and that was working out okay until someone almost blew my head off.

I was sitting on my bed during yet another party when a bullet tore through my wall and whizzed by my ear like an angry wasp. It stopped in my little practice amplifier. Turns out, some idiot was showing off his new .45 in the living room and accidently fired it while pretending he was a gunslinger. Cody couldn't stop laughing about the look on my face. I couldn't stop thinking about how stupid it would have been for my whole life to come down to being shot through the skull by some drunk dumbass. That's when I decided I wanted out.

Leander helped me set up the emancipation. Talked to my parents about signing off, telling them it would be better all around. They had never heard of emancipation, and they mostly saw it as me thinking I was too good for them. But in the end they signed off, because what difference did it really make? The judge determined that it was in my best interest and that I'd proved to be self-sufficient. And just like that, I was a seventeen-year-old legal adult and could live on my own.

We'd been driving in Leander's Cadillac for a while before he said anything else. "So that's it, then?"

"I guess so."

"What's your plan? Work in my store for the rest of your life?"

"What's wrong with that?"

"Nothing *wrong* with it. I like having you there. It's fine with me if you want to spend the next twenty years giving boogery kids guitar lessons and spending your lunchtimes eating with an old man."

"Good, because that's what I want to do," I said, even though it felt bad to say.

Leander braked at a stop sign, but then he didn't get going again. We just sat there. "Now that I'm old, I look back on my younger self, and I realize the number of chances a person gets to change their life—I mean really change it—there ain't many. And most times, it ain't even any."

"I missed the flight," I reminded him. Now, I had some idea that I could call the producers and beg them to get me another ticket. Maybe they could do it. I didn't really know. I'd heard that out in Los Angeles, people in TV just threw money around like it was confetti.

But I couldn't bring myself to pick up the phone. Asking for another ticket felt the same as saying that I was just some back-woods guy who had messed up before anything even started. What was I gonna say? *Hey, sorry I missed the flight, got arrested for being at a drug party. Can you just send another four hundred dollars?*

I told Leander, "It's over."

"There's more than one way to get to California."

"Maybe I don't want to hear what those people think of my sing-ing anyway."

Leander nodded again, like I was making some kind of sense, but then he said, "I think you're lying to yourself. I think you do want to know. You think it's common to have the kind of talent you have? That promise, it's in your bones, and if you don't let it out, it's gonna burn you up. And I don't feel like sitting around watching it happen. So you're fired."

I smiled, assuming that he was joking. "C'mon."

"That's right." He gave me a look that said, *Cut the bull*. Then he pulled the car up to my house and held out some cash. "Here's two hundred dollars severance pay. That should be enough gas money to get you to LA. Don't think it over another second. You get out of my truck, and you leave town right this minute."

When he wanted, Leander had a way of talking that cut right into me. So when he looked at me with those wise hard eyes of his and told me to *leave town right this minute*, that's what I did.

Twenty hours later I wish I'd at least stopped by a store to pick up some new shirts and maybe some provisions for the trip. Still, just driving through all that empty space has made me feel like I'm expanding. I want to keep driving. I don't really ever want to arrive.

7

It's one a.m. when I walk through the doors of the hotel, only thirty-eight hours later than I was supposed to be here. It's definitely not the Motel 6. The lobby reminds me of the inside of one of those science labs where they solve crimes on TV, except there are a bunch of cute girls hanging around instead of nerdy scientists. I mean, there are more good-looking girls in this one hotel lobby than in all of Calumet put together.

The desk clerk looks me up and down before he types my name into the computer. "Mr. Buckley, you're with *Spotlight*?"

Nobody's ever called me Mr. Buckley before, outside of school when I was in trouble. "Yes, sir," I say. "That's me."

He picks up a phone, dials, and has a quick conversation. ". . . no, he's here now. Yes, he's standing right in front of me. Okay." He hangs up. "The producer will be right down, Mr. Buckley, if you want to have a seat on one of the lounge chairs."

The last part of the drive out I'd been filled with weird confidence. Felt like the whole city was waiting out here just for me. But now, looking around at this crime lab with the attractive girls and the DJ playing his bleep-bleeps and boops, I start feeling pretty nervous.

They aren't gonna let me in this thing. I didn't even call to tell them that I was making the drive. I didn't even call them after I missed the plane. What if I'm disqualified already? I probably am. Stupid. What was I thinking anyway? I don't even have enough money to make it back home. They're probably sending a security guard down to throw me out of here.

"Ford?" A woman's standing in front of me in a silk robe, like I woke her from sleeping. She doesn't look as old as I thought a producer would, but she does look pretty annoyed.

"Sorry I'm late."

She puts two fingers to her eyebrows like I've given her a headache. "Where the hell have you been? You made me feel like some soccer mom who lost her overgrown kid at the mall, you know what I'm saying? I had a PA talk to the guy at your work—"

"Leander?"

"I guess? He said you were 'going to be here, he guaranteed it.' But there was no way to reach you. There are these things called cell phones."

"Yeah, I don't have one right now." I shrug, then ask, "What's your name?"

"What?" She seems to awaken, and looks at me in surprise.

"Your name."

I swear she's acting like I asked her what she wants for Christmas. Finally she gets over the surprise and says, "Catherine."

"Hi, Catherine, nice to meet you. Like I said, sorry I'm late. I got held up on account of some family stuff."

"We've been trying to decide on a replacement for you all day. You know, I was one of the ones who really fought for you because I thought the show could use a little hayseed—no offense," she tells me. "You made me look bad."

I look her in the eyes. "I'm real sorry, and that's the best I've got.

If you let me compete, it won't happen again. I'll be punctual."

She studies me, and I can sense she's starting not to be annoyed anymore. "Did you buy your own ticket?"

"No, I drove."

"You drove out here?"

"On my motorcycle."

She jumps up and down one time like a little girl. "We should get some footage of you on the motorcycle! It will kill in your video package, set up that whole personal narrative of an outsider rolling into town on a cloud of dust. I'm picturing dirt. Torn denim. Maybe we get a tumbleweed." She seems so suddenly excited that I get excited too, thinking I'm back in.

But then her expression goes flat as fast as it lit up and she says, "I've got to talk to my executive producer. Hold on."

She steps away to make a call on her cell phone. It's in a sparkling case. She looks over at me as she talks. Then she hangs up, and instead of coming back over, starts typing away.

Suddenly I want to grab her and beg for mercy and explain that this is life or death for me. A momentous feeling runs through me. The kind you get sometimes when you realize the weight of something while it's still happening. This lady and whoever was on the other end of that phone are about to make a decision they'll probably forget about in a week, but I'll be living with it forever.

She walks back over. Her expression hasn't changed. "Welcome to Hollywood," she says. "Let's get you a room."

The room is bigger than my house. It's a little weird, though. There's a chair shaped like a hand and a black-and-white photo of a nude girl shown all curled up on a floor. You'd need a pilot's license to turn on the sink. I guess in LA they just like simple things to be complicated. I throw myself on the bed, trying to calm down, but I can't, so I decide to go to the roof and look at the city.

A bartender getting off his shift tells me the whole roof is normally like an outdoor club, but now it's so late that everyone's gone home. When I get out there, it's quiet and abandoned.

I walk over to the long narrow pool that makes it look like you could swim right off the edge of the building. Except for the lights under the water, the patio area has gone dark. Beyond it, Los Angeles is hard to take in. Hard for me to understand. City lights go to every horizon. Where do you even start in a place like this? All those people, and for them Calumet may as well not exist at all.

"Hello, Los Angeles." I say this out loud, not sure why. I lean on the railing and watch a helicopter fly off around the corner of a skyscraper.

"Sorry, it's not going to say hello back."

I turn around. I guess she was there the whole time, a girl sitting behind me in a strange egg-shaped chair. Just sitting there. I can't help but think right off that she's pretty. But the kind of pretty where pretty seems like a wrong, too-soft word. Her hair is dark, long, with these two thin braids in the front of it. I think she might be my age. She doesn't look like I imagined girls in Los Angeles would, all platinum-blonde hair and diamonds in their ears or something, but she's nothing like the girls from home either.

"Hey," I say. "I'm Ford."

"Hi," she says, but doesn't give me a name. It's seeming like people are cagey about that around here. But I'm not letting her off the hook.

"What's your name?"

She sits up and forward and gets this determined look on her face like she's suddenly decided to get involved with talking to me. I'm not sure what I did to open her up. "Magnolia."

"Huh, that's a nice one," I say. "I have a cousin named Marigold, but she doesn't look like a Marigold—she looks more like a thorn-bush, if you know what I mean. Rough. She's locked up for trying to blackmail a guy." I don't even know why I'm telling her about anyone in my family. I should be starting out new.

"My mom named me after *Steel Magnolias*, the movie," Magnolia says. "She loves Julia Roberts."

"Why didn't she name you Julia, then?"

"Middle name."

I laugh, and the sound of it in the air makes me realize I'm tired. "That's a mouthful, Magnolia Julia."

"Your drawl just gave it another syllable." I think I can see her barely smile in the dark. I've racked up some experience making girls smile, but this almost feels lucky. She twists the chair a little from side to side, like she's trying to shake more conversation out of herself. "Where are you from?"

"Arkansas. I just got here. I've never been before. I'm supposed to be on a TV show."

"*Spotlight*?"

"You too?" Her too.

"Me too."

"How nervous are you?"

"I'm going to approach this thing with a lot of energy."

"What?" I look at her sideways. "Come on, that's a cop-out. That's like a robot answer." I break into a robot dance for her for a second, doing a robot voice. "I-have-en-er-gy."

She regards me with such seriousness. "Your robot is so bad that I'm not sure they have robots where you're from."

"Now, I thought we were being friendly."

"I am being friendly! And energetic."

I think about what a girl like her would think if I took her out with me in Calumet. The way the other girls would give her suspicious looks, how small potatoes it would all look to her. The difference is just in the way that everyone's come up. It runs through everything everyone does. A girl like this could barely grasp at the feeling you get when you're born and raised in a town so small that people still hold you responsible for shit your grandparents did.

"It's different where I'm from." I look out over the endless lights. "That's for sure."

"Different how?" she asks.

If I wanted to explain why to her and do any kind of a decent job, I'd have to get into my background and my family. And telling her about Marigold already feels like enough of a stumble.

"I really don't think you'd understand," I say, and as soon as I've said it, I can hear how it sounds. It sounds like I'm blowing her off.

The look in her eyes changes, like she's suddenly given up on whatever she wanted out of our conversation. She gets up out of the egg chair. She does the Robot—and she's good at it.

Then she walks off, her high-tops squeaking on the pool deck. I watch her, outlined against the night, and I keep my mouth shut just in case being mysterious can save me.

Magnolia

8

The producers originally wanted the ten of us to meet while arriving at the mansion so cameras could be there when we took in the size of the bathtubs. But we have to do it instead at the vocal coach's glass house in the Hollywood Hills. Or at least what's supposed to be the vocal coach's house for the purposes of the show, since I don't know if this is actually where she lives. I'm kind of suspicious because I haven't seen personal photos anywhere. Also, she keeps saying things like "This is so cute" and "Cute, cute, cute, I love this" every time she notices a vase or a little statue on a shelf. Either she's just really, really appreciative of her belongings every morning or else she's never been here before either.

There's no filming yet, so Catherine, the head producer, says, "You can just be yourselves for a second."

We've been asked to sit still on the white leather sectional while a cameraman checks the lighting under our faces. But the guy I met on the hotel rooftop, Ford, has gotten up to go stand at the window while he waits his turn. He was in my dream last night, and it was one of those dreams where your brain tricks you into thinking you're so close to someone you don't even know in real life that you wake up sort of devastated, like you've actually lost him. And all we were doing in my dream was collecting marbles together.

Anyway, this lingering feeling is making it hard for me to look at him, so I'm ignoring him instead.

Besides that, I think I'm doing great at coming out of my shell. Normally, I would be the one standing over at the window. But here I am, sitting on the couch with the group and keeping my eyes wider than usual so I don't seem withdrawn.

Catherine stands in front of us and claps her hands together once as if she's going to lead us in a prayer. I can smell her perfume, which is like oranges if oranges were mostly made out of metal.

"I'm going to need you all to pay attention to the rundown because I will open a wrist if I have to repeat it. Dress rehearsals are on Tuesdays. Live PST performance show is on Wednesday nights. Live eliminations on Friday nights. Do you know what it means that they've put us on Friday nights for a limited run? Hint: Friday night is the anus of the television week. It means we're plugging a hole until the network unfurls its new awkward genius crime solver. Do you know what *that* means? It means viewership expectations aren't very high. And what does that mean for me? It means I could really shine."

When she says "shine," she separates her hands like she's accepting rays of light from heaven.

"Bright like a diamond. But back to the schedule. Mondays through Wednesdays will be your heaviest days of scene tapings."

The show's casting notice originally caught my mom's eye because the new idea behind *Spotlight* is that it's part singing competition and part reality soap opera. On the live shows, our performances will only take up half the hour. The other half will be scenes of us bonding and having fights. I'm more nervous about whether I'm going to bond than I am about getting up onstage and singing.

"You will know when the cameras are in the house," Catherine says. "These periods will be limited, and you will not be taped without warning, because some of you are considered children, and I will have the child labor people deep in my Friday-night anus if they think I have kids on tape around the clock."

"The ladies don't think I'm a child," says McKinley, the youngest on the show. He's fourteen. His angelic mom, Shannon, is with him, and she keeps on fixing the curl that's supposed to fall over his right eye. (It wants to go straight down the middle.)

McKinley also has this habit of winking if anybody calls him by name. When a PA was taking roll to make sure that everyone made it over here from the hotel, the rest of the contestants said, "Here," but McKinley just winked while the PA was looking at her clipboard, so for a second she got scared we'd lost him.

"I don't think the sixth graders commenting on YouTube are ladies," Catherine says. Then she continues, squinting one eye as she asks, "Are these scenes going to be real?" as if this is a really tough question coming from someone else. "Mooooostly. We're not going to invent story lines out of thin air, like a cancer scare, for instance. But there will be gentle guidance so we end up with something to use. And all that means is say if you, Dillon—"

She gestures to Dillon, who's twenty and comes out of some pretty big Midwestern Jewish temple where he sings rock songs, except he just swaps out lyrics about boyfriends or girlfriends for God. On the van from the hotel, he told us he got into rock singing when his temple decided to try to compete with all the local mega churches, but before that he'd personally been more into rap. The thing is, he looks a lot like Jesus.

"Happened to get into a fight with Belinda—"

To Dillon's right is Belinda, twenty-one, who definitely looks like a hippie on the outside, but then when you make eye contact with her, you're not so sure there's a hippie on the inside too. There's something sharp behind her pupils that's especially surprising after you first take in her long, flowing skirt with tiny bells and her long, flowing hair. The color of her hair is so soft, it's almost peach.

I used to go to Disneyland all the time as a kid, and often you'd see the same eye thing in the women they hired to dress up as the princesses. They would kneel down next to you (well, it was more like they'd kneel down *near* you because of their gigantic hoopskirts) and smile and say, "You're so beautiful, you must be a princess too!" in the most singsongy voices.

But even when I was little and was supposed to believe they were real, I could look into their wide eyes and see a college girl who was baking in the sun and tired and bored and maybe even resented you a little bit for putting her in that position. And I totally got where she was coming from.

With Belinda, it isn't so much that she seems tired and bored, but it still seems like she's in a costume.

"Nah, why would I get in a fight with Belinda?" asks Dillon, giving a gentle elbow in her side. He seems good-natured.

"Maybe I'm going to eat your food," says Belinda.

Dillon smiles like he thinks she's making a joke, but at least to me, it's clear she's threatening him.

Catherine shrugs. "Maybe she's going to eat your food. Different personalities coming together, coming apart. Things are just going to emerge, like maybe Ricky is going to be the one who has a problem with you."

Ricky, who is eighteen, shakes his head. "My personal philosophy is that anyone who has a problem with somebody else needs to look at the *man in the mirror.*"

Ricky has got on a shiny glove like Michael Jackson used to wear. He's also got the start of the same skin condition that Michael Jackson had, but Ricky isn't wearing the glove because he wants to hide the white patches. The first thing he told me at breakfast was that he's proud of them because they mean that he's closer to Michael than your typical fan. He said, "Sometimes I like to think of myself like Michael reincarnated," which is tricky when you consider that Michael died after Ricky was born.

But I didn't point out that paradox because one, I didn't want to crush him. And two, when you're trying to change how others see you so you can see yourself differently, I think you have to start from scratch. Which means you have to be on from the very first impression.

Catherine pretends like she's a contestant interviewing to camera, using a different voice from her regular one. "Ricky spends all his time looking in the mirror. His ego has gotten *so* out of control!" She returns to her normal voice. "Just spitballing. But you see how there's a natural story to be pulled out of everything. We'll work with you. There are certain aspects of you that we might choose to emphasize, and then certain other aspects of you that we might choose to chop. . . ."

This chopping is already happening to Nikki from Hawaii, who I initially assumed was in high school because she showed up with a rough-looking woman who seemed to be her chaperone. But then we found out that Nikki's nineteen and that woman is her serious girlfriend, Rebecca.

I overhead the producers talking to Nikki about how she might want to keep Rebecca a secret while she's on the show. Not because she's in a lesbian relationship, but because Rebecca's pushing forty and kind of looks like the type who might accidentally set her house on fire when she falls asleep with a lit cigarette in her hand.

I mean, that's my best description of her, not theirs, but you can tell the producers are thinking along those lines because I've already heard them say things like "We're just suggesting that showing Rebecca might be . . . confusing."

To that Nikki asked, "Confusing, how?" but all Catherine was able to explain is that trying to put the two of them together requires a whole back story that the show doesn't have time to explore.

Now Nikki just shakes her head at Catherine and looks over at Rebecca, who's standing in the kitchen, talking with my mom. And maybe Nikki sees herself in her girlfriend, meaning that in her eyes, Rebecca is a dream hula girl straight from a movie beach party. Or maybe she sees Rebecca in herself. Like maybe Nikki looks at herself in the mirror and sees a lady bus driver who's starting to resemble the vinyl on her seat.

I really like the idea that love can transform you.

Catherine goes on. "That's where our story consultant will come in, to help make sense of what we're seeing of you. If there's been a fight, he might ask you to have it all over again when we're doing scene taping, which I think could be very healthy and cathartic. But no one's going to ask you to start a fight you weren't already going to have. No one's going to ask you to be the good twin"—Catherine's eyes sparkle with the next possibility—"or the evil twin."

She's talking about the eighteen-year-old twins with long weaves in pigtails, Mila and Felicia, but I can't tell them apart yet. It's not that they're wearing completely identical outfits (although they're both in denim cutoffs), but they do have the very same face. They went in the other van, so I haven't really met them yet, although one seems to be more the type that bounces off walls, while the other seems pretty quiet.

"And no one's going to force the two people in the house who are obviously the most dark and tortured into a satisfying dark-and-tortured romance." Catherine is not subtly staring between me and Gardener, who's wearing all black. On top of that, his hair is dyed black and it goes to his shoulders.

Today I'm wearing a white bustier top with blue jeans, on purpose, for America. It's not like Gardener and I are an obvious match, not like we're two Goth kids peering out at Catherine from under a shared velvet cape. And how about my last boyfriend, who looked like a goddamn ray of sunshine? But I'm not here to think about Scott.

"You think I'm dark and tortured?" I ask. "I'm not dark and tortured."

"Yeah, no, she's a ball of energy," Ford suddenly pipes up from over at the window.

To that I say, "If you want tortured, you should ask Ford what it's like where he's from."

Catherine blinks at me and then she says, "Bunch of characters on my hands. What, are you trying to junior produce? We'll get to that in his video package. Which reminds me . . . Madison?" She calls to a junior producer talking on a cell phone in the dining room. "Did we secure the ocean?"

Madison calls back, "There's a chalk festival on the boardwalk."

Catherine laughs. "I'm sorry, what?" To us she says, "Sit tight," and she goes to talk to Madison while still laughing about chalk.

"I swear, I don't think I'm going to fight with anybody," Dillon says to the group.

"Of course you aren't," I say, like a comforting presence would. The group starts talking about what it's going to be like once we get in the mansion, and it's not that I'm not interested, just that there are so many people talking. Rebecca's excited and one of the twins talks a mile a minute and Ricky keeps making those "Ow!" and "Whoo!" Michael Jackson sounds when he agrees with something.

It's like when you're on the Pirates of the Caribbean at Disneyland, and you enter into the pirate town part. The ride has this soundtrack of overlapping voices piping in from speakers in all directions so it feels like you're in the middle of a lot of hubbub. But you can't really make out what's being said.

Hubbub is such a weird word. If you just repeat it over and over.

Hubbubhubbubhubbubhubbubhubbubhubbubhubbubhubbub.

And hey, what's with all the Disneyland memories resurfacing today? My dad used to take me all the time up until the year before he died because the brokerage he worked for gave out corporate passes. I think the place is deeply knit into my formative understanding of things. . . .

And just like that, I've gotten lost in my own head and haven't participated in the conversation for at least five minutes. At this point it seems too unnatural to just jump in, so I decide I'm going to start over with the next one.

I look over at Ford by the window, and he's got his head tipped back a little, like he did when he was looking out from the roof. He seems to only take in views from the bottom of his eyes.

His hands are halfway slid into his pockets and he's got a

grin on his face as he looks out at the panoramic view. It's like he's alone with it, like none of these other people are around and someone just gave him the whole valley as a present.

Now that I'm getting a better look at him in daylight, I can tell he keeps his dark hair combed back with a little bit of gel. He's got the very beginning of a widow's peak. I heard he's only seventeen, but I'd assumed he was older, because he showed up without a chaperone and also, he has this sort of bruised quality around his eyes. I don't mean that he's actually got bruises, like he's been fighting. Although he does have a small bruise on his right cheekbone. So maybe he has been.

Fight or no fight, there's this slight purpleness under his eyebrows and under his lower eyelashes that makes him look like he's been up late every night for his entire life. But anyway, word in my van was that he's his own legal guardian. I don't know why that is.

He glances back over his shoulder and sees me.

"Come over here a sec," he calls over the other voices.

"Why?" I call back.

"Just come here."

"I don't need to say hello to Los Angeles. I live here, basically."

"I want to show you something. Activate the walk function on your control panel."

Since last night, I've revisited my feelings about being called a robot. The first thing that pops into your head when you hear you're robotlike is that you're a distant, unreachable husk who's impossible to connect with. But then I woke up today and asked myself, *What kinds of people have I said are robots before in my life?* And it's always been the people who are so upbeat and positive that they practically have little birds singing around their heads. So by the time I got out of the platform bed, I'd come around to the idea that Ford's first impression of me didn't have to be dispiriting.

Although I had just woken up from that dream where the two of us were collecting marbles together, and I can't say that didn't factor into my outlook.

Maybe out of lingering fondness for the dream version of Ford, I pretend to press a button on my back, and I get up from the couch. I walk over to the glass and stand next to him.

I see a bunch of treetops. "What is it?"

Ford nods at the window. "The wonder of nature."

From the awed tone of his voice I think he's about to point out a couple of squirrels or something even more mysteriously beautiful, like a family of deer passing by. Instead he hooks a finger in a belt loop of my jeans, pulling me toward him so that I can look out at a different angle. I'm surprised by the intimacy of that move.

Now I can see past this house's terrace to a neighboring backyard that's a little bit down the hill. There's some sort of fight going on between a blonde woman in a checked one-piece bathing suit and a bald man in a business suit. The woman is standing up in the hot tub, even though it's summer. And he's got a jacket on, even though it's summer.

Ford says, "She keeps scooping up water from the Jacuzzi with her hands and throwing it at him whenever he tries to talk to her."

The man starts gesturing with his hands. The woman bends and takes both her hands and pushes a wave at him. It soaks his loafers.

The man wrings out the bottom of his pants. He kicks over a fancy urn that makes an echoing clang on their patio. It's so loud, we can hear it softly through the glass from this distance.

I laugh. I've never seen a fancy urn go bouncing. "Can you tell what it's about?"

"Lovers' quarrel."

The way Ford says this is so Southern that the words sound like they're curling in on themselves. I copy his accent. "Lovers' quarrel."

Ford takes on my flattened Southern Californian accent. "Lovers' quarrel."

He sounds like a jokey imitation of a sun-bleached surfer. I mean, he kind of sounds like he's making fun of someone like Scott. The man now storms off back into the house, slamming a door we can't see.

"Are they broken up? Is it over for good?" I ask.

Ford watches the woman in the spa, who just stands there, frozen. "It's up to her," he says. "He kicked the urn 'cause she still gets to him. Watching them makes me feel right at home, except for them being too civil."

I think I'm about to hear him talk more about home to make up for last night, but all of a sudden Catherine is behind us, peering over our shoulders. One of her huge hoop earrings actually touches my face.

"What was that noise?" she asks. "Please don't tell me someone's doing construction in the neighborhood. Do I have to go stop a bathroom add-on?"

"Lovers' quarrel," Ford and I say almost at the same time.

Catherine sighs. "Oh, good." She pats the side of my thigh. I've never owned a horse, but still, I think this is the kind of pat you might give your pony. "Change of plans. We're doing introductions at the beach because I realized the couch is making it look like everyone's gathered for therapy at a drug addiction center. So we're skipping to taping vocal coaching segments now. Magnolia, you're up."

"Okay."

Her phone rings. "One sec," she tells me, and steps into the kitchen. I see my mom beam at her.

Ford and I remain there, keeping an eye on the woman in the bathing suit. She seems okay, not about to drown herself in the Jacuzzi or anything.

Finally Ford tilts his head down toward mine like he's going to share a secret. "I wasn't trying to be rude with you last night. It was just that I could have told you more and more things, but they wouldn't combine into anything that comes close to the whole picture."

I let that sink in for a second.

Then I have my say. "Nobody ever understands someone else's life in any kind of complete way, but oh my God, people should still *attempt* to piece something together for each other." Ford's chin jerks up in surprise. "People still *attempt* to talk about, like, their childhood dogs or some really great Halloween they had eight years ago. I mean, what are you supposed to talk to people about if you can't ask where they're coming from? Really, what were we supposed to talk about last night if the only stuff on the table was from when we met onward? Like, the moon? Did you want to have a conversation about how pretty the moon was?"

"You don't think it was pretty?" he asks slyly.

"Beautiful. So crescentlike. So yellowish," I say.

"So moon-shaped."

"So up there, in space."

He quickly touches under his eye, unconsciously, I think. Now that I'm closer, there definitely is a bruise. "It was bad where I'm from, okay? A bad run. So I'd rather start out fresh here without that on my back, following me around."

That's all I have to hear to understand what's going on,

even though I don't know a single specific about what's actually going on. But now I get it.

Out of curiosity I ask, "Have you ever thought about how it might be *you* following you around?"

Ford looks at me. He says, "Yes."

Then Catherine is back from her phone call and right away she takes my hand, steering me away with her.

9

My mom has this issue where she gets worried that black people won't like her. Not that she's ever explained this to me out loud, and I don't even know if she's really aware of it herself. But whenever I've been around her and she's been around a black person, she seems to work extra hard to come off like a cool lady, or at least what she thinks of as a cool lady, because she's nervous about being perceived as a sheltered white one. And that's because in southern Orange County, the truth is that sheltered white ones are mostly what's running around.

So as Stacy, the vocal coach, has me do some warm-up scales at the piano and can tell right away that I'm not trained, my mom jumps in and says, "Natural emotion is what produces a really cool tone in the voice, though. That's what makes Aretha Franklin so amazing."

At this point, I start hoping that she's not going to rattle off a list of black singers she finds amazing. One of the cameramen is filming us from the other side of the piano. His name is Hector, and he has a cigarette behind his ear.

"And Whitney Houston . . ." Mom continues. "My God, was she gorgeous. I listened to 'How Will I Know' a million times before my first date with Damien."

Damien was my dad. This is the first detail I've ever heard about that night. My parents had a habit of never talking about their pasts, and I barely know anything about them outside of what I was around for. Interest takes over my embarrassment. "Oh yeah, where was he taking you?" I ask.

"Stevie Wonder," my mom keeps going, even though I can tell she definitely heard my question.

Stacy decides to pull the plug on the list before we have to listen to a roll call of the entire Motown catalog. "If they sent Aretha in here next, I'd make her sing scales too," she says, then takes a last sip of the Frappuccino she's got sitting on top of the piano's high keys. She put her drink there for convenience when she realized I wasn't going to need them. She told me, "You've got one of those singing voices that sounds like there's always a tear hanging in the back of your throat," but it didn't seem like that was a good thing.

Now that I've done some scales, it's time to talk about my song choice for the first show. I have to pick a hit from the year I was born.

Stacy gives me a once-over. "This is the song that's going to introduce you to America. But it's not just a song. It's a movie you're putting into America's heads about your life. You open your mouth, and you want them to see a whole world built around you instead of just that cheesy-ass stage. They should see you getting up in the morning. They should see what you make yourself for breakfast. They should see you opening your closet and getting dressed for the day—"

"So half of it is picturing the audience naked, and then half of it is helping the audience picture *me* naked."

"She's kidding," my mom says to Stacy and the cameraman. "Sometimes people can't tell when she's kidding."

"I already know that about her from the way she sings," Stacy says. She evaluates me up and down. "There's an edge to you, and that's what we've got to play up so that people know who you are." Pulling out a list of old hits, she turns over her right hand and knocks a gold ring that goes across all four knuckles against a title.

I look. It's "Just a Girl" by No Doubt.

"I don't think that's the song," I say.

Stacy shakes her head once. "No, that's it. Edgy and cute at the same time. It says to America, 'I'm saucy, but don't worry, I'm still going to be a lot of fun.'"

"But the song isn't transparent. I want to be transparent."

"But people think it's fun."

"But I don't want there to be distance between what I'm singing and what I actually mean. Like I want to get up there and have people just, like, know me. Like I'm an open book."

My mom and Stacy are staring at me.

I try again. "I don't want to put on an act."

"Yes, that's exactly what you want to do," Stacy says. "You go up onstage to put on an act. That's what stages are for."

My mom, who's been sitting sideways in an armchair with her legs dangling over the arm, drops her head back in annoyance. She says my name, but like this: "Magnoliuggggggghhhhh."

Instead of just rejecting their ideas, maybe it's that I have to be more positive and offer something of my own. I take the list from the piano and look it over.

"There's some Hootie and the Blowfish on here," I say. Not really my kind of music, but has anybody ever seemed more approachable than that band? Also, Hootie and I have a similar vocal range.

Stacy takes her fingers and massages her jaw. "I'm going to take a break and see if they can get me another Frappuccino. Why don't you come get a drink with me?" she says meaningfully to my mom, which is code for, *Why don't you come give me a tip on how to manage this one?*

They walk out, comparing rings. Hector lowers his camera and follows them, pulling his cigarette from behind his ear.

I sit down at the piano and pluck out the first few notes of the only song I know how to play, Wham's "Last Christmas." When I was thirteen, my mom hired a piano teacher to teach it to me before a holiday party. I wasn't learning how to play the piano, just how to play the song. We didn't have a piano until my mom had a white baby grand delivered two days before the event.

After a couple of hours of cocktails, my mom turned down the stereo system, and I came downstairs and played "Last Christmas." The guests, some of them already drunk, danced in slow motion like huge nerds with swinging arms. Snapping and everything.

They all knew my dad had died two years earlier, but no one was acting like that had happened because one, my mom. And two, after a few months, that's over for other people. But sitting there on the piano bench, I was still unable to grasp that my dad was in a crypt. We'd never see each other again? It seemed impossible, maybe because you just don't picture attending your parent's funeral until you're an adult yourself. You don't imagine that you'll be in braces.

After "Last Christmas," I went back up to my room, shut the door, and listened to a call-in show on the radio about personal problems. We still have the piano.

"*Shit*, it's that time of year already?"

I look over my shoulder, and there's a sleepy-looking guy

I haven't seen before in the doorway. He's got on an oversized football jersey. His hair is a dark bob, if men can have bobs, and he has really bad posture.

"Kidding, kidding, I know what season it is," he says.

"I know," I say.

"I just had a baby, so that was new-parent humor about the confusion of time. Those kinds of jokes are mandatory." He wipes crust out of his eye with his ring finger. "I'm Lucien. I'll be figuring out what's going on with you during any given week and turning it into a piece of drama."

"You're the story consultant?"

"That's what they're calling me so they can pay me less, but yes. You're . . . Magnolia."

"Right."

He takes out a pocket notepad and looks at it. "Seventeen, from Dana Point, kind of rich but not *rich*-rich, here with your mom (who I just met outside), good grades in English but Yale's not going to take you because of your other iffy subjects, went through a semi-recent breakup—"

"Who told you that?"

"They gave me a file. I don't know what comes from where."

I say, "Oh cool, it's *1984*."

"Shit, it's that year again?" Lucien breaks into a big, purposely dumb smile. It's jarring because he goes from being half awake to crazily beaming like a cartoon bear. Then he yawns and says, "I was good in English too."

He starts to walk out. "Okay, well, I wanted to introduce myself. We'll sit down together tomorrow, and you can tell me whom you like, whom you want to destroy. Being around all these people all the time is probably going to be hard for you because you're an introvert."

Hair practically stands up on the back of my neck. "It says that in the file?"

"No." He puts the notepad back in his pocket.

"Then how do you know I'm an introvert after talking to me for two seconds?"

"Because you look more exhausted than I do."

10

When we get back to the hotel at night, I think about where I can go. I can't go to the lobby because it's impossible to be alone there, plus the DJ is loudly playing what sounds like mermaids rapping. I can't be alone on the rooftop because the bar and the pool are open until much later. I can't stay here in the room because my mom is lying on her side on the other bed, wearing a new shell bracelet, saying to me, "Mag, maybe you should give Stacy a call and smooth over this song thing. I got her number for you. I've heard that this business is more about making friends than even being good."

"I know, you're right," I say. "I'm going to go down to the lobby to see if anyone's still hanging out."

"You want me to come with?"

"You should go have a drink on the roof. Maybe that actress is there again."

"Only if you're not just going to sit here by yourself. I'll stay with you if you're lonely."

"No, I'm going downstairs."

My mom starts taking out her ponytail holder, saying, "My hair is so crazy from the ocean air. I'd have to get ready. . . ."

While she sits on the floor to evaluate the nighttime tops in her suitcase, I grab the hotel pad and pen on the nightstand next to the bed.

"See you in a little while," I say, and duck out the door. "Have fun, Mom."

The door clicks shut after me, and I walk past the elevator and the stairwell, down to the room where there's a sign that says ICE. It's the best option I've got. How many people really go through the effort of getting themselves ice?

Once I'm in the ice room I sit down against the wall behind the door. I smell like the beach. They had me spend the afternoon walking along the shore in a bikini top and a leather skirt. I thought about birds tweeting around my head and hoped it would show on my face.

Now I give myself over to the hum of the ice machine, which is incredibly comforting, and I put the pen to the pad. I start writing the next episode of *Ships in the Night*. Seeing as how I don't yet have a vocab list from the on-set tutor, I just pick up with one of my favorite characters, Warren Gettysburg, the rebellious son, letting him do whatever he wants.

I scribble in really bad handwriting: *Warren puts out his cigarette on his dad's gymnastics trophy from college. It leaves a mark, and Warren likes the message that sends to his family about how little he cares about his own health.*

Someone coughs.

For a moment I think I've gotten so absorbed in *Ships* that I'm hearing sound effects from Warren in my head. Then I lean over to see around the other side of the machine. One of the baby-faced twins is sitting back there with her knees up and her arms draped over them. She looks kind of like Rihanna before Rihanna became herself.

"Mila," she says.

I say, "Thanks," because I had no idea which one she was, only that she obviously isn't the twin who bounces off the walls. It must be really strange to share a face with someone else.

We stare at each other for a few seconds, neither of us seeming very motivated to say anything.

Finally I ask, "Did the story consultant tell you he thinks you're an introvert?"

"No." Mila rolls her eyes. "He said he thinks I have an attitude problem."

I nod and lean back against the wall, returning to my writing. Mila goes quiet except for occasionally kicking the ice machine, but it's clear she doesn't want to talk. We hang out like that for a couple of hours. I think we might be friends.

FORD

11

No one has picked out my clothes since I was probably about nine years old, and it only happened rarely back then. My mom would just toss me one of my brother's hand-me-downs when she noticed long sleeves were hitting at my elbows. That's why getting dressed by the wardrobe department makes me feel like a kid.

Still, it's a good thing they have stuff for me to wear, because I only brought two shirts, my black Led Zeppelin one and a plain white tee. I guess I figured I could wear the black shirt when I was rocking and the white shirt when I did one of those songs you sing from atop a stool in a lone spotlight.

Not saying the audience wouldn't notice that I was the guy who kept a rotating wardrobe of two shirts, but what's the big deal? The Beatles wore the same suits for, like, all of 1964. And they did all right.

I already met Robyn, who's the wardrobe department girl, earlier in the week by accident. On our first day on the lot, I was wandering around during the lunch break. She was trying to drag some racks, and it didn't seem to be going so hot because she was wearing some of the highest shoes I've ever seen in my life. The heels were so sharp, Sissy would consider using them as shivs. Robyn's one of those people who looks so cool that it's almost intimidating, but she seemed to need help, so I helped.

After that she told me, "I'm going to look out for you, kid." And I took that to mean she wasn't going to put me in anything too terrible.

When I walk into wardrobe today, Robyn's in the middle of arguing with some tattooed-up guy. At least she's *trying* to argue with him, but the guy just leans back and grins at her, all confident like he knows she can't stay mad. He goes in for a hug, but she crosses her arms.

"You can't just show up here without calling first. This is my job, Spider." Yeah, he does look like a guy who'd be named Spider. Not because he's skinny or anything, but because he looks like something you don't want to find in your house. When Robyn sees me, she gives an apologetic look and holds up a wait-one-second finger.

I amble over to the far side of the room to give them some space, stepping around what seems like hundreds of pairs of shoes. To seem like I'm busy, I start looking through some of the clothes. The outfits are complicated flashy-looking stuff. A lot of rivets. A lot of foil too—not the kind you use to cook, but thinner stuff. I can't imagine myself wearing half of it, but then I couldn't have imagined most of what's happened this past week.

I can't remember having this much attention paid to me ever. After we all officially met each other for vocal coaching, we spent the afternoon filming our "video packages" down by the ocean. When they were fixing my hair, this guy Lucien introduced himself and started reading from his notepad the things he knew about me.

"Dad's been in jail before, mom's been in jail before, siblings been in jail before. . . ." He looked up at me. "Well, shit, it's like you came straight from *The Outsiders*."

"Something like that," I said. He told me we'd have to have a discussion later about whether I wanted to come off as a Ponyboy or a Johnny.

Then it was time for my first interview on-camera, and I told the truth about myself, mostly. Except I might have misled them a little about my family. Like, I might have told them my family was all dead.

Maybe that was the wrong thing to do, but it's hard to explain the whole emancipation thing to people in a three-minute clip. *I love a good pizza and playing the guitar and oh yeah, I got myself legally emancipated from my family due to gross negligence. You know how that sort of thing goes.*

After I finished the interview, Catherine called Lucien over and they huddled, talking in low voices, looking over at me every once in a while. I wanted them to just say whatever it was out loud.

Was Catherine disappointed with the interview? Did she know I was lying?

Skip, one of the cameramen, leaned out from behind his equipment. He was wearing an old Metallica concert shirt also owned by my dad. That just shows you how music can travel.

"Condolences," he said.

When Catherine and Lucien broke up their whisper session, she had Skip film me riding my motorcycle down to the end of the pier. She was really excited about this, even though it didn't make any sense. I'm pretty sure piers are more for fishing off than cruising on. Then I was supposed to just idle there and stare out at the ocean, like I was thinking of riding straight across it. It's pretty hard not to start laughing when the director's yelling at you to gaze out over the water with a "dreamy expression." I'd just try to look like I was concentrating on something far away. And then he'd yell, "Dreamier!"

It all made me wonder if Johnny Depp has trouble not laughing on set when he's supposed to be acting all serious about something. Probably not, though. He's probably real professional.

Right when the producers wanted me to pick up a dried starfish like I just happened to find it on the deck, I noticed Magnolia watching me from the side. I knew the starfish thing was corny. I felt real stupid holding it.

But Catherine said it was a metaphor, like I was pondering becoming a star. She told me to think hard about looking hopeful, but honestly, all I was thinking about was that I didn't want that girl watching me right then.

Earlier I had seen Magnolia getting ready for her shoot. She didn't seem as blown away by all of it. She has this sort of presence about her—maybe that's why they let her just walk naturally along the shore. They didn't need her to be standing on a pier, gawking like some white-trash kid who's never seen an ocean.

The important thing is, I'm trying to keep it professional like Johnny Depp, and I do everything they ask. I mean, if gazing at things dreamily is a part of a career path that doesn't include digging ditches or flipping burgers, then just point me at an ocean or a mountain or whatever, and I'll gaze at it like it's Keira Knightley.

What's harder to get used to are the production assistants, who I now know are on the bottom rung of TV jobs. They're always trying to fetch me bottled water, or following me around like store detectives who think I've just shoplifted. This one guy, Jesse, he's constantly hanging around about ten feet away from me, reporting my every move over his walkie-talkie.

"I've got a twenty on Ford. He's on the move, heading to the cooler. Over."

Look, I know it's his job, but I feel a little embarrassed because these people are older than me, and college graduates shouldn't be wasting their day tracking my hydration.

I've been trying to give Robyn and Spider some room to yell at each other, but they just keep moving my way. When it finally becomes obvious to the guy that she isn't going to suddenly forgive him for whatever, his laid-back attitude turns ugly fast.

"You think I need you?" he asks. "Because I don't." But instead of leaving, he starts trying on jackets, roughly, like it's the jackets he's mad at.

Spider moves to the rack next to me and looks me up and down. I guess he would be handsome except he has these really crazy, intense eyes—bright blue with a darker blue outline around them. Maybe that sounds nice, but trust me when I say that they make him look crazy, kind of dangerous really. There's something in them that reminds of my uncle Red, who's serving a fifteen-year sentence for armed robbery. Uncle Red is nuts.

"What are you doing? You can't treat this place like your personal closet!" Robyn says, but Spider pulls on a purple sports coat from the rack anyway.

"Chill out." He doesn't look at her. "I'm just going to borrow it for the meeting with this designer. She needs someone to do her new look book."

Robyn tries to take the jacket off him. "Property of the show. If you need something nice to wear, I can loan you money—"

It's pretty obvious that Spider doesn't like that idea because his face immediately twists up in anger. "I don't need your money!" he yells, and goes to slap away her hand. But he's a strong guy. He almost knocks her over.

"Whoa, take it easy, man," I say, putting a hand on his upper arm.

"Who the hell are you?" Spider turns on me like he's only just noticed I'm in the room, even though he looked straight at me before. I drop my hand pretty fast.

"I'm Ford."

For a second I think he's gonna take a swing at me. It's hard to tell what a guy with eyes like that is thinking.

"Ford? Why don't you mind your own business?"

"I will," I say in a real measured way. "Just take it easy, okay?"

He shakes his head like he can't believe anyone would want

him to calm down. "What are you, a contestant? You think you're a celebrity or something because of this ridiculous show? Another kid who thinks he *deserves* to be famous. I got bad news for you: you don't deserve shit. You thought you were gonna hop off the bus and everyone in Hollywood would be just waiting for you to arrive?"

"I didn't take a bus." I shrug. This just seems to make him angrier.

He takes a step toward me, and I think, *Here we go.* Story of my life. I tense up my hands. Either I find the trouble, or the trouble finds me.

But then Robyn pulls me back gently by the shoulders. "Stop it, Spider. Just take the coat and go before you get me fired."

"Oh, that's right, you're afraid I'm going to mess up your mini-career. You get a job dressing Justin Bieber wannabes, and now you're too good for me? You wouldn't be anything if I hadn't booked you on that first job. Don't forget that."

"How could I? You bring it up every five minutes."

Spider looks at me like this whole thing is my fault. "Good luck with the singing. You know no one's going to remember you in two months, right?" Then he backs out the door, giving Robyn a betrayed look as he exits.

"Oh, man," Robyn says, and sighs. "Sorry about him. Embarrassing." She rolls her eyes toward the ceiling. "I probably look like a serious idiot now."

"Nah, you just look like someone who's too good for whoever that guy was," I say.

"Ex-boyfriend." She glances around and grabs a measuring tape off a table. "I mean, he's supposed to be my ex-boyfriend, but our breakups never stick. Somehow he always ends up back in my life." She wraps the measuring tape around my waist.

"How long have you been together?"

"Forever. He's a photographer, and we met when he pulled me from the boutique I was working in to style a spread." She writes down some measurements on a card.

"Photographer, huh? Hard to imagine him working the Sears portrait studio."

Robyn laughs, measuring my neck. "Not that kind of photographer. He wasn't always a jerk. He used to be really fun. When we first got together we did all these celebrity shoots, like this big one in London with Vin Diesel right before *The Fast and the Furious*. Then Spider pissed Vin Diesel off—he was using his name to get into restaurants—and that was that. He's been booked a lot less since. It's no good anymore, but we just keep getting back together anyway. Pretty lame, right?"

I shake my head. "I know what it's like with people who are bad for you. Everyone thinks you can just walk away, but the bigger the mess, the harder it is to get untangled."

"Yes!" She holds her hands out like I just gave her a trophy. "It's such a mess, but every time I end it, somehow he guilts me right back into the relationship."

"He's probably just angry at you for succeeding where he failed. Back home, some people I was close to, they didn't like it so much when I tried to go in my own direction. I guess they thought that I was somehow judging them just by existing a different way. With some people, you being happy makes them miserable."

She stops measuring and gives me a serious look. "Ford, don't take this the wrong way, but you're smarter than you look. I mean, good-looking guys, not always so bright, y'know."

"Well, as long as you think I'm good-looking." I grin.

"A little young for me, though. You have a girlfriend?"

"The last one was a few months back, but her parents wouldn't let her see me anymore. Her dad's the 'Mattress King of Northeast Arkansas.' I guess I wasn't up to the standards required to become the Mattress Prince." I shrug. "But I don't blame him. If I was her father, I wouldn't have let her date me either."

I almost explain to Robyn about my family's reputation back

home. Then I remember I'm not supposed to have a family who's alive to cause trouble.

Robyn looks angry again, like she did when I walked in on her and Spider. "Well, she's going to feel like a total idiot because you are gonna be world famous in a couple of weeks. Then she's going to be begging you to take her back. Her stupid Mattress King dad too."

"It's okay, I wasn't in love with her anyway." I tip my head back. "But you think so? About being famous?"

"Yep. And I'm gonna do everything I can to help you win this thing by making you look uh-mazing. Don't tell the others, because there's not supposed to be favoritism among the crew. But the truth is—" She drops to a whisper. "I always play favorites. I have a favorite parent. I have a favorite sister. I bet when I have kids, I'll even love one more than the rest."

I let that one sink in. "So . . . what do you think of the other contestants? Have you met Magnolia?"

"The girls don't come in until this evening. Why, who's Magnolia?"

"Just another contestant."

Robyn gets an excited, intrigued look on her face. "The one contestant you're asking me about . . ."

"She's just the one whose name I remember best," I say, playing it down. "Unusual name."

"Uh-huh." Robyn nods, but her eyes aren't buying it.

Once she gets to work bringing me clothes to try on, it doesn't seem like she's ever going to stop. This isn't the kind of stuff you might buy at your local JCPenney. She's got me putting on a purple puffy vest with bleached-out skinny jeans and chunky neon tennis shoes; a fur-lined leather parka and giant gold rope chain necklaces and a red baseball hat; a leopard-print jacket and short pants that stop halfway up my shin.

"Are you sure these aren't just long shorts?" I ask her, but she holds out her pinky, wraps it around mine, and swears that they're pants.

She has me trying on a big scarf that half covers my face (like you need a scarf in Los Angeles) and some kind of army coat with the sleeves ripped off. Black leather jackets and white leather jackets and red leather jackets; thin black dress ties and medallions and big belt buckles.

I'm trying to figure out which of these outfits looks like it belongs on a guy who's capable of winning a million dollars and an American stadium tour. I'm staring at myself in a tight Navajo-patterned sweater, silver pants, and weird sunglasses that look like somebody's covering your eyes with their hands, when doubt starts to set in.

I can tell that Robyn's really good at her job, but I'm just not so sure I can pull this stuff off.

"I'm sure some people would look great in this. But I don't know," I say, taking off the hand glasses. "It's like Halloween. I usually only wear a T-shirt and jeans. I feel kind of stupid."

"T-shirt and jeans are cool. That can be very cool. But hear me out, Ford." She gets serious, and I'm reminded that she said she was going to look out for me. "In this contest, you only have a few minutes to make an impact. After you win, you can perform in a garbage sack and people will think it's cool. We don't have to go all crazy." She pulls off the Navajo sweater. "But we should at least pick out one thing that's, y'know—"

"Memorable," I finish.

"Yeah. I want you to be yourself, but it's just showmanship, man. Y'know. Theater." As she says *theater*, she uses her hands to dramatically reveal her face, like she's a magician.

"Showmanship."

"Look at it this way: you didn't come all the way from Arkansas just to be what you've always been. You came to reinvent yourself, yeah?"

I step over to the racks to look through my choices again. "I guess

I do think this jacket is kind of cool." It's slick black satin with a red silhouette of a ram's head on the back. "I mean, I'm an Aries."

"Now we're talking. Take it with you, sleep in it, make it yours."

"I do think I'm going to pass on these pants, though." I gesture at the silver pants. "I don't want them exploding if I microwave something." We smile at each other.

"Don't worry, dude, I'll get you some real jeans. Without rhinestones or anything."

Another one of the contestants, Dillon, walks in for his wardrobe appointment. I talked to him for a while yesterday when we were waiting for vocal coaching to start, and he strikes me as an earnest but good guy. We give each other a slide handshake and shoot the shit for a couple of minutes while Robyn takes his measurements.

When she goes to the other side of the room to grab Dillon a pair of shoes, he asks me softly, "Did you see my wardrobe yesterday at the beach?"

"No." They'd split the group up into two different camera crews so everyone could get done in a day. Dillon was with the bunch on the other side of the pier.

"I don't want to complain, but they put me in a Tommy Hilfiger shawl-neck cardigan," he tells me. "How many Jews do you know who wear Tommy Hilfiger?"

I laugh. "I don't know any Jewish people except you," I say. And that makes Dillon laugh too.

Robyn presents Dylan with a pair of velvet slippers, and I head over to check out my new outfit in the mirror. Studying myself, I try to imagine the Mattress King, with his purple robe and his scepter made of mattress springs, bowing down before me.

12

As I'm pushing the button for the elevator, I catch my reflection in the mirrored doors. The feeling is like I'm one of those guys in a movie who's jumped into someone else's body.

They trimmed my hair and now it lays different somehow. Zara, the hair stylist, said it was her version of young Elvis. I know it's only a new hairstyle and a fashion magazine jacket, but I have this odd sensation of not recognizing myself. What's more, I can't say if I'm excited or freaked out about it.

The mirrors slide away and reveal Magnolia. You know that rush of adrenaline or whatever it is you get under your chest that lets you know that you wanted to see someone more than you'd even realized? That's what I have right now.

"Hi," she says.

"Hey," I say.

"Are you getting in?" she asks at the same time I'm asking her, "You getting out?"

She shakes her head. "The past couple of nights I've told my mom I'm hanging out downstairs, but I've actually been going to the ice room. For personal space. I make sure to at least make the stop down here so it isn't a gross lie." She has this habit of talking with her hands, demonstrating what's up, what's down for me as if she operates on her own compass. It's pretty cute.

I step into the elevator. "You hang out in the ice room?" Her floor is pressed, and I hit mine.

"It's not much to look at. But the ice cubes don't suggest new choreography to me." She leans against the opposite wall, her hair falling down around her face. "You looked like you were getting pretty close with that starfish yesterday."

I look doleful. "She left me for a sea urchin."

The elevator chimes because we're at my floor. I take a look at Magnolia. I feel suddenly compelled to hook a finger in the loop of her jeans again and pull her near me, but I just say, "Have a good night." I walk out.

"Ford—"

I turn, and she's blocking the sensor with her hand so the doors won't close. "I heard a rumor going around that both of your parents are dead."

All the adrenaline from first seeing her plunges down into my stomach like it's a fist. "Right," I say. "That's true."

"I'm sorry." Her face transforms, and she looks like she could almost cry. The change startles me.

"No, it's okay—"

"No, that's just what you say."

I nod.

"My dad died from cancer a few years ago, so I know too." She removes her hand from the sensor. "I just wanted to say that I'm sorry. We don't have to talk about it now. Or ever." The elevator doors begin closing. "Since I'm assuming that's a big part of what you're trying to leave behind."

We look each other in the eyes. Doing that makes me want to tell her what I've done. I could just tell her I made up a stupid lie. But then the next thing I know, I'm just looking at myself in the shiny door, and she's gone.

13

For the first show I'm going to be singing "Where Did You Sleep Last Night?" Nirvana made it popular in the nineties, which is why I can use it, but it's a much older song. No one even knows who wrote it. It just appeared out of the mists of the old Appalachian Mountains almost a hundred years ago.

I love songs like that. They seem ancient and mysterious to me, like they have secrets I'll never totally understand no matter how many times I hear them.

The lyrics are all about this guy demanding this girl not to lie to him, to tell him where she slept last night. The answer goes:

In the pines, in the pines,
where the sun don't ever shine.
I would shiver the whole night through.

Now, I don't know if he's singing about his girlfriend or a daughter or what, and I don't even know what's meant by "in the pines," exactly, but it sounds like a dark and lonely place. Like she's gone someplace or seen or done something too terrible to even speak of.

The way Kurt Cobain sings it really makes me catch my breath.

When he sings, you know the pines are a kind of place you can't come back from, or at least you don't come back the same kind of person. You know the people in this song aren't ever gonna be the same after this. At least, that's what I hear when I'm listening to the track alone in my hotel room tonight. Leander would just call it the blues.

If it turns out the audience wants to hear something more upbeat or more danceable or whatever, then it'll be me who's "in the pines." For me, the pines are back home in Calumet, where the sun hasn't really ever shined on me so much.

But I'm going with this song anyway because one, I love it and two, the producers want me to play up what they're calling my "roots." They want me to bring out my guitar (well, not *my* guitar, which Cody pawned, but the one they've given me), and they want to project some kind of rural tree scene on the stage behind me while I sing. Stacy, the vocal coach, says I have to show my soul.

Since I'm working on being professional, none of this is a problem.

Magnolia

14

"Sorry in advance if I hurt your head, but we've got to get this out quick," Zara says.

There's less than an hour until the first show goes live, but ten minutes ago, after I was already in full makeup and wardrobe, the producers decided that I should be something more exotic than a brunette. So Zara, the hair stylist, basically poured on some dye.

"Yes," I said when they first made the suggestion. "Definitely."

I really like the idea that it could be possible to change from the outside in. Bright hair. Bright outfit. Bright eyes. And then there will be actual brightness from the spotlight, of course.

Maybe I could be the kind of person who gets energized by being in the presence of lots of other people. You can't be the girl who's drawn to the corner when you're the girl who sings on a stage. And if other people see you as the second girl, then maybe you can actually move around as her in your life. You can meet people as her. They won't know any different. And then you don't have to feel like such a fraud for adopting this outward exuberance. You can become the kind of person who other people enjoy, if you can just get over your voice sounding tinny in your own ears.

My hair's supposed to turn out a shade of magenta (Zara described it to me as "not red, not purple, and without the baggage that burgundy carries with it"), but I'm taking her word for it because she's been keeping a warm towel wrapped around my head.

My mom has already been seated in the audience. Before leaving, she took both of my hands, held them to her heart, and said, "I can't believe I made you. I'm really proud. I'm really, really proud." She was practically glowing, and it wasn't because of makeup.

I had the thought that even if I can't win, maybe I've done something for her. I didn't notice so much when I was really little, but once I became more aware of people's feelings, I could tell how badly she wanted to be chosen. It's like she's been waiting and waiting for the world to Red Rover her over to the side of the people who are watched. I know being here as my mom is only second best. But it's something.

Now Zara's violently shampooing me. It's like my skull is her piggy bank and she's trying to shake out her last penny.

We're out in a trailer on the back lot, and the sun is just starting to set, so the light coming in through the windows is blurring everything with goldenness. I have such anticipation about what tonight is going to change for me that I relax by imagining that Zara and I are two girlfriends in a doublewide in a field somewhere in the South, just doing hair. And I guess I'm imagining somewhere in Arkansas, where Ford is from, even though I've never even seen that part of the country before.

I can't help it, the last couple of days I've been thinking what his life back there looked like. Both of his parents are dead. Did he live alone?

"It's looking so good!" Zara shrieks with the underwire of her bra pressed right against my forehead.

"I'm excited!" I say. I mean, hair changes are no joke. Hair is an emotional thing. Look at Samson. Look at every girl who's ever cried because her hair got cut too short. Look at how my mom acted when she found her first gray one night while she was plucking her eyebrows.

"I've never dyed my hair before. I mean, I messed with Sun-In once in seventh grade, but I wouldn't count that."

"I think you're going to love it."

She does one last rinse and then sits me up. I can see myself in the mirror across from the chair. Even though my hair is still wet, the color almost glows off it like some kind of unreal halo. Like there's a mist made out of fruit punch and grape soda evaporating around my head.

"This is *great*," I say.

Jesse the PA throws open the door to the trailer. He's visibly sweating. "They need Magnolia back in wardrobe ASAP—they want to switch out her shoes. Also, they're sending McKinley over to you in two seconds because his mom wants you to work on that weird curl he has."

Zara says, "Shit!" and grabs a hairdryer so fast that you can see she probably wouldn't be all that bad with a gun if you dropped her into one of those old saloons.

There's the South again, I think.

I flip my head upside down for her and stare at my feet.

"What's wrong with these shoes?" I yell. Zara doesn't hear me. They're iridescent high-tops that have lights in the soles when you walk on them. Bright shoes.

She straightens me up and dries my hair with her fingers while leaving it sort of undone like I've just rolled out of bed in time for the show. Then she pushes me outside to go back to wardrobe.

I head across the lot. Crewmembers are going about their jobs in golf carts and sunglasses like it's an ordinary afternoon. Up on the hill, the tram that gives tours of the studios wraps around a corner. It is incredibly weird to think that after tonight, next time the people in the tram see me they might go, *Hey, we know her.*

Mila is suddenly walking beside me in a white sequined minidress.

"Hey," I say.

Even though we've been hanging out in the ice room the past couple of nights, we haven't really had a full conversation yet. Last night all she said was, "My sister won't stop talking," and I said, "My mom, either," and that was it. But I would say there's a certain understanding between us.

I know she's got this reputation for having a bad attitude—like when the choreographer wanted us to practice holding the mic, Mila said, "I've had a hand my whole life," and left for lunch early. But if you pay careful attention to the subtleties of how she acts, I don't actually think she has a chip on her shoulder. I think it's just that she really hates to bullshit.

"Hey," she says. "Did you also get called back to wardrobe?"

"They don't like my shoes."

"Your hair looks good."

"Thank you," I say, knowing that she's not the type to say something like that just to be nice. "Yours too."

They've kept her hair in long pigtails, French-braided at the scalp, maybe because she insisted. There's something very resolute about her.

She says, "Belinda the hippie is smoking salvia in her dressing room."

I'm blown away by this information. I only know about salvia because of all the press Miley Cyrus got when she had to explain it wasn't weed in her bong. I've never gotten into casual drug use, probably because I have control issues. "What?"

"Belinda's an intense girl."

"I know, but she's about to perform on national TV. That seems like it would really put a lot of additional pressure on you, you know? To possibly be going out of your mind while you're trying to sing and hold the microphone in the right way?"

"I've seen weirder preshow routines. My sister always spends the half hour before she has to perform in a headstand. She thinks the blood in her head gives her more energy. Like she needs more."

I raise my eyebrows in agreement.

"She's been doing it since we were five."

McKinley passes with his mom, coming out of wardrobe, and he winks at us. Mila shakes her head at him like she's saying no to the wink.

"She's been performing since she was five?" I ask.

"Both of us, since we were two. We were child stars," Mila says, opening the door to wardrobe.

"There's my guh-irls!" shouts the show's stylist, Robyn, over rap coming from her laptop as we step in.

Surprised by what Mila just said, I study her profile and imagine her as a kid, trying to place her from some old sitcom or movie. This isn't a hard thing to imagine because like I said, the twins have got the kind of face that makes it seem like childhood was just over for them yesterday. While I'm looking at Mila, Robyn places a pair of black Doc Martens in my hands.

"Put these on," she orders. "They said they wanted you to have a more rock look." She rolls her eyes. "They have no idea what rock is. They think it's a skull temporary tattoo from the mall. But okay, sure, I know how to interpret their language."

Mila grabs a hanging sea-foam green dress that belongs on an ice skating rink and starts to change. "I found out my sister's wearing sequins," she explains.

I look at the Docs. "I'm trying to go . . . light. I'm trying to go bright."

Robyn shrugs. "I think they're concerned your song is a little, like, drippy and so they want to edge you up."

"Drippy!" I say. "Drippy?"

A ringtone goes off that's the chorus of Kanye's song about being a douchebag. Robyn says, "Ugh, I have to take this call—it's my boyfriend," and then she ducks out of the trailer to talk.

I sit down in a chair and stare back and forth between my high-tops and the Docs. "So you've already been famous before?" I ask Mila.

"That's debatable." She turns around for me to zip her.

"Why is it debatable?"

"You get called a child star if you were a child and you had regular paying work. It's like being called a porn star."

I know what she means. A teacher from my high school was fired after someone's parents found out she was a "porn star," and all that entailed was a gross couch in a video on the Internet.

Mila turns and goes to look at herself in the mirror on the

wall. "This is very black-girl Tinker Bell," she says, fluffing the skirt.

"Did you and your sister used to do that thing where you played the same kid?"

"All the time. When we got older, we auditioned for everything as twins—like to play twins. Then Felicia started getting called back for things I didn't, because people like her better in a room. When I was a small kid, I thought I wasn't socially well adjusted because I never went to normal school. But then I had to realize that Felicia didn't either." She takes off the white heels she was wearing and starts going through Robyn's shoe racks for a new pair. "Did you ever hear about the *The All-New Mickey Mouse Club*? It used to have Britney Spears and Justin Timberlake and Ryan Gosling and all those people before they were famous."

When I was younger, in the days back when my parents were still together, my mom would show me clips of *The All-New Mickey Mouse Club* online and say things about Spears and the rest like, "They all started early. Maybe if someone had started me early . . ." She's a pretty creative person, but I know she always dreamed of having a specific talent that other people could point to in her.

Anyway, from what I remember, that show was canceled before the midnineties. Mila's only a couple of years older than me, and I don't think the club ever had a baby as a member.

"Aren't you too young to have been on that?"

"The one with Britney. But a couple of years ago they were going to do *The New New Mickey Mouse Club*. I learned how to do backflips for the audition. Felicia's personality is a double layout triple tuck whatever whatever that's followed by ten double pikes. So they cast her. I can't compete in a room." She shrugs to herself.

"I only casually watch gymnastics during Olympic years. But I get what you mean," I say. "I'm surprised they let her be on this show. Aren't we all supposed to be amateurs?"

"That pilot never made it to air."

"Oh."

"I'm a big enough person that I can admit that made me a little bit happy."

I stand to go take a look in the mirror alongside Mila. During my fitting the other day, I really pressed for Robyn to put me in something upbeat. The producers wanted me to show some skin, so the compromise that resulted is what you'd technically call a tube top, and it's made out of shiny leotard material that's iridescent like the sneakers. I turn one way, it looks pink. I turn another, it looks green. It kind of has that rainbow effect, and who could ever say a rainbow is dark and tortured?

My white pants are very tight with a high rise, so you can only see the barest sliver of skin, right under my ribcage. The outfit isn't something I'd wear to school and it's not something you'd wear to your grandmother's house, but it's making me feel hopeful.

And I want to keep my matching shoes.

I say, "I'm keeping my shoes."

"Okay, get down with your bad self." Mila looks at me curiously. "Is that like a journal or a diary that you're always writing in when you're in the ice room?"

"It's not about my life, but kind of."

Jesse, now sweaty, runs into wardrobe, out of breath. "Catherine wants everyone waiting in their dressing rooms. Now," he says. "Need you two to head over this second."

Robyn still hasn't come back from her phone call, but Mila shrugs and says, "We look finished to me."

"But is a person ever really finished?" I'm joking, but I'm also not joking.

"Well, here's a bracelet," Mila says, and she hands me one off her wrist, but she's kind of joking too.

15

Tonight I'm singing "Wonderwall" by Oasis. Stacy the vocal coach isn't a fan. The past few days she's been telling me every chance she gets that it's too depressing, it's too abstract, it's too British. Now I find out that the producers think it's drippy. But out of all the songs on the list from the year I was born, this is the one that speaks to me.

The recorded version starts off kind of bratty, with singer Liam Gallagher sounding like he's ready to abandon whomever he's singing to. Like he hopes she gets the trouble she deserves. You think he's angry and maybe even uncaring, but then he comes to the line about no one else feeling the way he does about her. And all of a sudden, you understand he's just said those first few lines because he's hurt.

So in a way, the song starts out as a lie because he's trying to hide how deep his feelings run for this girl, but as he sings, his defenses break down. He can't keep up the lie anymore. I know exactly what that's like because I have a tough time with pretending to be something I'm not too. That's why I've had to stop talking to Scott.

It's been almost two weeks since I hung up on him, and

I've successfully resisted picking up the phone at least three times. I came closest to calling him after the first day of introductions. I just wanted to talk to someone who knows me. Because I want to believe he knows me under the good face I put on for him this summer, trying to seem like I was a mature person who could handle separations without getting too upset. But I've reminded myself that that's the reason Scott couldn't stop calling me—because he wanted to feel known too, even if he didn't want to admit to the strangeness that had settled between us—and that it's not enough.

So anyway. Then you come to the chorus.

Liam's voice loses the brattiness, and it's initially replaced by what I hear as helplessness. Helplessness that sets in because he wants to get through to this girl so badly, and he wants her to grasp what she means to him, but he's really nervous that he's not going to be able to do it. And then finally, at the end of the chorus, he desperately says that she's his wonderwall. And what's so moving is that there's actual wonder in the way he sings that word. He's trying to show her the wonder he associates with her by dragging that experience out of himself, by turning it inside out. That's what gets me.

I really like the idea that love can have so many complicated layers.

When I was printing out the lyrics to learn them, I found an interview in which Liam's brother, Noel, the writer of the song, described it as being about "an imaginary friend who's gonna come and save you from yourself." And isn't that something that everybody wishes they had in their lives? And doesn't that make the song the very opposite of abstract?

16

Mila and I hustle to the backstage area, where people in headsets and a bunch of guys in faded concert shirts are yelling and
pointing and just generally being the embodiments of stress.
You can hear the hum of the audience and the bass from the
hype music playing on the other side of the walls. We squeeze
by and continue down a more muted hallway to the row of
rooms with our names posted on the doors.

Earlier today I heard that the skylights are back in, so we're
moving into the mansion after the after-party tonight. Mila's
about to go into her dressing room when I feel like I should do
something to cement what I think is a burgeoning friendship.
Talking to her has reminded me that hanging out doesn't have
to be this massively pressured group thing. You can just like
someone's company. You can just sense that you don't have
to perform for each other because everything's already there.

"I wanted to ask you something," I say.

"Sure."

"Do you want to be roommates?"

It's an optimistic feeling to have accidentally stumbled into
this friendship.

She looks like she might be thinking the same thing. "Yeah," she says. "Definitely."

"So do I."

"Done. See you out there." Mila presses the lever to go into her dressing room. But as I'm turning from the door, she pokes her head out. "One more thing. Don't think differently of me as a person after you see me onstage." Then she shuts the door.

"What?" I say to myself.

The contestants haven't been allowed to watch each other in individual rehearsals, so I have no idea what Mila or anyone else actually sings like. We're going to be seated on the side of the stage during performances because Catherine says they want to "capture the experience of newness on your faces. Like those videos on YouTube where a fat-headed baby gets a load of a sneeze for the first time."

"Maggie," Ford calls as I'm continuing down the hallway. I look over.

"No one really calls me that," I say, but in a friendly way. I'm feeling very friendly all around this evening.

"Well, maybe I'll be someone by the time this whole thing is over." He catches up to me. "Look at you," he says, meaning my hair.

"Well, look at you too." They've put him in a jacket, kind of like the shape of a letterman one, but in black satin, and a pair of jeans that are tighter than what I've seen him wear of his own choosing. His hair is also maybe a little higher than usual in the front.

He leans against the wall, his body turned toward me, and for some reason this reminds me of how guys will stand against a locker while they're waiting for you to get your books. It makes me start to run through a theoretical idea of what it would be like if we'd met at school. What would I think of him? What would he think of me? The answers are hard to sort out because we met on top of a weird hotel in the middle of the night in disorienting circumstances. So everything I come up with just seems imaginary.

"Do you have anyone out there to see you?" I ask. He's got to have someone in the world. I mean, relatives, friends, someone.

He keeps his eyes on me. "No. Doesn't matter. I'm excited."

My mom's out there in the third row with McKinley's mom and one mature, leathery girlfriend of a contestant. I know she's got to be very, very thrilled right this second, the theater filling with people talking around her and the neon lights running along the stage and top 40 playing in surround sound, even from the rafters.

And I get this jolt of excitement too, this feeling of something really being about to happen. It comes over me like the world's most forceful crush. It makes me want to say crazy things to Ford that have no basis in reality. Things about how I wish I could have met him in what I'm imagining as his South (which in my head is mostly based on having read *Where the Red Fern Grows* in elementary school) because I wish I could already know him. That doesn't make any sense, I know, but it's kind of like that feeling of seeing something you really want in a window, so you just want the glass to drop away.

The air feels like it's whirring or buzzing around me.

"What's going on?" Ford kind of smiles and tips his head back to look at me out of the bottom of his eyes, like he does.

"If only we could . . ." is all I can think to say. That's it. I don't have the rest.

"Could what?" he asks, but now he's really smiling at me like he knows something I don't. The music in the theater gets louder in the background. There's applause.

I don't know how he could have some idea of what I was going to say when *I* don't even have a clue, so that makes me say to him, "What? What is it?"

The stage manager comes running down the hall, yelling that the show is about to start and she needs the girls lined up for our introductory walk and waves. The air is quivering, if air can quiver.

I ask Ford again, "Seriously, what is it?"

He comes off the wall, and I would swear he's looking at my mouth. I'm looking at his mouth back, because the way he's looking at me compels me to spend a few seconds on the shape of his lips.

Then the stage manager puts her hands flat on my back and practically does my walking for me. "Batter up," she says, moving me toward the door to the stage. I look away from Ford because I have to. The stage manager and I step into darkness, but then, as I round the corner, I can see the stage glowing violet through the slots of the wings.

I'm put in the front left wing, and then I see the host, Lance Thrasher, run onto the stage with his mic in hand. He has a shit-eating grin that doesn't budge, and his suit is so tight, it fits almost like a woman's.

Over the music he says, "Turn on the spotlight!" It lights him up. It's so bright. And I think there's no way I could go out there and come back the exact same person.

FORD

17

My shoulders go limp as the final chord of my song rings out into the dark theater. From out of the black, rising applause swallows the chord, takes over the room. The house lights fade up a little, revealing the audience is actually on its feet. *This feels good.*

The audience's approval is like a ray of comic book energy hitting me in the chest, a supersizing beam causing me to grow gigantic right in front of everyone, like I could keep growing right through the roof of the theater, then stomp off through LA, an unstoppable hundred-foot-tall monster throwing buses and tearing through power lines, rampaging until the police, the Air Force, and maybe Will Smith are forced to team up and machine-gun me from the top of the Capitol Records building, the whole mess ending with Naomi Watts weeping over my giant dead body.

This feels really, really good is what I'm saying.

I look to my side because I need to share this with someone who isn't out there in the audience. I spot Magnolia. She feels so close to me. I've finished the song right next to where the other contestants are seated onstage. From her stool, she's clapping with a look that says, *All right, okay, not too shabby.* I walk the rest of the way to her, scoop my hand behind her head, lift her up, and see the slightest surprise cross her face before I kiss her.

Kissing her feels better than really, really good.

Lance says something in the background on the sound system about me being a ladies' man. I barely hear him. The audience makes catcalls and whoops, but they seem so much farther off than they are.

When I pull away, Magnolia's kiss lingering there on my lips, her eyebrows are raised and her mouth is almost open like she's about to ask me a question.

Lance sidles up to us. "I really hate to interrupt you two, but we do still have a show to finish," he says into the mic. The audience laughs over the thumping music that has kicked in.

He escorts me over to the center of the stage, right in front of the judges. Oh yeah, the *judges*. What's wrong with me? How could I forget about the judges? Their four votes alone control 50 percent of my fate; America's call-in vote makes up the other half.

I look to the three strangers who will probably decide how the rest of life my plays out. There's Davey Dave, the DJ record producer, eyes hidden behind his trademark aviator sunglasses. Jazz Billingham, who's already made a fortune selling records even though she's only eleven. When she stares at you with these eyes that are just too old for her face, it's kind of unsettling. And, of course, there's never impressed, brutally honest Chris James. It's strange to see that famous silver pompadour of hair right sitting right in front of you after all the years you've watched him tear apart movies on his review show.

"How do you think you did?" a bored-looking Chris James asks me.

And I'm back to reality. My hundred-foot-tall feeling shrinks down to nothing under that gaze.

How *did* I do? I desperately try to replay the performance in my head.

Seconds before my entrance, my usual nervous energy started to build, ratcheting up and up until I almost couldn't stand it. So by the time Lance took the stage and introduced me, I felt just like a slingshot pulled all the way back.

Leander tells me that when I make an entrance, it's always like there's some kind of emergency. This time, I started singing almost before I hit the microphone. It took the show's backing band half a line to kick in with me, so my first bit was a cappella. I think it sounded okay, even though it's not how we'd rehearsed it.

Then I think I did something weird. I was chewing gum, wasn't I? I'd forgotten to get rid of my gum from before, so I turned my head and spit it halfway across the stage without missing a beat. Why the hell did I do that?

My brain works different onstage, fires off new kinds of messages. It tells my body to do bizarre stuff. Leander tells me I get all convoluted, like I'm having a seizure, and maybe I am, because when I'm performing I partly feel like someone else is controlling my body.

But now the other judges are talking to me. I've been answering them on autopilot, lost in my own head. I can't focus on their questions, I'm too busy interrogating myself: *Was I terrible? Did I look stupid? Do I look stupid now? Is Magnolia going to be pissed?*

"You might have chosen the wrong song, bro."

You choked.

". . . intense emotion. But out of control."

You're going home.

". . . natural talent, but no polish."

Who did you think you were fooling?

"I thought you were going to hurt yourself up there."

You don't belong here.

You don't belong here.

You don't belong here.

Then Chris James swoops back in once the other judges have finished giving their comments, and I hear him say, "I thought it was the best performance of the night."

My head goes silent.

18

Cameras line the pathway into the after-party. The club is in an old theater on Hollywood Boulevard, and it's packed. Every person I squeeze by smiles at me as though we know each other. It takes about fifteen of those smiles before I stop trying to figure out if we do.

This isn't like any party I've ever been to. I guess it's more of a press conference, except for the bass-heavy music and snacks floating around every five seconds. The food is always something simple combined with one weird ingredient. Like mini grilled cheeses except they have shrimp in them. A waiter who looks about my age offers me one of those from a tray after a reporter asks me to say, "America, could I be your next superstar?" into the camera.

"No, thanks," I say to the waiter. I'm thinking I could easily be him.

The lights on all the cameras make the rest of the club seem even darker by comparison, and I look around for Magnolia from where I'm pinned in this corner. One of the twins passes (not sure which one), and I bend close and ask if she's seen Magnolia so as not to make a whole production about it.

"She's back that way with her mom," the twin says.

Before I can search for her, Catherine takes me by the arm and leads me to a corner where a bunch of entertainment reporters are doing interviews. I recognize most of them; they're famous for asking famous people questions. There are all kinds of famous, I guess. In person, they have the whitest teeth I've ever seen.

I just do interview after interview. The *Spotlight* camera guys, Skip and Hector, are filming the reporters filming us contestants, and almost all the questions I'm getting are about Magnolia. "Is this a new showmance?" "Is she a good kisser?" "What happens next?"

I don't know if there's a right way to answer any of this. I try to laugh it off.

I turn my head, looking for her bright, shiny top somewhere in the crowd, and then I realize that's not what she's wearing anymore. They changed all of us after the show. It's like my heart is seizing just a bit at every Magnolia-maybe girl I can make out between the lights in the dark. The next reporter steps in front of me and beams a gigantic smile in my direction. Finally I get a different question for the first time in an hour.

"Ford, is it going to be weird living in a mansion, considering the life that you came from?"

"Oh, man, it's crazy! It feels like I'm dreaming." As I answer, I realize that while part of me is just being honest, another part of me is listening in and working hard to be what the interviewers want me to be. I have to say, I don't fully know which of those parts is running this show.

19

From the driveway the mansion reminds me of the Alamo, if the Alamo had been built in 2003 and had six bathrooms and a waterfall pool. Even though it's extremely late, you can see the house plain as day, they've got it so lit up: red roof tiles, arched windows, spotlights reflecting yellow off the thick plaster walls. They don't build them like this at home, these Spanish-looking houses that seem solid enough to ricochet a cannonball.

I look at this place before me and I'm blown away, but I'm also thinking it's going to be hard to get comfortable, what with the first elimination a day away. Someone is going to have a real short visit.

Dillon and I get out of the last van. Our shoes touch wet ground, and I ask, "Did it rain while we were in that party?"

"What, you don't watch *The Bachelor*?" he says. "On these shows they really like to spray the driveways down with water. Looks better on camera."

Sure enough, the camera and sound guys are set up ahead of us, waiting to capture our first reactions to the mansion. I try to put on an awed country boy face, feeling like that's what they must want. Looking ahead, I see Magnolia already standing at the door with the rest of the group since she came in the first van. She leans against the wall with the glowing doorbell.

"Come on, man," says Dillon. "We get the inside of it too."

We walk up the rest of the driveway, and Catherine gestures to the crew that we're ready for the next shot. They disappear around the side of the mansion. She goes up to the front double doors. I look at Magnolia. Magnolia looks at me. I can't read her, not even a word. We look away from each other.

Catherine claps. "Okay, guys, I'm going to need high energy. I'm going to need *Tiger Beat* kind of lunacy, but it's a house you're losing your nuts over, like you love it so much you want to date it. So it's open mouths and a lot of *oh my Gods*. Pretend like it hasn't already been a long night. Got it?" She pokes her head in one of the doors to make sure the crew's ready on the other side, and then she stages McKinley to be the one who lets us in.

He presses down on an iron lever, and we walk in with our mouths already open.

I don't say anything. I can't.

Because the first floor of the mansion is the size of California. I honestly don't know what one family would do with all the space (play really long games of hide-and-go-seek or something?). There are framed photographs of girls at the ocean and hot orange sunsets and galaxies in space about six feet tall, no kidding. And I have no clue what the paintings are supposed to be, but they're just as big and just as overwhelming. The leather and see-through furniture is the kind you see on TV that nobody actually owns. Suddenly everyone's going crazy, even though we're exhausted. It's like a summer camp with no counselors in here.

Nikki takes off sprinting down a long marble hallway, laughing, and the twins and Ricky are already running upstairs. McKinley grabs one of the furry pillows from a couch in the open living room and hits Belinda in the head with it. She's still seeming kind of fried from tonight—her performance was really out there, and I suspect, from my vast experience, that she might have been on something. Either way, she starts laughing like a maniac. Even Gardner cracks a smile when he looks in the built-in aquarium by the stairs and sees it's filled with a bunch of black fish.

Magnolia heads off toward the glass doors that lead to the backyard. Dillon says to me, "We've got to get the best bedroom!" with real panic in his voice, so we head up that way. Hector follows right behind us, his camera at the back of our heads.

I think I'm starting to be able to tell the twins apart, so I'm pretty sure it's Mila who is already fighting with Ricky over a bedroom. Hector goes running into that room to capture the drama. I pass by one of the bathrooms and there's Felicia (pretty sure) doing gymnastics. The bathroom is that spacious. Dillon says, "You're so flexible" to her, and then he takes a running jump into the tub that's the size of a boat.

While Dillon's taking a soak in his clothes, I leave that bathroom and walk by myself down the upstairs hallway. I come to what I guess is an entertainment room, and sit down on a luxurious couch that feels like it was taken out of its store packaging just a second ago. And I just know I'm the first person to ever sit here. I let myself feel it.

Back home, our stuff was *used.* Even my family's living room couch has a complicated history: it belonged to Grandma Tilda for thirty years before she died and gave it to Aunt Rose, whose son Brad slept on it for two years before he traded it to his friend, David Barr, for a rusted-out '86 Camaro with no engine. When David got a job cleaning up after an oil spill in Texas, he gave it to Sissy, even though she had turned down his marriage proposal about five times, and then one day there it was in my parents' living room with the same fading flowers I remembered from when I visited Grandma Tilda when I was a kid. Y'know, *used*.

I take a second, alone in this room, to look around at where I am.

I finally say, "Oh my God." But it's not caught on camera, so it's like my proverbial tree falling in the forest.

Still, I heard myself say it.

20

"Hello, Cheboygan! Are you ready to rock?" Dillon asks the full-length mirror in our new room, pointing a finger at an imaginary audience as he sweeps his arm to make sure the whole fantasy stadium feels included. Still just as wired as he was last night.

He's working on what he calls his "stage posturing." He says that growing up performing in a giant mega temple, you learn that you can't do things just for the people in the front row. You want them to see your moves up in the cheap seats. You've got to go big. For him this means standing with his legs spread really wide, swinging his arms in giant circles, and throwing in a jump kick after a high note.

I try to point out to him, "We're really performing for the cameras and they're taking close-ups half the time, so maybe we don't need to *overdo* it." But he's in the middle of another jump kick.

"I'm going to the kitchen. You want anything?" I ask.

"You're gonna go look for the Superstar." Dillon points at me, smiling like he's caught me at something.

Last night, after every room in the mansion had been explored, Catherine called us back downstairs. We were nearly delirious, they'd kept us up so late. Jazz Billingham was standing in front of the leather couches in a tiny tux kind of thing, but she wouldn't look at anyone until Skip was in place and ready to start filming. It seemed like it should have been way past her bedtime.

Once the camera was on, Jazz came alive. "Somewhere in this house there has been hidden a silver statuette called the Superstar. . . ." She took a dramatic pause. "And the one person who finds the Superstar can use it *one time* to stop herself from getting sent home."

"Herself?" panicked Ricky. "It's only for the girls?"

"No." Jazz sighed. "But person is singular, so it needs a singular pronoun."

Catherine stepped toward Jazz from out of the shot and motioned for a new take. We could hear Catherine muttering to Jazz, "Jesus Christ, just say 'themselves.'"

So we reset, and Jazz did the announcement over again, even though it seemed painful for her.

On the flat-screen TV, Jazz showed us a picture of the Superstar, which to me just looked like a silvery, genderless six-inch alien with a shooting star in its hands. She told us the rules. If the losing contestant produces the Superstar, then the next-to-last loser has to go home. And we're not allowed to hurt each other while looking for the Superstar, or the involved parties both lose the Superstar privilege. I listened, half-asleep. But when we wrapped, right away people started to poke around, myself included.

Just now, though, I wasn't being sneaky about going to the kitchen.

"I'm really going to the kitchen," I promise Dillon. "Seriously. So you want anything?"

"I want to rock! And maybe some Cheez-Its." He launches off his bed and goes spread-eagle in the air. Twenty-four hours a day this guy is performing at Madison Square Garden in his head. Other than that, he's not a bad dude. I leave him alone with his millions of fans.

Once I step out of our room, I'm still thinking about the Superstar, but even more than that, I'm thinking about Magnolia. Since yesterday's show and move-in, they've been shooting us nonstop. But we've been given the night off, so maybe I can finally talk to her without a camera in our faces. The house is so big that sometimes you really have to go looking if you want to find someone.

If you do find someone, though, you might not even be sure what you have to say. The kiss is already starting to feel unreal.

Still, if it didn't really happen, I don't know why I'm so damn conscious of who's in a room from the second I walk in. Like when I stop by the entertainment room, I instantly know she's not in there, even before I know who is.

The twins and Ricky are dancing to an Azealia Banks video playing on the giant flat-screen. The twins look like a mirror image, nailing every single one of the moves in perfect time. Ricky is really doing his own thing, which is mostly a lot of crotch grabbing.

I sit on the arm of the couch to watch for a second, maybe thinking someone else will come in. And then I realize that I've started involuntarily nodding a little because watching the three of them dance makes you feel like you have to dance too.

"You looking for Magnolia?" Felicia (I think?) asks, and gives Mila (90 percent confident it's Mila) a sly glance. The twins have this way of looking at each other that makes it seem like they can communicate full thoughts through eye contact alone. It makes you feel like you're with people who speak a different language.

"No." I try to sound casual. "Just messin' around."

"She's not here anyway. Some guy came to see her," Felicia says.

"Really? What guy?" I ask, forgetting to act cool.

"Don't know. This white, blond guy. I guess *some* people think the 'no guests' rule doesn't apply to them."

"Hmm" is all I got. My face feels hot as I stand and walk away. Where are all these feelings coming from? I mean, what did I think was happening here anyway? I barely know this girl. All I should be thinking about is the competition. It might be the only chance in life I'll ever get. But I can't deny what was there just a second ago, a knot in my stomach and a burning in my face. I jog down the stairs.

On the first floor I pass a bathroom and see Nikki applying eyeliner to Gardener. Laying it on pretty thick. I grin at them. Nikki beams back. Gardener just gives me that blank stare of his.

In the kitchen I find McKinley sitting at the counter, texting, looking all serious and grown-up, while his mom makes him a PB&J. I poke around the cabinets a little and end up just grabbing an apple.

"I said no crust, Mom, *c'mon*," McKinley says like he's talking to his personal maid. He slides the plate back over to her, shaking his head at me like, *Can you believe moms these days?* His mom starts slicing off the crusts without complaint.

My mother would have been slicing off my eyebrow if I pulled a move like that. I don't know if that makes her a worse mother or a better one.

I walk out the doors to the back patio. The night is still warm. The grounds are lit up by small lamps along the pathways. The place smells like I imagine the Garden of Eden would, with purple jacarandas and white honeysuckle growing all over the place.

The pool throws disco ball lights around the yard. It's more like a waterpark than a swimming pool, though, what with the giant waterfall pouring over fake boulders that are slides too. Would they have hidden the statue outside? Jazz didn't say if the outdoors counts. If anybody is gonna need that Superstar to get through this thing, it's me. These people have singing voices trained to do everything except the dishes. And, honestly, as much as I'd like to win without a cheap freebie pass, I'm not above using it. I'd use it in a flat second.

So I should be searching for that thing like I'm Indiana Jones and it's the Lost Ark, but I'm feeling crazy trapped. Like I need to escape. Where do you go to escape from the place you escaped to?

I get an idea, and continue around to the front.

My motorcycle is parked outside the garage, light reflecting off its silver gas tank. The producers have made it clear that they don't want us leaving the grounds. But all I want to do is go for a ride so my nervous energy will just vibrate out through the handlebars.

I push my bike quietly to the side gate. I'm not supposed to know the code to this number pad, but I watched the pool guy punch it in this morning. The gate silently swings open. I hop on the bike and point it downhill.

The headlight shows another mansion's gate just across the street. There's so much money up here. The Hollywood Hills have mansions on top of mansions, most of them hidden behind walls and hedges. Seems like rich people want to live as close together as possible but never actually see each other. The streets up here are tight and twisty, like a rat's maze. And I guess these are the rats that got all the cheese.

Leander used to tell me stories about the band he was in in the late sixties, the Escalators. He'd show me their old photos—a young whip-thin Leander with dark hair cut like he was in the Rolling Stones. A devilish grin. He hadn't always been an old grayhead whose sad eyes seem like they see everything in slow motion. It's hard to imagine time could change anyone that much.

One of their songs hit it big in Texas and then started getting play in California. They came out to LA to go on one of those TV shows where teenagers danced around while the band lip-synched its hit song. It seemed like they were really going to make it.

But after they got back to Texas, their lead singer overdosed on drugs and things just fell apart. The band members all drifted off and ended up working at gas stations and diners and such. I think it took Leander a lot of years to realize that it was all over.

Still, while they were in LA, they played at a place called the Whisky a Go Go on the Sunset Strip. It was a famous venue back then, and a lot of rock legends played there: Jimi Hendrix, the Doors,

Led Zeppelin—all the big ones. Leander said he even hung out with Janis Joplin one night.

I asked Jesse the PA about the place earlier, and he said it was still there. The winding streets from the hills all descend onto Sunset Boulevard, and from here it isn't supposed to be far. Sunset Boulevard, Melrose, Mulholland Drive—even the streets in this town are famous. I pull onto Sunset, heading west.

Broad curves wind between slick hotels and strip malls. But it's the thirty-foot-tall palms leaning wildly over both sides of the street, like crazy cartoon trees, that make me really feel where I am.

A police car speeds past me, sirens blaring. I'm imagining some fictional movie cop like Denzel Washington in the driver's seat. The Chateau Marmont hotel rises up on my right (famous for having some famous guests act up, mistreat the furniture, even die there, Jesse told me). Multistory buildings pasted with billboards of eighty-foot-tall Victoria's Secret models. You can't not look at them, but I don't know how you can see them straight without running into the back of the car in front of you.

Then, on a corner across from a gas station, painted completely over in a red so dark that it's almost like it doesn't want to be seen, is the Whisky. I park on the street and get out to take a look.

It's not what I expected. After all the years of listening to Leander, I guess I thought it would somehow be stuck in its glory days of the sixties. Hippies lounging around outside, Jim Morrison's ghost hanging from the roof by his fingertips. But it's a quiet Wednesday night, and there aren't many people around, living or dead.

Still, I like to think about young Leander being here, in this very spot, in those days when everything was going right for him.

"Ford, hey, Ford, over here!"

I look over in confusion and see a very large black guy videotaping me. A light is in my face. I think he just said my name—is he talking to me?

"Ford! How's the show going, buddy?" the guy asks from behind his camera. He is talking to me. I think maybe he's one of those paparazzi guys. I'm shocked to realize that something is already starting between the show and the outside world. The first episode only aired last night. But it's in motion. He knows who I am.

"Fine," I say, wondering if I'm even supposed to talk about it.

"What's going on with you and Magnolia?"

That question knocks me off-balance. I guess I expected that sort of thing back at the studio and the party, but from some random guy on the street? It feels like I accidently left my journal out and the whole world's reading it.

I mean, I get why he's asking, but that doesn't make it feel any less weird. Like, I know we were on television, but up until this very second, I haven't been able to grasp what that means in a larger way. We've heard the producers talking about ratings being surprising, but those are just numbers. Thinking about ratings is like trying to feel something for a problem in a math book. I don't know what I imagined those TV cameras were connected to, but it turns out there were people sitting on the other end.

I realize now that the kiss is something a bunch of strangers have an opinion about.

"Magnolia and I are just friends," I say, trying to walk away.

"I wish I had some friends like that." The paparazzi guy has a stupid grin on his face.

I don't want Magnolia to think I used her for a prop, to get attention for myself or something. It wasn't that thought-out; nothing I do onstage ever is. If I could just find a way to talk to her, I think I could explain myself.

Suddenly someone's got their arms around me, and I assume I'm about to get mugged; I know from TV that these cities have muggers in every alleyway. My fists tense, and the thought occurs that maybe Sissy's got the right idea, always carrying around a screwdriver. Then I feel warm lips on my cheek. When I turn to face the person tackling me, the lips move onto my lips. I pull back.

Two girls, around my age, with their moms. One is taking a photo of the other one kissing me. They're dressed in flouncy short skirts and colorful tights. They've also got on Hollywood tourist T-shirts, like they just went shopping on the Boulevard together.

"Ford! We love you! You are so, so cute. Can we take a photo?" But they are already taking photos. I'm astounded again to realize these girls have seen the show. And all it's taken is one glimpse at me, one song, and they already think I'm someone they love? They feel connected to me, just like that. *Holy shit* is all I can think.

"Thanks," I say, because it's hard to know how to respond to someone being so aggressively complimentary. I'm stunned. I try to move back toward my bike.

"What's Magnolia gonna say about this, Ford?" That's the paparazzi guy, still filming.

"Magnolia sucks," one of the girls says.

I stop and look her in the eyes. "No, she's really good," I say.

"We hate her," the other girl says. This is crazy.

I'm suddenly aware that all this is going to be on the Internet.

"I have to go."

I break free of the girl holding on to me, and jump back on my Triumph. The girls and their moms keep taking photos next to me as I put on my helmet and start the bike. The video guy's still filming. I don't even know what his face really looks like because I haven't seen the whole thing.

"What happens if you and Magnolia are the final two?" he yells over the bike engine.

I push the Triumph back out into the street, and accelerate away. I'm light-headed with the strangeness of what just went down. Driving back to the mansion, I wonder how much trouble my little field trip is going to get me in. With the producers, with Magnolia.

Those girls wouldn't have looked at me twice normally. I won't say it doesn't feel good to be seen as something besides a local screw-up, but whatever this attractive new vibe is, I don't feel like it really belongs to me.

It could all go away the second that stupid paparazzi video goes online and the producers find out I already broke the rules. All I had to do was hang out in a sweet-ass mansion, but no, I needed to do my thing. Maybe it's true—maybe failure is in my DNA. Maybe that's why I'm all worked up about Magnolia instead of thinking about winning the competition. It's as good a way to self-destruct as any. Then I remember about Magnolia and this supposed white, blond guy, and I think maybe I'm not the only one who doesn't have their head on straight.

But underneath all that, I know I don't want to lose. I'm so tired of having nothing. So how about maybe I could let myself try to win just this once? This one time. I promise myself that after tonight, I'm gonna be all business. No more distractions.

I drive back up into the Hills, the moon hanging over my shoulder. When I get to the edge of the mansion's street, I turn off my bike and walk it past the neighbor's gate so that no one at the mansion hears me coming. If I'm going to get hell for this, I'd like to save it for tomorrow.

But when I round the curve, I see two people coming back down the hill toward the house. I stay put, duck a little. They pass under a streetlamp, and I see her. Magnolia. She's walking with the blond guy. And there's something about the way their faces are turned toward each other's that puts the knot back in my stomach.

I balance my motorcycle on its kickstand.

Then I get real angry at the knot for being there. This feeling is a traitor, a thing in me that would rather focus all its attention on another lost cause than on the chance I have.

Here I am, a thousand miles from my home. Finally far enough away that the heavy feeling I've had my whole life has started lifting. But the vote tomorrow could put me right back there like none of this never happened. And there's no one who's going to save me from that. I have to do this alone.

Something's ringing.

I think it's coming from inside my head at first—that it's my anger at myself—but then I realize it's in my pocket. It's the phone I got from the producers. I step back around the curve and think, *Great, the video is probably already up on the Internet. They want me to pack my bags.*

"Hello," I answer.

"Well, well, if it isn't our own damn TV star." My spine crawls when I hear that familiar voice. It's not the producers. It's worse.

"Hey, Cody," I say. I have no idea how he could have gotten this number, but I'm not surprised he did. Cody can pull almost any con he sets his mind to.

"We all watched you last night. I gotta tell you, you kicked some ass, bro! Even if you stole half those licks from me."

"Thanks," I say, knowing Cody's never given a compliment in his life without some kind of string attached.

"But then we see most of the other people have their families out there with them, and we got to thinking—it ain't right for you to look like some kind of orphan, man. I know you were joking when you told the people that your family was dead, kid, but I don't think the people out there really picked up on the joke." He's talking about my video package.

It seems stupid now, but I was just hoping I'd get lucky. I was hoping the night the first show aired, my family would be passed out. Or someone would have thrown an ashtray through the television screen. There were an incredible amount of things they could have been doing instead of watching and paying attention.

Cody's still talking. "We're thinking about maybe making the drive out there, see Hollywood and everything."

I close my eyes and take a deep breath. I feel an ache when I think about Magnolia, probably about to fall into the arms of someone she actually has a real history with. It only gets worse when I imagine what she'll think when my real history shows up. They say your past has a way of catching up to you. I just thought it would give me a better head start.

Magnolia

21

Earlier tonight I had a sit-down with Lucien to discuss, as he put it, "what we're going to do with this romance that sprang up. Like a goddamn tulip."

"I wouldn't call one showy kiss a romance," I told him.

"But we can make it one," he said.

I asked him if he ever watched television or movies, and if he believed that every time an actor kissed an actress, they were in real-life love.

He laughed, rubbed his eyes, and said, "Okay, do you have a better idea for yourself?"

I told him anything else. Anything else besides a romance or doing a weepy package about my dad.

We decided on a light story about how Mila and I are becoming friends, with human interest details like Mila discovering I don't move at all when I sleep. Which is true.

When I came out of that meeting, Felicia, leaving one of the upstairs bathrooms in a robe, said, "Magnolia, there's someone yelling your name from the street."

"What?" I said.

"Yeah, I'm in the bathroom relaxing in the tub, and there's some guy out the window going, 'Magnoooooooolia, Maaaaaaaaag.'"

"Like a ghost or a real person? Because it sounds like you're doing a whoo-whoo ghost voice."

Felicia smiled at me quizzically. "A real, live person with longish blond hair."

I guess I already knew who it was going to be when she said that because there are no other significant blonds in my life.

I went out the mansion's front doors barefoot, and jogged down the front walk. When I got to the top of the driveway, that's when I could tell it was Scott standing on the other side of the gate. In the scheme of things, there are very few white people who still wear Baja ponchos. And also, even from a distance, I'd know him anywhere.

The last time we'd seen each other in person was the night we broke up. When I saw him at the gate, I had this feeling of not being prepared, kind of like if I'd shown up to class and had no idea there was a test. It was that kind of sinking uneasiness. I guess a feeling of wishing I'd had more time to get my head right.

Scott spotted me and jumped up on the bars of the gate, hanging there, smiling. I walked down the driveway. Once I was facing him, I could tell he'd been in the ocean that day because his hair was pretty stringy and wavy from the salt.

"This is a big house, Tiny," Scott said.

"What are you doing here?" I asked.

"You hung up on me."

"A couple of weeks ago."

"So maybe you've had some time to cool down."

I could have banged my head on the gate. "It's not like I'm actively mad at you. Us talking just wasn't very good for me."

"What did I do?" Scott asked. But as spacey as he seems to people who don't actually know him, I knew that he understood. Scott is an everything's-always-cool! kind of guy on the outside, but what's really happening is that he's a person who can't handle anything negative. The positivity doesn't go all the way through him. From the very beginning I think that's what I was so drawn to about him. I felt so sad, and he wanted to be the hero who cheered me up.

That's also why the breakup was doubly painful. Because one, we were coming apart. And two, it felt like he had given up on wanting to fix me.

My sense of it was that I became an uncomfortable person for him to be around. I didn't know this right when we broke up, but I think I've figured it out since. Before, I made him feel like his best self, but then, once he became nervous about his future and what he was going to do with himself, he saw me as a negative presence. I held him accountable. I asked questions. I was the kind of person who made him feel like his worst self. So he tried to cut me loose, but he couldn't do it completely because you can't always force yourself to break a bond. That's why he still called me. That's why he was standing at the gate.

Coming a night after the show, Scott being there felt like concrete proof that I'll never escape myself. You can change where you live, you can change your hair, you can change everything that's going on in your life, and still you'll project your you-ness, which is what's left underneath everything else.

And again, that's why Scott was at the gate, because he knew that I couldn't get rid of the part of me that connects with him.

"How did you know this address?" I asked.

"I talked to your mom earlier and she gave it to me."

My mom loved Scott from the first time she met him because he always talks to her like she's his age. Early in the relationship, she started calling him my "brotha from anotha motha" until I told her to please stop because she was grossing me out. Sometimes, when he ditched his last few periods, he'd go to our house to wait for me, and I had a suspicion he'd heard things about my dad from my mom that I never had. When he cares about you, he makes you feel like you want to tell him things. It's a natural gift. When I told my mom we broke up, she cried.

He shook the bars of the gate a little. "But there's no intercom, which I didn't count on."

"Why are you here?" I yelled suddenly, even surprising myself, my eyes going wide without any effort. "What do you want?"

Scott held his hands through the bars and made a step out of them by interlocking his fingers. "I just want you to come take a walk with me."

I stared at him for a few seconds.

And then I gave up—not to him, but to myself. I pulled up on the bars of the gate, putting my bare left foot into his hands. There's a code to the keypad, but I don't know it. I swung my right leg over the top of the gate, avoiding the sharp parts, and then Scott helped me down on the other side. I could smell sunblock on him as he was lowering me.

Maybe change isn't a sudden lightning bolt that goes

through you. Maybe it's small little increments that you don't even notice until one day you're on the other side.

Anyway, that's the story of why we're now walking slowly up the hill together when two weeks ago I told him we shouldn't talk anymore.

22

"This doesn't mean we're going back to talking," I say. "This is just for right now."

"Cool, whatever," Scott says, and nods, then, "I saw two dolphins when I was out surfing this morning."

I kind of laugh. This is an old joke between us. There have been a bunch of times when he's come back from early morning surfing and told me that he saw a dolphin while he was out there, and I've never believed him. I mean, he doesn't go out that far. I just can't believe there's this one rebel dolphin that likes to swim inland and watch the bros get up on their boards. Scott always used to say I should go out there with him so I could see this dolphin for myself, but I could never make myself get out of bed before six a.m. Now he's added another dolphin, which is really upping the ante.

"Can you have sunstroke when the sun isn't totally up yet?" I wonder.

He makes the sign of the cross, which doesn't do much for his credibility considering I know he doesn't believe in religion. It separates people, he says. "Tiny, I swear. Two free, beautiful dolphins."

"Did they talk to you?"

"I think I heard a soft . . . like a soft *eeeeeee*."

"And no clicks? Not a single click?" My voice chatters.

"Hey, are you cold?" Scott asks. "Do you need my poncho?"

"Yeah," I say, and he takes off the poncho and hands it over. When I put it on, it's like putting on a time machine, the way it smells and feels to be in it.

We shoot the shit like this for a while. We come up under a streetlamp. The light shows the creases he's getting around his eyes from being such a squinter and spending so much time at the ocean, and it's like I can see an older version of him for a second. I think, *I wonder if we'll know each other then.*

"So I watched the show," he finally says. "You were good up there."

When I sang my last note, I thought I'd been good too. Meaning that I thought I had really connected with the audience, even though I couldn't see them. It was just this feeling. I sang to a bright green light far away at the back of the studio, a glowing green little planet. I was hit with this quick exhilaration that I had just *been* different. That I'd just experienced some new adaptation of myself that was going to mark the beginning of everything easy and simple and light. I looked down, and my high-tops were blinking under me like when you reset a clock.

Davey Dave was the first judge to speak. I couldn't see his eyes. He took a sip of his Big Gulp and said, "I found your performance style strangely depressing. Even though you're dressed in shininess and white, I still felt as if I was watching"—he thought—"a sad little bat in a cave."

Chris James looked at me hawklike, making the whole show suddenly seem very serious. He ran a hand through his big hair as if he were a weary philosopher. "You're the girl I have to coax out of the coatroom at a party. There are many parties for which you couldn't be blamed for feeling that way, but the fact is, you needed to show up big to this one."

The air hummed like it had before I went onstage, but the quality of the humming was totally different. Instead of feeling excited, I began to feel as if the air was squeezing me.

Last were the comments from Jazz Billingham, who's so young, she makes me feel like I'm babysitting her and we're just playing at being a judge and contestant on a singing show. She said, "I find you interesting. . . ." The in-studio audience gave a lukewarm clap to this, as if they were saying, *Yes, interesting is a good, safe word for this performance we were not very interested in.* She waited for them to go quiet before she spoke again. "But also alienating, and alienation brings about a darkness of the soul that I do not believe is in the realm of the artist."

Lance was holding his microphone in my face like I was supposed to say something back to that. I was so stunned by this feedback that all I could think to say to Jazz Billingham was "I enjoyed your Christmas special last year."

I honestly had. It was kind of charming, what with the puppies in snowflake sweaters and the number from the penguin exhibit at the zoo.

Jazz leaned in delicately toward her microphone. "Thank you, but this is not about me," she said.

I think that tomorrow night there is a very good chance that I'm going home. Mostly this has made me feel heavy with disappointment directed toward myself. I would have said there's no chance of me staying except for how Belinda barely made it through her song.

"Thanks," I say to Scott.

He looks into my eyes. Deep down in his, I can detect

something unsettled. "And you must have been pretty shocked when that guy kissed you out of nowhere, right?"

And then there's the matter of the kiss, which I have barely even begun to process.

I look back into Scott's eyes, and I know he's here partially because he's jealous, and partially because seeing me on TV just made him realize that I've entered a new phase of my life that has nothing to do with him. He's realized I wasn't kidding on our last phone call. Even though he will pretend like I was.

"Right," I say. "Shocked."

23

The kiss:

I mean, I don't know the reasons behind why Ford kissed me. I can't even begin to tell you if that kiss was actually a real thing between us. When the reporters at the after-party asked me if there was a burgeoning romance, I said that it was nothing, just showmanship. And maybe what I said to them was actually true, and that was just Ford being an entertaining person for the people at home. But there was the way he looked at my mouth before the show, and the way I was drawn to his. So there's also the possibility that he actually meant it. Maybe it *was* real, but he only kissed me during the show because it was the atmosphere of the show that carried him away, like what happens when couples who barely know each other get married at four a.m. in Vegas because the lights and the *ching-ching-ching* sounds do something romantic to their brains.

As for whether that kiss was a real thing from my end, I temporarily forgot I was on a stage. I felt like a warm hood had been pulled up over the back of my head. I wanted to be there. I moved my mouth. I kissed him too. Does any of that make it real?

Why do I not know the answer to that?

Anyway, that's the entirety of what I know about the kiss.

Scott tries to fish, saying, "You looked surprised when he kissed you."

He wants to know where I stand. We are not going to sort through my feelings together. I refuse to do that. "Yeah, I must have," I agree.

Scott stares at me for a moment, like he can't believe that things are really going to be this stiff between us. Then he pulls and stretches out the collar of his T-shirt in frustration. "I'm jealous, okay? I'm jealous!"

Even though this truth doesn't come as a surprise to me, hearing him admit it does. And it makes me really angry instantly, because here Scott is, changing before my very eyes, acting different, showing a new side, when I just seem to be stuck in my old behaviors and feelings and thoughts. He's come here to make sure I didn't feel anything when Ford was kissing me? To make sure I'm the same person who used to cling to him, even though I'm living a different life on this show? And it turns out that maybe I am that same person, because here I am, walking next to him, aren't I?

"Well, good for you, Scott!" I say. "Good for you!"

"What does *that* mean?"

"It means your need to express yourself isn't my problem," I tell him, and then I leave him to walk back toward the house.

24

It's seven a.m. the morning after our first elimination show, and I'm awoken by the sound of Belinda the not-hippie hippie throwing a suitcase down the stairs, wheels clanging against the wrought iron banister.

I open my eyes. My first thought is that I can't believe it wasn't my name. When Lance said Belinda's last night, I could hear my mom's gasp of relief from the studio audience. I knew it was her, even in the dark. It took me a good few seconds to begin to grasp that I wasn't going home.

"America couldn't see that it was next-level. Assholes!" Belinda yells, and then I hear a sound like a dead body sliding down one step at a time. I hope this is just a heavy duffel bag and not her.

On the other bed in the room, the down comforter starts moving. Mila rolls over and gives me a bleary stare. "What?" she just says.

"Belinda's leaving," I tell her. My speaking voice, which is already kind of low to begin with, sounds like it's bending to get under a limbo bar in my throat.

From somewhere underneath our room Belinda screams,

"Peace out!" and then, for good measure, "Assholes!" I don't know if this time "assholes" is the rest of us, or if it's still America. The front doors, both of them, open and slam.

I can't say that I'm going to miss her, but she's not wrong that her performance was next-level. I guess the problem was just that not enough of the viewers at home were hallucinating too, so they couldn't join her on it.

The salvia she smoked in her dressing room was in effect by the time she hit the stage. She was supposed to be singing Lenny Kravitz's "It Ain't Over 'Til It's Over," but it really ended up being more of an interpretation. At the after-party something started going on with her facial expressions. Sometimes it looked like she was trying to touch her upper lip to her nose, and in other moments she kind of looked like her head was on backward, if you know what I mean.

I had figured the viewers might send me home before her, since I think you see depressing pretty often, but it's not every day that you can watch possessed.

But here I am, lying in bed, and Belinda's out the door. Maybe America saw something in me?

"Assholes," Mila repeats, and laughs to herself. She sits up in bed and unties the silk pillowcase she keeps over her weave while she sleeps, and her hair comes down. Last night she made me laugh because her head looked so tiny surrounded by a pillowcase that was also surrounded by a pillowcase.

I roll over and look at my own pillowcase, which is turning pink from my fuchsia hair.

"She didn't really say bye," I say. When we got home from the results show last night, Belinda locked herself in the garage; that was the last I saw of her.

Mila sings, "It ain't over 'til—" and does an "oh, shit" face that makes me laugh. Then she turns serious. "Well, I'm still here."

"Mila, there was no way that you weren't going through."

Now I know what Mila meant when she told me not to think of her differently after seeing her perform. She sang "Come to My Window" by Melissa Etheridge, but her voice wasn't raspy like the original. She sings like a pop star. She's all breath and charisma. But it's more than the shininess of her delivery; it's that she completely becomes someone else when she's up there. She's "on" in the way that the princesses at Disneyland are "on." Like the world's most impressive animatronic girl. But the girl on the other bed across from me is the most dry and down-to-earth person you could ever hope to share a bedroom in a mansion with.

So it's like Mila is her own twin too. She doesn't have to worry about me judging her though. Because I just find it impressive.

"Okay, I trust your opinion," she says. "And you don't have to worry for a while either. No one's sending your tortured ass home, now that you're in a romance."

"I'm not going to say it again. One televised kiss isn't a romance."

I had to explain the same thing many times over to Lucien during our story meeting. Before he gave up, he'd crossed a foot over his knee and flipped open his notebook. "It could be like a *Wuthering Heights* thing. Ford *is* homeless, in a way, and so maybe you're the moodier one, which is sort of a character reversal, but it still works."

"I'm not moody," I snapped at him.

Now Mila gives me a skeptical glance. "You haven't seen Ford looking for you in a room?"

"No."

Ever since they moved us into the mansion, things have been so chaotic that it's pretty impossible to tell if Ford and I are actually avoiding each other or this is just what life is like now.

"He's constantly doing this—" Mila's eyeline slips away from the conversation and searches in the distance. She puts on this pining expression that's supposed to be Ford. "But you've usually got your mom glued to your side."

"Oh yeah, my conjoined twin." I actually know that what Mila is saying is true. I'm just playing dumb because I don't want to sit around and analyze it another second. If I let myself analyze, I can analyze into infinity. I'm trying to teach myself that no good comes of that.

There was one moment late last night when I could have gone and talked to Ford alone. The camera guys weren't around. My mom and McKinley's mom had gone to sleep in the guesthouse. Nikki and her girlfriend, Rebecca, were sitting at the kitchen island eating leftover desserts from the party, trying to have a date. Everybody else was upstairs, except for me, and Ford, whom I saw through the dining room window sitting out on the patio by himself. He was facing the pool, watching the fountain. His guitar was on his lap, but he wasn't playing. His right arm just hung over it and he was leaning back in the chair.

I could have taken that moment, but I didn't, and so now I'm shoving myself to move forward mentally.

"Okay, I can tell you don't want to talk about it. We won't talk about it," Mila says.

I nod at her with gratitude. It seems simple, but really, not that many people are able to back off without hurt feelings when you shut down. Part of why I already feel so close to Mila is that she's so comfortable with being quiet together.

And we get to hang out quietly lying in bed for all of a minute before Felicia pops into our room—pops exactly like a kernel bouncing out of the bag in the microwave. She has so much energy. Every sleepwear item she's wearing says *PINK*.

"Hey, guys!" She sits on her sister's bed. "Oh my God, Magnolia, I just saw Ford look over at your guys' bedroom door when he was finished brushing his teeth like he was thinking of coming in here, but then he saw me coming in here and he went downstairs. Did I just ruin your life? Do you think he brushed his teeth because he was going to come in here and grab you and kiss you again?"

I look at the twins sitting there like the living embodiments of those drama and comedy masks. Felicia has her mouth wide open, and I'm tempted to grab one of the peppermints on the nightstand (I took a handful from our dinner at the restaurant last night) and try to land it in there.

"Mila and I just decided to take a break from talking about Ford. Let's pick another topic."

Felicia pretends I'm speaking another language. "As you know, I think what's happening between you two is cute, totally cute. Still, maybe you should be careful about that kind of thing."

"What kind of thing?" I'm not sure if she's talking about kissing in general or getting involved with Ford. Maybe she knows something about him. Like maybe it's about someone from back home.

"It's different for girls and guys on these shows because it's all these young girls at home who are doing the voting. So you want to watch out when they get the impression you're the crush of the guy they're getting a crush on—"

I interrupt, "Okay, cool, I'm really done talking about this now."

"Are you hesitant because of the blond guy at the gate? Is that your secret boyfriend?"

"No. He's not even a friend." After Scott yelled that he was jealous and I yelled back at him, I left him standing outside. Things feel like they've come to a real end. It took three miniature breakups to add up to one that finally would put us out of each other's lives. My anger stepped on most of my sadness. That's what it took.

"Okay, well, listen. When Ford kissed you, he became very desirable to all those girls watching. But the more desirable he becomes, the more they'll want to believe he's free for the taking. Even if that isn't, you know, realistic because they're thirteen and living in Wisconsin. So just watch out."

"This is crazy," I say. It's very hard for me to believe that these imaginary girls would have fallen in love with him through their TV sets overnight. I'm pretty sure love at first sight is something that happens in person. It involves eye contact and signals between actual physical bodies.

"Craaaazy in love," Felicia sings.

"Okay, time for you to get out of here," Mila tells her twin.

Felicia turns around to look at her. "What? We're just getting started with this conversation."

"We're going to meditate," says Mila.

"Since when do you meditate?"

"You know how sometimes when you're talking and talking and you say my eyes goes blank?"

"Shut up!" Felicia says, and smacks her sister in the head—not too hard.

"I want to. That's why I'm trying to get rid of you." Mila smacks her back.

I roll back over on my pillow and try to clear my mind for the day ahead.

★ ★ ★

The vans show up at nine to take us to the studios. On my way downstairs, I pass McKinley trying to casually knock on a wall, as if he's just a guy walking along without a care in the world, rapping his knuckles against the hallway. It's pretty obvious he's trying to find the hidden Superstar. I've been keeping an eye out, but I'm not going to extraordinary measures to find it. I want to be on the show because the audience is latching on to me, not because of a trick. I pat McKinley on the back and go out front.

Catherine is practically floating around on the driveway, she's in such a great mood. Final ratings for the week are in, and the show's doing better than anyone expected.

"Off we go, cuties!" She giggles like a completely different person. Of course, Ford and I are put into different vans. The drivers take us over to the studios, past the soundstages and to the back lot, where we stop on an exterior set that's built to look like a suburban cul-de-sac.

We're here to film a fake-charity video package for the next show. It's going to look like us nine remaining contestants are all working together to fix up a house for an underprivileged family. The producers want the show to seem conscientious. But what's really happening is that we're pretending to fix a house, and the house is actually a façade. It was built for a sit-com that never got picked up.

I don't feel great about this charade, not great at all, and I just get more down when Catherine divides us into two groups for the shoot. Once again, Ford and I aren't in the same one. I don't understand why she's splitting us up when Lucien says she's excited about something happening between us. If she's going for tension, then she's successful. Because I feel tense. When Ford goes off to hammer the finished roof, I'm put with McKinley, Ricky, and Nikki to plant again when we're done.

Ford doesn't look over at me when Catherine splits us. I'm
watching as he goes, and he doesn't. Noticing this means I
have to admit I care. I guess I was hoping that we'd at least
pass each other today, and we would flirt or stare at least
once. And then I might know that he liked me and it wasn't
just the show.

But he goes off and climbs up to the roof, joking around
with a tool belt like he doesn't have anyone on his mind.

For the rest of the day I'm sent back and forth between pretending to plant tulips and studying with my tutor at a folding
table they've set up on the side of the set. For an hour Hector
films me patting down the dirt and talking to Nikki about how
nice it is to get flowers. I tell the anecdote about my dad and his
feelings on carnations because I want to say something true. It
feels so skeezy to have to plant these tulips from four different
camera angles for a family who doesn't exist, so that's why
instead of lying about what these tulips mean to me, I talk
about how my dad loved carnations because they're a flower
you give to your little girl. I don't care that I have to tell it ten
times so they can get the sound right.

Then it's an hour with the tutor, Felix, who's walking me
through how to graph ellipses. I'm trying to pay attention to
him, but my mom keeps coming over every second, happily
reading to me from her iPhone. She's tracking every single
conversation about me on the Internet, since to her that's
more important than passing Algebra II. But I don't want
to fall behind and mess up my life in some bigger way. It's
weird for me to think about everybody back in real school,
which has quickly become an alternate universe in my mind.
I wonder if my classmates are confused about seeing me on

TV. One day I'm there, one day I'm gone. I didn't announce it or anything.

"This girl likes the color of your hair. But this girl wants to pull it out because, quote, 'Ford is dreamy and she needs to keep her hands off him.'" My hands were never on him, but potato, potahto. It's pretty shocking to learn how emotionally invested some people are in the show when it's only been on a week. Maybe these are the same kind of people who can feel connected to almost everyone they meet.

"But then, look! There's a whole message board group that's sprung up to discuss how they think the two of you would be cute together. Mag, I think it's all good news because you're a topic of discussion." My mom gives me a look. "And next performance, you'll be more bubbly and upbeat."

Anyway, the day goes by like that, tulips and graphs, and then the van takes us back to the mansion. I'm feeling weirdly low by now, and all I want is an evening to be myself, to write some more of *Ships*, to not have to talk. I'm so tired of acting, which I don't even think I'm decent at, and I'm tired of being filmed.

But the producers have the cameras follow us into the house to tape a "making pasta dinner" scene. And I just can't take any more show stuff, so I slip out onto the patio while they're checking everyone's light. It's a busy shoot, so no one notices. I'm wearing a black cropped tank top and jeans, but there's no way I'm risking going back inside to get my bikini, so I walk into the pool, just like that.

I duck under the water and shut my eyes and it feels so great, really comforting and still and removed, and I swim underwater until I get to the other end and have to come up for breath. The sun is going down, and the sky is tilting purple. It looks and feels like fall is coming. It feels like I should be in school.

Before anyone spots me, I duck under again, eyes closed, and start swimming back across the pool.

Then there are lips on mine.

I open my eyes underwater. The chlorine stings them. Ford is pulling back from my face. He's in his clothes too. We stare at each other, finally, finally, finally where no one else can see us. I hold on to his shirt, pull myself up to him, and this time, I kiss him.

FORD

25

When we were kids, Sissy and I were the movie addicts in the family. We could watch three or four in a night. After she got her permit, she would drive me down to the video store, and we'd argue over what to rent. She'd insist on renting one of those teenage romance movies from the eighties, like *Pretty in Pink* or *Some Kind of Wonderful.* Those movies where the cool/rich guy falls for the awkward/poor girl. Or where a nerd takes off his glasses, slaps some mousse in his hair, and suddenly he's the hottest person in school. Or where someone finds out the person they really loved was right in front of them all along. Those kinds of movies.

What Sissy loved about those movies was the big romantic moment: that scene where a guy makes a fool of himself to win the girl back, usually by making a speech in front of the whole school, or waiting out in the rain like a wet stray dog.

"I hate the guys in this town," Sissy would say. "Not one of them would do something like that for me." But I know for a fact if a guy showed up outside our house holding a boom box over his head, blasting music like John Cusack in *Say Anything*, Sissy would do something terrible to him. She likes to sleep.

Now that I've had a couple of girlfriends, I've learned those movies are not a trustworthy guidebook for romance. I'm telling you, that stuff usually doesn't work. In real life, the big romantic moment often just ends up being embarrassing for everyone involved. I've always known better than to go around holding my heart up over my head.

But this once, I didn't even have to think about what I wanted to do. The big romantic moment just happened on its own. I couldn't have done any different. All I know is when I saw Magnolia walk into the pool with all her clothes on like a lunatic, I didn't stop to think it over. I just found myself diving in.

I swam until I found her, and I kissed her like I was supposed to. When we came out of the water, we went separate ways so we wouldn't have to answer bothersome questions. But later that night, when everyone else was asleep, I went and got her. Without saying anything, we started again.

26

Now that we've started, we can't keep our hands off each other. Whatever animal magnetism is, that's what we've got.

I pull Magnolia into the little photo booth at this producer's house. He had the whole *Spotlight* cast over for a fancy dinner. I thought he was trying to show us some West Coast hospitality, until we got there and saw that the table was surrounded by lights and cameras. It was more like a high-pressure performance than a dinner. People cranking their personalities up a notch for the cameras.

Everyone else is upstairs in his insane white master bedroom, sitting around his grand piano, listening to him play songs from the old days. But Magnolia and I have snuck off downstairs. In his front hallway he has a booth like the ones in malls back home, the ones that print those strips of black-and-white photos. We hit the button and wait as a beep counts down to . . .

Flash! Making faces into camera.

Flash! Pretending to strangle each other.

Flash! Flash! Making out. Making out until we hear the printer drop our photos into the slot outside the booth. Making out until we hear the piano upstairs stop and footsteps coming overhead.

We step out of the booth and take the evidence. The last two photos are basically of our hair and hands.

27

It's hard to believe that we weren't always like this, her and me.

28

Monday morning, the cameramen are back with Lucien. The three of them walk in on Magnolia sitting on the edge of the pool table, me between her legs, our mouths interlocking perfectly.

"Uh, this is a private moment," I say.

"Great. Passion! Obviously, we're going to do the romance story line, since this is now clearly happening," Lucien says like he didn't hear me.

"I don't think so," says Magnolia.

"Come on, it's showmance time!" Lucien bounces his eyebrows. He's making fun of the term. "That's Catherine's favorite word. But it'll be good for you getting votes. I promise."

I think about that.

"But are you going to make us cheesy?" asks Magnolia.

Skip and Hector are already setting up their equipment while joking around.

"Oh, Ford, your body is so amazing," Skip says in a girly voice.

"No, *your* body's amazing," Hector says back. Admittedly, his fake-sexy voice sounds pretty funny coming from his big round body.

"No, yours is totally more amazing."

I throw the cue ball just to the right of Skip's head, purposely missing.

"Well, now I'm confused if you're a lover or a fighter!" Skip laughs.

"You can give this footage whatever voice-over you want, but I'm not talking about my feelings!" Magnolia yells. It's pretty cute, and I could kiss her, but instead we just frustrate the three of those guys by sitting there and talking about our newfound connection without saying one nice thing about one another.

"I get along with Ford because he's an idiot. And that makes me feel more secure about myself," Magnolia says.

"And Magnolia reminds me of this pet lizard my brother used to have, always wanting to hide under rocks and such. She has the same cold-blooded charm."

I think the people at home will be able to see what's going on between us no matter what we say, though. How could they not?

Of course, it gets around to the rest of the group. Up until the shoot in the game room, we've done a pretty good job of sneaking around. But now we figure there's no real point in even trying.

I pull Magnolia into my lap on the downstairs couch, where Felicia's flipping through a celebrity magazine, and Felicia says, "How am I supposed to do research in here with your guys' phero-mones flying back and forth?"

Gardener comes through on his way to go take a run in his bizarre version of workout clothes: a cut-up black tank top, penta-gram headband, black pants that are half pleather, half lace, and black boots. He stops and looks at me and my girl. "Love will tear us apart," he says. "Again." I think he's quoting something.

But mostly everyone is cool about us. They're in good moods. Things feel different around the mansion since elimination night. For one thing, with Belinda gone, there's less incense smoke in the upstairs hallway. But the bigger change is that the rest of us are still here—if that makes sense.

Now it's like we're survivors, like we've all jumped off the same cliff and lived (except for Belinda, RIP). Last week we were like nervous kids the first day of high school, and now everyone is lounging around the mansion like overconfident seniors.

I guess your sense of being home accelerates when life gets this weird.

29

I wish I could say that all the making out has left me so dizzy that I don't know who I am. But there's still the living ghosts of my family rattling their chains inside my head.

The good news is I haven't heard from them since Cody called. I'm praying, even though I'm not close to religious, that this means he was drunk and forgot about it the next morning. I tell myself that driving to California is exactly the sort of thing my family will sit around on the couch talking about while they're wasted, but never get it together enough to actually do.

Even though this is probably the truth, I still feel the threat of them every time Magnolia confides in me another memory of her dad.

"This is his sweater," she says tonight. We're sitting facing each other on the stone bench in the flower garden in the yard. Her legs are on top of mine. We're supposed to be in bed, but the mansion isn't exactly Alcatraz. The producers are pretty relaxed about curfew when we're on grounds, or when they're making us go to promotional-type parties. Then they don't care when we come home. I got my ass handed to me by Catherine for my TMZ appearance at the Whisky the other night, though. She threatened to throw me off the show if I take out my bike again. She says it's an insurance nightmare.

Magnolia is wearing an oversized sweater that looks like it belonged to a guy who was nothing like my dad. It's a really nice sweater. Like the kind I've seen pretend dads wearing in those department store circulars that come with the Sunday paper.

"Did you save any of their clothes?" she asks. She means my parents.

"Some stuff, sure. Things that meant the most." I look down at how she's pulled his sweater sleeves over her hands. It makes her look vulnerable in a way she usually doesn't. I feel like a piece of shit. Why am I continuing this lie to her? Why can't I just come clean?

Well, it's because I feel so great when I'm with her. Because I don't want her to go away. Because I feel like someone different when I'm with her, and I really want to be that person.

"He would wear this a lot on the weekends," she continues. "Even when it was too hot for it."

"My dad used to have a sweatshirt like that," I say. I'm such a fraud. He's still got it, still wears it. Has an eagle and an owl fighting on the front, God knows why.

"Wearing it is like my version of visiting his grave. Or sometimes I talk to him in the car. It's not like I believe in ghosts, but I can get this feeling when I'm in the car like I could say something out loud to him. It makes more sense there. That sounds wacky, I know—"

"Nah. I get it."

"Do you visit your parents' headstones?"

"Mmmm," I say, and that's just my bullshit way of sounding like I'm telling her yes when really I'm saying nothing at all.

Since we got together, I've learned so much about Magnolia's dad. Every day she tells me a little more. I know about how he would listen to music in the middle of the night because he had trouble shutting his brain off. Couldn't sleep. I know that Roxy Music was one of his favorite bands. I can even picture him lying in bed with his headphones on, like Magnolia said he did. I can see him.

I have to get off this subject or I'm not going to be able to look at her face.

I shiver. "Didn't think it was supposed to get cold in California. False advertising." I'm wearing a T-shirt. I put my hands underneath the hem of Magnolia's sweater.

"You're supposed to layer here. Southern California weathermen have been preaching the virtues of layering my whole life."

"And my whole life I thought my only choice was jacket or no jacket."

"Stick with me," she says. "I'll teach you things."

I slide a hand up into her magenta hair, tugging at it while I lean into her and kiss her. I close my eyes and I lose track of everything: time, the garden. Hell, the planet. I'm only aware of the shape of her lips and her legs intertwined with mine. It doesn't make any sense at all, but I feel like I belong here.

What gets me is this feeling when she's in my arms. I have a hard time saying anything is meant to be, but there you go. I've never felt anything like it before. How else could I make any sense of it? It's like a red carpet rolling out in front of me that I have to follow.

We hear voices coming from the other side of the pool, and glance over. Nikki and her girlfriend are out searching. They look around nervously as they flip chair cushions and peek under planters, looking for the Superstar. I had lost track of everything. Even that we're in a competition. Inside me, a cold wind shakes the walls of the warm little world I've got going with Magnolia, making it feel like a cheap movie set of plywood and glue. There are things trying to wake me up from this dream and drag me back to myself.

They go inside, and Magnolia leans her head back, tossing a few strands of hair out of her eyes. She stares into the sky. Above us reach the black silhouettes of the palm trees, blacker than the sky. The LA sky doesn't get truly dark at night—it's just a big purple smear, washed out by the city lights. You can only see a handful of stars, only the brightest ones. Unless some of those are airplanes?

Her eyes are heavy-lidded and dark and deep, and when they meet mine again, I can't look away, even though it's almost too intense to keep this up. I feel that I'm gone for sure.

"It's so weird," she says. I know she doesn't mean the purple sky. She means us. She means how big this feels. I'm right there with her.

"That we like each other?"

"That we ever even met. That we're us."

"I need to tell you something," I say. My voice is slow, like I've finally fallen in line with my family and become a drunk. There's this second where I think I'm going to come out with it. I'm going to tell her about my people. Lying to her has become excruciating.

But the words change on the way from my brain to my mouth.

"I had them put drugs in your hair color, like mind control drugs," I say. "You got no choice but to like me."

"That feels close to the truth."

We kiss again. And again. I can only liken it to a form of short-term amnesia. It's new every time.

30

I jump off the stage at the preshow rehearsal. Instantly the anxiety I've been keeping at bay comes raging back.

Magnolia's been taking up so much of my brain, there's been little room for the fear to hang out. But now that we're hours away from Wednesday's show, the importance of making it through is closing in like an unstoppable reality. It rolls right over my little fantasy world like a tank.

I need air.

I walk out into the alley behind the stage where a weathered New York street set has been left to rot. I sit down on the stoop outside a brick building that's really only six inches deep. Behind the front door, there's a whole lot of nothing.

I'm just not feeling as prepared to go up there as I did last week. I feel less focused. The joke of it is if being distracted by Magnolia gets me voted out, I don't just lose the show, I lose her too.

Sure, we could talk on the phone. E-mail. But then what? She's going to come to Calumet and throw rocks at the water tower on Friday night? Right now we've only spent time together in music fantasy camp.

"Hey," I hear from behind me, and I turn around. It's Magnolia's mom. She's about to go in the stage door.

"What are you doing lurking around out here?" she asks.

"I just like to be alone sometimes, when I'm thinking."

She gives me a puzzled look that I think means she finds it highly unlikely that any human would choose to be alone. She blocks the sun from her eyes with her hand, and her bracelets jangle. "You're not avoiding Magnolia, are you?"

Now I'm the puzzled one. "Why would I be avoiding her, ma'am?"

She gets a visible shiver. "Oh God, don't call me ma'am. Di, Ford. Di."

"Sorry, ma'am. I mean, sorry, Mrs. Anderson. I mean, I guess I'm used to calling my friends' moms by something besides their first names."

"Is that what you guys are: friends? So the whole romance thing is for the show?"

The way she carries herself, it's more like I'm talking to Magnolia's suspicious friend than her mom.

"What does she say?" I ask, surprised to find a little doubt sitting in my chest.

"Oh, we haven't really had a chance to talk about it in depth. Mag's a pretty private person. You know. Sometimes she can get a little touchy about this kind of stuff."

I just nod. "Oh."

Di's energy picks back up. "Listen, I wasn't born yesterday. I wasn't born *superlong* ago either, but it definitely wasn't yesterday. I can tell there's chemistry. And Magnolia's not stupid. She knows that a show relationship is a ticket to the finals. So don't worry, this stunt totally has my blessing. It's cool. I'm not trippin'."

"You think it's all about the show?" I ask.

"That's not a bad thing," she says.

My phone vibrates from my pocket. I pull it out. It's a text from my sister.

> Watz up, kid? Buckleys r in Cali.
> Can we sleep on ur floor?

I swear, my heart stops.

If I thought I was feeling anxiety before, I didn't know what I was talking about. Now blood pounds in my head like a drum. I wave down the stage manager, Patty, to ask if she's seen Catherine, and she points toward the control booth without so much as a pause in the conversation she's having on her headset.

You're always in someone's way backstage. The grips are pushing massive pieces of staging around on wheels, and I have to press myself against a wall to avoid them.

I have no idea what I'm going to say when I find Catherine: "You're not going to believe this—it's a miracle! My dead parents have come back to life. Can you pay for their hotel?"

Right now I can't even understand why I had to go so far as to lie and say they were dead. It's not that I don't have love for my family. It's just that family love is supposed to feel like a warm embrace, but for me it's more like being wrapped in a heavy chain. The weight makes it hard to feel anything but the weight.

I stop and stare at the control booth. They keep the air cool in here, but I'm sweating.

Where did it all go wrong? It's tough to say exactly when things went south for the Buckleys, but the fortunes of my hometown and the fortunes of the family have been declining hand in hand since before I was born. Not that we ever had a family crest or a grand estate somewhere, but things used to be better.

My grandparents owned a farm and a grocery store, but that's all gone. The grocery store burned to its foundation, and the farms had to get big to survive. Ours was just regular size.

The town is vanishing anyway—banks are gone, the theater is gutted, you have to take a bus to another town to go to school now. The only things downtown that aren't vacant are Leander's music shop and the liquor store, and only one of those makes any money.

I see small American towns in movies sometimes, and they look all quaint and lively, but I've come to believe those towns must be a complete fiction. On my bike ride out west I did not see one small town that wasn't peeling, rusted, and shrinking, that didn't look like its best days were behind it.

There's a lonely feeling that lives under your skin when you grow up in a town like that.

I can even feel it now, as I'm walking up to the booth. I take a breath and step in to find Catherine ripping into Jesse over a mix-up on her lunch order. Something about a missing salad. I try to help him out by lightening things up.

"Should I call the salad police?" I joke.

She spins around. "Try to imagine how you'd feel if your fried Twinkie sandwich didn't show up, or whatever the hell it is you people eat in that mayonnaise-and-corn-dog state you're from."

Jesse takes the opportunity to sneak away. I have a pang of bad longing because it's what I wish I could do too.

Instead I manage to go on with it. "I need to talk to you about something," I say.

"Well, walk with me back to the office." She sighs, already walking before she even knows if I'm coming along.

I follow her as she heads out through the elephant doors—the giant doors that stages have so they can fit big set pieces through—and out onto the asphalt of the lot.

So far there have been fewer actors walking around dressed like gladiators or superheroes at the studio than I thought there would be, but today we walk past a group of people in creature makeup out for a smoke break. The sight of them makes me happy, just for an instant.

"What is it, Ford?" Catherine asks as I catch up to her side. "You and Magnolia break up? I don't have time to play summer camp counselor."

You could tip me over. "What? No. I mean, we haven't even actually discussed if we're boyfriend-girlfriend."

"Good, stay together. Hector was quick enough to get you guys kissing on his phone camera, which saved our asses because you two are way zzzzzzzz talking about the romance in the game room. The phone footage isn't supersharp blown up, but we slowed it down and now it eats up twenty seconds of the package."

I'm not sure how Magnolia's going to feel about the clip, but what does it matter when my reveal is going to make her feel worse? "No, it's nothing about that relationship. It's about my family."

"I think we'll work that angle more as we get near the final vote. Don't want to overplay the sympathy 'little orphan Andy' card too early. No offense."

"None taken." I feel an actual adrenaline rush when she talks about the final vote, like she thinks I'll be around for it. "But that's just it," I say. Here goes. I loosen my shirt from my chest. "I don't think people are going to be too sympathetic when they find out my family isn't actually dead."

"What?" Right away Catherine stops and makes certain eye contact with me. "How not dead are they?"

"They're all the way alive. And they're on their way here." I wince at the thought of it. My stomach churns.

She puts her fingers to her eyebrows and stares at me, wide, out from under her hands. "You lied to me? When there's been all this trust between us? Here I thought you were a sweet hillbilly, and instead it turns out you're a cynical media manipulator!"

I take slight umbrage to the former description. "I'm not a hillbilly. I'm from the delta. Anyway, it's complicated with my family. I wasn't trying to make anyone feel sorry for me. The truth is, we're estranged. I haven't lived with them since I was sixteen."

"You shouldn't have lied to me. I don't care if they abandoned you in diapers at a fire station doorstep and just came back the day before you left for LA! I could have helped you." Catherine shakes her head. "Now, I don't know. Maybe I should just go get a margarita, decide this isn't my problem, and throw you to the wolves."

I feel awful, I really do. She gave me that shot after I messed up in the beginning, and now I've just proved to her that she shouldn't have. "I'm sorry I caused you trouble," I say. I reach out and put my hand on her elbow because I want her to really hear this. I want her to know it's true. "Thank you for everything you've done. Thank you. When you put me on the show, it felt like a chance. I only wanted to make a new start."

Catherine still has that stare on me, but something about it is changing. She doesn't say anything for a moment.

Then, "Impromptu life lesson for you, Ford: it's not that easy. Your past will follow you whether you like it or not. The best thing you can do is learn to live with it."

I wait for her to tell me to get lost while she goes for that margarita, but she stays.

"You're going to need an angle on this reveal so everyone in the country doesn't want to strangle you. Let's go back to the office, and this time I want to hear everything about your screwed-up bumpkin childhood. After I fire the guy who did your background check."

31

It's an hour before show time, and my reflection in the dressing room mirror is as pale as a ghost. I try to shake out the nerves through the ends of my fingers. Catherine has decided that the best plan is for me to come clean about my family, live, on camera tonight, in front of millions. First I'll sing, and then Lance will hold me onstage as he calls up the Buckleys. To make time, they're going to trim my video package down to nothing much more than the kiss.

The mere thought of this event makes me want to disappear off the earth. Change my name, bleach my hair, hop on a train like a dust-bowl hobo and ride it to Timbuktu, or wherever is farthest away from here.

I'm supposed to say that I lied about my family being gone because they're very private people from a quiet town, and I didn't want anyone to come bothering them. That's the story that Catherine has decided is most sympathetic.

The light bulbs around the mirror reflect off the lacquered surface of my guitar as I distractedly practice my song for tonight, "Home" by Edward Sharpe and the Magnetic Zeros. This show's theme is a song that represents "who you really are." The truth is, I have no idea.

But I like the country stomp of "Home," and it seems right for what I'm feeling tonight. Maybe because it gives Arkansas a shout-out right in the first verse—Arkansas doesn't get too many shout-outs. And maybe because the song is asking, Where is your home, really? Is it the place you were born? What if that place is fading right off the map—well, where is it, then?

The song is a duet, but we're not allowed to sing with anyone else, so Stacy has coached me on doing both parts. Lately I feel like two people anyway. There's the person I thought I had to be, and the new person I'm trying to become. Split right down the middle.

In my mind, as I picture it, home is where you feel like you belong. Like there's an empty space in your exact shape already there, and you just fit right into it. In the song, home is when Edward's with that one right person. I haven't had that feeling with my family for a long time.

The truth is there are only two places I feel like that: one is onstage, playing music, and the other is new. It's when I'm with Magnolia.

Magnolia. Shit, shit, shit.

Magnolia.

A knock comes at the door. I stop playing. I get up and open it. Jesse is standing there carrying a bouquet of flowers.

"Came for you," Jesse says, pushing it into my arms.

"For me? Who sent them?"

"Don't know. A fan? I get fired if I read the cards. Good luck tonight."

He hustles off, and I close the door. I open the card on the flowers. They're from somewhere called the Children's Relief Association. A brochure inside the envelope explains that they're an orphan aid society. The card itself reads, *You've been a great role model for orphaned kids everywhere. We're all cheering for you!*

My face goes all hot. Now I'm going to disappoint a bunch of orphans? I might as well grow a thin black mustache and tie a girl to a railroad track. The night ahead of me suddenly seems even more impossible than before, and it already seemed intolerable.

I think about all the people out there hearing my confession, the orphans and the associations and anybody who ever believed even a little bit in me. But mostly I think about Magnolia.

She's going to find out on TV like everybody else.

I put down my guitar and pace the carpet. The dressing room has no windows, and it's making me feel like I'm in some kind of mirrored trap. No matter where I look, I only see myself looking back. A sham. That's the real me. I don't know why everyone hasn't seen it already.

I sit down in the chair and put my face in my hands. So what if it all falls apart now? Everything will return to normal, I guess, and I'll go back to my proper place. Just go back where I really belong.

But there's this other voice inside telling me if I can just talk to her first, explain everything, maybe then things could be okay.

Then I'm running down the hall, dodging between people in headsets and backup musicians on their way to the stage. At her dressing room door, I knock maybe a little too hard, waiting with my hands resting on the doorframe.

Maggie first looks surprised when she opens the door. She's wearing a top with cut-out parts so I can see glimpses of her skin down the sides. Then she looks concerned.

"I needed to see you," I say.

We're kissing before we even have the door closed. I back her into her dressing room and we're unsteady, our brains neglecting basic functions like balance. I just hold on to her to keep from kneeling to the floor. She picks up on my desperation, and we grab at each other like we have to stay tight or risk being pulled apart by the vacuum of space.

I take off my shirt with one arm bent around the back of my neck, and then I'm unzipping hers and pulling it up over her head. She doesn't seem to care about being ready for the show. Then we're falling down on her couch, me on top of her. Her warm skin against mine sends that electricity up my spine. I feel like we're going to pull each other right through our skin.

I slide my hand down to her hip, the most beautiful hipbone I have ever had my hand on in my life. The silk type pants they've got her in dip underneath the bone. I look up at her.

There's one knock at the door, but before we can tell whoever to get lost, it swings open.

Jesse averts his eyes to the floor, but he doesn't leave. We all freeze in place, waiting for someone to make a move, like a Mexican standoff with no guns. I'm personally waiting for Jesse to get embarrassed and shut the door.

"Sorry, guys. I didn't know, you were . . ." He trails off. "But, Ford, there's someone named Cody here to see you. And he's making a pretty big scene about it."

Magnolia

32

Lance straightens his thin tie and puts his hand to his chest like this is a personal moment for him. Dramatically, he says into the mic, "Step on up here, Buckley family," and I'm still thinking that this is some kind of really dark joke that's gone on too long. Mila's sitting on the stool next to me, and she looks over to see if I know what the deal is. I make a confused face to mean that this has got to be a dumb bit. Out of the corner of my eye, I can see my reaction on one of the camera's screens on the side of the stage.

Ford is turned so I can't see his face. But he wasn't smiling when Lance said there was something that needed clearing up. I caught a miserable look in my direction before he stood and went over to the mic.

Ford leaned over and began talking about his parents, in present tense, like they're still alive. Like they're still up and around, and not in the ground. And he talked about a brother and sister I didn't know he had. He said, "I made some stuff up about being alone because, you've got to understand, my family isn't used to this kind of attention. I got worried it would be overwhelming for them."

"But then they made it clear they want to come out and support you, right?" Lance prompted. He had his hand on Ford's shoulder. In profile, Ford's visible eye looked especially bruised underneath the blue overhead lights.

I thought, *This is really terrible comedy*. It had Catherine all over it. I couldn't believe she would drag Ford into doing this kind of shitty bit. I thought Lance was going to say, "Well, let's meet Ford's family!" and then some bales of hay were going to come rolling out from the wings.

Except after Lance says, "Step on up here, Buckley family," four people actually stand in the first row of the audience. They're all in shirts and jeans except for the younger of the two women, who's in a tank dress with pony beads hanging off the fringed bottom. They jog up the stairs on the side of the stage. They've all got both hands in the air, double waving hello to everybody out there. Two of them look like a mom and a dad, the right ages, I mean, and there's even some resemblance to Ford. You can kind of understand how features from those two faces could combine to make up his. And the other two look like they really could be his older brother and sister. They feel like real people. They've got this comfort in their own bodies that says they're not acting. Even the best actors, if you really watch them, give off something that says they're acting.

And maybe these four people are a little animated in terms of where I set my personal energy levels, but I'm really watching them, and they don't look like jokes.

When Lance passes the dad figure the mic, I can see from here that the guy has some prison-looking tattoos on his knuckles.

Those tattoos finally bring it home for me. That's Ford's real dad.

Ford's dad says, "I just want to tell everybody that I'm nothin' but proud of my boy. There's no hard feelings." Ford, facing away from this side of the stage, awkwardly hits his dad on the arm with an open hand. It's like a theater slap. It makes a loud sound in the mic, but it seemed like his hand barely connected.

I just stare at Ford's family, my scalp tingling like they've walked straight out of their graves. Graves marked by red ferns. (Look, I can't help it, that's just what I pictured.)

I stare at the side of Ford's face, which has immediately become stranger to me than an actual stranger's. In another couple of seconds, when I belatedly accept the obvious truth that's right in front of me, that's when the really hard feelings come rushing in. They're such bad feelings. They're so overwhelmingly bad. So that's how I realize that I've fallen in love with Ford. Because it's incredibly painful to realize at the exact same time that I'm in love with him and that being in love with him doesn't even matter anymore, now that we're done.

"Did you know anything about this Ford family intrigue?" a fluish-looking reporter on the press line asks me outside the studio after the show. She looks like she should have stayed home in bed. There's a chill in the air, like cold weather is actually coming to Los Angeles.

"I don't feel like answering questions," I say. I wish I had a coat. I'm practically in a leotard.

Catherine is walking behind me at just this moment, and she pulls me back from the reporter.

"Uh, yeah, answering questions isn't an optional part of

the night," she says, looking at me like I'm crazy. "This is part of your job. People ask you things, and you tell them things."

"I'm not a robot." As soon as I've said it, I'm remembering the night I met Ford.

"It's all been such a great opportunity," I hear Nikki, standing next to us, answer a reporter. "Gets kind of gnarly sometimes back in the house, like, just accommodating different personalities, but yeah, still way cool."

"I know you're not a robot," says Catherine. "Because I had a Teddy Ruxpin, this talking robot bear, as a kid, and he would be doing a better job on this press line." She walks me back up toward the reporter. "Ask her again," she commands the woman with the probable flu.

The reporter coughs and clears her throat. Then she goes back into the same tone of voice she had before, like we're girlfriends dishing, like she hasn't asked this already. "Did you know anything about this Ford family intrigue?"

"Nope," I say.

"But aren't the two of you close?"

"Nope."

I'm sitting in the walk-in closet of what's supposed to be the maid's room. But we don't have a maid living in the mansion. There's a service that sends a different team of cleaning people every morning, and they seem like they've been instructed not to look anyone in the eye.

As soon as the vans dropped us off, I slipped away up here even though everybody's supposed to be practicing the group number for tomorrow's elimination in the living room. The song is a last-minute thing. Last week, when this was a show without high expectations, elimination night was mostly filler with performance clips and a ridiculously drawn-out reveal. But now that it turns out people are actually watching, Catherine suddenly has more money from the network. This week we're singing "Feel So Close" live. And we're supposed to dance too, kind of. It's not full-on choreography, but there are moments when we're supposed to be stepping side to side in time or looking at each other.

I'm not in the mood to be singing about feeling close to people. Only Mila saw me ducking out, and she jerked her head toward the stairs, meaning, *Get away while you can.*

Ford has been taken over to the Venice hotel, where his family is staying, to shoot footage of them being a family together. The show is trying to spin this new development into some kind of amazing reunion story, instead of what it really is, which is that Ford just bullshitted everyone.

When I was looking into his eyes and telling him stories about my dad, how could he not have cracked? When I was telling him about this hole in my life? When I was telling him about what it was like to have a dad gone, how you feel like one of your very earliest signposts in the world just went and evaporated, and he was saying that he knew? When he was looking right at me? Even just some unconscious part of him. I mean, even if his eye had twitched. Then I could look back and say I'd seen the real him.

For a minute there it seemed like we'd magically found each other. With Scott, it was more like we formed a balance. He had what I didn't emotionally, and the other way around. But with Ford, the pull felt more like we were somehow the same underneath, despite having almost nothing in common besides that. I mean, you think you've lucked into a connection. You think, *Wow, it's easier than I thought to talk to someone for hours and get the hell out of my own head.* You think, *I can't believe how great this feels; no wonder other people work so hard to find this in each other all the time.* And also, you think, *Oh my God, it's addictive to be this happy in the presence of another person.*

But you don't care that it's addictive. Until you find out that the person was running scenes with you and you just didn't know it.

The sliding door to the closet opens. My mom is standing there. "Found you," she says.

I've felt like I could cry since about five seconds after I saw the tattoos on Ford's dad's knuckles, but I've been keeping it together. When my mom finds me, though, the tears start pressing uncomfortably against my eyes. It's not because I feel like it's okay for me to cry in front of her. She makes the tears come to the surface because I know she's not going to be what I need.

"I just want to be alone for a little while," I say.

"Come on, gloomy. Is it the Ford thing?"

She invites herself into the closet and sits down across from me in a cubby that's meant for lots of shoes. This closet has an intense organization system installed. It looks like a secret level of Donkey Kong. My dad loved arcade games. Once in a while he would come home from his investment firm early, which meant nine, and he'd take me to a pizza parlor for dinner, still wearing his suit. He'd play the old-school machines beside the kids in Little League uniforms and the dorky, hunched teenagers playing the fighting games.

I always liked the game where the plastic chicken spins around clucking, and then drops out a prize in a bright egg. I know there's no skill involved, but there was some weird stuff in those eggs. If my egg had a piece of cheap jewelry, I'd give it to my dad and he'd wear it for the night.

"Mag?" my mom says. "You're not talking to me."

"He could have at least told me before he told the audience. At least."

She shifts to tuck her knees underneath her, and the shiny discs covering her minidress make a crunching sound. "Yeah, the pair of you were supposed to have this insta-deep connection, right? Okay, I have an idea. You ask to tape a scene at the mansion where he's trying to plead with you, and you're walking away from him. And then he comes running after you and takes you into his arms. To an amazing song. People love that moment where the guy runs after the girl in movies. They love it! I love it. I've heard you say you love it when we watch movies. You only need that kind of thing because I've been reading a lot of the feedback online, and there's definitely interest in that story. If you could just build up the love aspect, it would really help you. People connect with you because the idea of you being a part of this emerging couple is definitely a softening thing." She starts patting the back of the closet wall like it's a false front. "But just in case, do you think the hidden Superstar could be built into the house?" she asks.

Right now I wish it were my dad sitting across from me. I speak slowly to my mom, like she's a kid. Which I guess in some ways, sometimes, I feel like she is. "I didn't mean that I'm worried about how tonight came off to the audience. I meant that *I'm* hurt."

My mom stops her patting, and makes a sad smile. "Oh, Mag, my supersensitive girl."

"I don't think this is a crazy thing to get sensitive about."

"He's embarrassed by his family, it's obvious. Don't take it personally."

The tears really push at my eyes. "But when you found out that dad was dying—not just dying, but pretty much almost dead—and he hadn't said a thing to you all those times that you guys talked about who was getting me for the first night of Hanukkah, or school supplies I needed or whatever, didn't that hurt you? That he was lying to you that whole time? That he could have said something to clue you in so you didn't have to feel so far from him when you found out? I mean, I know why dad didn't tell *me*. Because I was just a kid. He didn't want me to worry. But he could have told you. And didn't knowing that make you feel lonely and hollow and terrible?"

Nightmarish butterflies hit my stomach as soon as I've asked this. I talk about my dad, but I never ask my mom to talk about him. Her expression is so panicked that I'm definitely finally going to cry if I look at her anymore. So I avoid her eyes.

After a couple of seconds, she says, "I wasn't involved with your dad when he got sick." Her voice is hard for me to take.

"But still, you were connected," I mumble.

"The relationship was over." My mom is already getting onto her knees so she can step up and walk out. She's the one not looking at me now. "I'm going to go call Lucien and talk to him about writing that scene for you. The Ford make-up scene."

"Please don't."

I don't know if she doesn't hear me over the rustling discs of her dress, but she doesn't answer as she opens the door to the closet and leaves. I just sit there for another couple of hours, thinking. I don't try to work on *Ships* or anything. It's more like a meditative state, except I don't think you're supposed to be extremely upset while you're meditating.

33

Lucien finds me during vocal coaching at Stacy's the next morning. I ended up missing the entire group number rehearsal, so she's teaching me my part. (Since the first time here, I've learned that this *is* actually Stacy's house. She's just continually surprised by the objects in it because she had an interior decorator choose them.)

"Dig in, reach for the note," Stacy commands as she hits a key on the high end of the piano. "You've got to put more heart into it or you're not going to get there."

"Noooooowwwwww," I try, not hitting it.

Lucien leans against the doorway. "Can I borrow Magnolia?"

Stacy sighs. "Is this show even about singing?"

It's definitely not. But I'm not going to be the one to tell her.

I join Lucien and we go out and sit at a table on the patio. He's got his hair in a low pony, a very thick pony, and baby spit on the shoulder of the usual football jersey he wears.

It's bright out. I put on a pair of Gucci sunglasses we got in one of the twenty gift baskets we've been sent since last week. The Guccis would be good for hiding puffy eyes if I had puffy eyes. I'm not even close to being in the mood to cry today.

When I woke up this morning, I had shifted into mostly being really, really angry. I saw Ford only once, in the kitchen grabbing breakfast. His back was to me. Anger surged through my chest, once again keeping away sadness. I walked straight out.

"So your mom called me last night about this Ford development," Lucien says.

"I don't want to have to go running to him on camera. And I don't want him to run to me either."

Lucien leans back and basks in the sun. "Yeah, I hear you."

I wait another second for him to argue with me, but that's all he says. I'm surprised because I figured he would definitely push for a more dramatic action than ignoring Ford.

"That's all?"

"I'd be pissed if I were you too."

"And?"

"Where do you want to go next with your story line? Do you want to do a variation on a young-woman-scorned thing? There's always a ready audience for that." He's looking up at the sky, speaking in that kind of back-of-the-throat voice you try out when you're a kid and you want to annoy your parents. But he's not trying to annoy me. He's bored, I'm realizing. "Or you don't have to do anything at all."

"Hey, are you bored by this job?" I ask.

He looks down. "Well, yeah. It's not my ideal project. It's not my *Moby-Dick*."

"What don't you like about it?"

"This job isn't writing. On a good day, it comes *close* to bordering on storytelling. If I get to structure a scene around something going on in the mansion or feed a good line, I go home feeling better about it. But I'm not creating you guys out of my head. I'm not getting to pursue the themes that most interest me."

"What are those themes?"

He makes a cross with his fingers and holds it in front of him like I'm a vampire trying to suck out information. "I don't think my job is to sit here and answer the big questions of my existence."

"Fine, the questions can be smaller," I say. "How old are you?"

"Thirty-seven."

"What's your baby's name?"

He looks at me sideways. "No, seriously, what's with all the questions? I'm not the one who does interviews. I'm the invisible one."

"I don't know. I just got curious about your life."

"Her name is Scottie."

It rings a bell. "Wasn't that also F. Scott Fitzgerald's daughter's name? We read *Gatsby* last year in English. Mrs. Corinthos turned it into a book about how Daisy should have focused on herself. She says Daisy got in that trouble by letting herself just be a pretty face."

Lucien shakes a finger in the air. "Mrs. Corinthos! Very reductionist, Mrs. Corinthos!" He switches over to pointing at me. "And, yes, that was Fitzgerald's daughter's nickname and the reason why my daughter also has it. He's probably my favorite author, depending which mood you catch me in."

"I like it for a girl. But my ex-boyfriend's name is Scott, so it makes me imagine him as a girl and as a baby." I haven't heard from Scott since I left him outside the gate. My anger toward Ford has pushed that night way into the background. It's become like a continually dimming star somewhere in the back of my heart.

"Do you like English class?" Lucien asks.

"I think it's the only class I genuinely do like," I say.

Lucien and I end up talking, as real people, for the first time since we've met. Usually our conversations consist of how Lucien wants me to come off on the show. The last time I talked to him, on Tuesday, the cameramen were at the house getting extra footage for the performance show. Catherine wanted what she called some "ambient stuff" to make a "pondering montage," which I came to understand was just us contestants in quiet moments alone thinking about whatever the show wanted to make it look like we were thinking about. My thinking face got intercut with Ford's thinking face.

Lucien wanted me to walk around the garden in (pretend) rain because that would convey a *Wuthering Heights* kind of romantic sensibility, and we had a small argument because I thought that would just bring up the tortured and depressed stuff all over again.

But now I tell him about Mrs. Corinthos and what school was like and all the semi-ironic roller rink skating trips that went down in middle school and how I socially cracked when I got to high school. I say I don't want to talk about Ford. Lucien says he doesn't blame me.

Lucien tells me about how he met his wife in the dorms at UCLA and how she made him like himself for once and how they actually used to live in the apartment where F. Scott Fitzgerald died in Hollywood. Lucien tells me that F. Scott died clutching the mantel of his fireplace, so Lucien used to knock on it for good luck every morning before he left for a meeting. I tell him that knocking on a man's death mantel seems like it might not be the best good luck charm. He tells me that yeah, it didn't seem to work because here he is, consulting on this show instead of getting his movies made.

I guess we talk for a really long time because eventually Stacy comes out, holding a fresh Frappuccino, exasperated.

"I've got an hour before I have to send you off to that movie premiere. Are you going to come work on this note or what?"

"Be there in a second," I say.

"I wish your momma was here to help me wrangle you," Stacy mutters before she steps back inside. My mom is at a salon getting her hair blown out for the premiere. It's a Pat Graves movie, and he's been her favorite star since I was a baby.

I push my chair back from the patio table with my legs. "Hey, why haven't we talked before?" I wonder.

"Context," Lucien says.

"What's that supposed to mean?"

"We were approaching each other from a standoffish context. I was the guy working for the show, making you portray yourself in annoying ways, and you were just another kid I had to convince to take a walk in the rain before I could go home to my own kid. Neither one of us considered trying to talk to each other in a real way. It was all *Spotlight*."

He opens his arms. "That's how the world works. It's hard to have the personal conversation because you get tripped up by the surface conversation you're *supposed* to be having. Not the one you'd get more out of. That's why you cracked in high school. You didn't know how to change the context. So you gave up."

I definitely know what he's saying. It connects back to everything I've been trying to reverse in myself. I get up and start back toward the house.

"So any feelings about your story line this coming week?" Lucien calls after me.

"I don't know if we have to worry that much about it. I think I might be going home."

"Nah, it's looking worse for Dillon. Even worse for Ford.

The girls on the message boards are unhappy with him. They liked the orphan spiel. They wanted to save him."

"Let me get back to you."

I head inside, and Lucien goes over to use the hose. He holds his shirt away from his chest to dribble water on the spit-up. I stop and watch him for a second. I feel like I've gotten more out of this talk than I have from actually being on the show.

★ ★ ★

I have this feeling like I should be thinking more about my performance than I am.

I should probably be running it over in my head.

I mean, it should probably pop into my thoughts at least ten times a day?

Twenty?

It kind of feels like there's homework I'm ignoring, but I'm one of those burnout kids who's completely content not doing it.

It was different for the second performance. During the first show, I went out there and hoped I'd become this whole new person. I was so discouraged when nobody else saw the new thing in me.

But last night, I don't know, I just wasn't concerned about starting over. I sang before Ford's family reveal, so it's not like I was distracted. The theme was "songs that we felt represented ourselves." I picked "Every Single Night" by Fiona Apple. I love that song. In rehearsal, Stacy had been pretty unhappy with me.

"You can't find the melody unless you listen to it five times," she said. "This is not an instantly enjoyable song. And the lyrics—no, no, no, no! You're going to sing about your breast busting open?"

"Yes," I said.

"No. No, no, no."

I said, "It's about how her brain won't ever let up. So she's caught in a constant struggle between being sensitive to everything around her and then also being tortured by all that activity." It really spoke to me.

Stacy just stared for a good few seconds. Then she asked, "Do you *want* to go home?"

I just wasn't worried up there. I don't know why.

34

It's my turn to walk the step-and-repeat red carpet at the Thursday night premiere. We're all here, judges included, because one, Jazz has a part in the film (as herself), and two, Catherine is thrilled about the free additional promotion for the show. The camera guys taped us getting ready because a story line for next week follows the disappearance of Nikki's curling iron and how she thinks Felicia hid it after Nikki used up her Moroccan oil. You'd think the two of them wouldn't want to play this out for the cameras, but each girl just thinks it makes the other girl look bad.

Anyway, the red carpet. All I have to do is smile, take a step, repeat, repeat, repeat, repeat, repeat, repeat, repeat, repeat, repeat, repeat, repeat, repeat, repeat. Then I can go into the theater and watch a movie.

This should be as simple as jumping rope in PE or like last year, in Mrs. Corinthos's class, when she made us repeat vocab words and definitions over and over in our vocab journals. She told us that's how she remembers names at a party. She mentally says a person's name and a defining characteristic a bunch of times, and then she's like, "Heyyyyyy, Jennifer!" when she sees Jennifer in line for the bathroom. After that I'm sure she's like, "Jennifer, honey, listen, I'd like to talk to you about the way you've been sticking to your husband's side this whole evening and how you could be better at partying if you just focused on yourself."

I've smiled for the cameras and stepped and repeated four times when I spot a flash of a ton of very red hair getting out of a curbside town car. I know who that is immediately. I check to make sure that my mom is still distracted talking to the director of the movie, and then I say, "Sorry, be right back" to the photographers.

Most people wouldn't know that my mom has been upset since our talk last night. It's hard to tell, but it's all I can see. Not that I really said anything unbelievably awful to her—I mean, I was just asking a legitimate question about my dad. But I know it messed with her.

Ever since then, something in her face has made her look unsteady. She's been quiet around me. She's been nervously shaking the bracelets on her wrists. I hate feeling like I'm her parent. I really, really do. But sometimes what feels worse is just the fact of seeing a parent be vulnerable. And you'd do anything to put her back on top so you don't have to linger in that dynamic a second longer.

I'm wearing a dark blue beaded jumpsuit and the pants on it are a little long, so I step on the hem a few times as I'm jogging to the curb. Catherine and junior producers are on the other side of the carpet hovering around Ford, making sure he says the right things to the press. Catherine is wearing a red tuxedo with her hair gelled back, and I can't explain it any better than this, but she looks like an abusive cotillion partner.

No one from the camp at the town car stops me from approaching the actress from the hotel elevator, because I'm not just an average person anymore. I'm on TV.

She's looking down, watching an assistant fix a streak of bronzer on her leg.

"Excuse me?" I say.

She looks up. She doesn't seem drunk today. Her eyes are clear and wide open. She recognizes me.

"Magnolia from *Spotlight*!" she says.

I say, "Well, that too. But I also met you in a hotel elevator once. Do you remember that time? I was with my mom?"

There's uncertainty creeping into her eyes. "The elevator?"

"I want to get a picture of the two of you together," says a man who I think is the actress's publicist. The request seems urgent, and I get the sense that he thinks it will help his client's fading career to release a photo of her with me, which is kind of mind-blowing. It's so incredibly weird that *I*, a random high school kid, could help her seem relevant.

We stand hip to hip and put our arms around each other like we're old friends. The publicist pulls over the WireImage photographer to shoot us.

"You know, the elevator," I continue. "You were really nice to us." It's sort of half-true. "I have a favor to ask. My mom's here tonight, and if you could come over with me and say hi to her, that would mean a lot." The photographer snaps us and we smile, repeat, repeat, repeat. "But if you could call her Di, like you remember her name, that would be even more meaningful."

The actress turns slightly, giving the photographer another angle. "That's it?" she asks me.

"That's it."

"Di, you said?"

"Right."

After we take a couple more pictures, I tell the actress to give me a head start and then to follow. I go over to where my mom is standing so the actress knows which person to approach. My mom's dressed in an emerald evening gown with a sheer panel at her stomach. The panel plays a trick on the eyes because it seems like you should definitely be seeing a belly button, and you can't figure out why you're not.

As I approach, my mom's bracelets are jangling on her wrists like wind chimes. Seeing her unsteadiness cements the feeling in me that I have to do something to fix it, like I have to take care of her, like I have to put her back together. So that's why I could kiss the actress for showing up to this premiere.

Walking up, I hear my mom saying to the director, "Spike Lee, his early stuff. Lee Daniels, I can't wait to see what he does next. . . ."

I don't think I have to explain that the director is black.

"Hey," I say.

My mom tries to beam at me, but it's not like normal. There's distance between us. "Magnolia, have you met Mike? Mike, I took her to see *Last Summer Resort* the night it came out. She loved it. I love the scene where Pat is leading everyone in lawn games and then suddenly that bear appears--"

"The bear scene!" Mike says, proud. He's bald and looks something like if turtles were allowed to join the army. He can just barely cross him arms successfully because his muscles get in the way.

"So Pat picks up the wife of the millionaire—that millionaire was *such* a douchebag, by the way—in his arms—"

"Di?" says a very convincing voice from behind us.

My mom turns. She sees the actress. My mom looks young. She looks doe-eyed. It's like I've restored her, and that makes me feel such phenomenal relief. "Lauren! Oh my God, hi! You remember my name?"

"Of course, the night in the hotel elevator!"

The actress can act. Lauren and my mom start talking like they're long-lost sisters, and my mom introduces her to Mike, which Lauren really seems to appreciate. It seems like Lauren would give up an organ to be in one of his movies. While the three of them are talking, my attention drifts off and I watch Pat Graves signing autographs for the fans in the bleachers; they've waited hours to see him walk the carpet. He smiles, and it's honestly pretty astonishing. I would need about fifty more teeth to manage a smile like that.

I notice one fan's face in particular—she has shining tears pouring down her cheeks, but she's obviously really happy. I wonder if that's real love, having so much feeling for someone that you only need the tiniest interactions to keep yourself going.

While I'm thinking about this, I feel someone's fingers drift up my spine. The jumpsuit is a halter, so it's completely open in the back. I know that it's Ford's hand on me. I just do.

I look over my shoulder, and his hand is still extended behind him, reaching toward me, even though he's moving away and facing forward. He's being escorted by Madison in the direction of Pat Graves, probably to meet him. I don't know what he thinks that touching my back is going to accomplish.

A whole new wave of anger comes. Let's put aside when I was looking into his eyes and telling him stories about my dad. What about when we were almost having sex before the show? What about then? What about when his hand was on my hipbone and he was pausing from kissing me and staring at me like I was all he needed? And he knew that in less than an hour, his family would be jogging up onto the stage. When he was staring at me like that, even if he hadn't known where to start, couldn't he have tried? Couldn't he have at least said something like, *Magnolia, I don't know where to start . . .* even if he couldn't get the rest out? And I would have said, *What? What?* and been completely frustrated and mystified, but at least I would have known a part of him wanted to tell me before the rest of the world.

I'm walloped by the sudden understanding of just how much Ford wants to get away from who he was. He wants it so bad that he even pretended with me, when we were alone.

But that doesn't change how pissed I am.

"You ready to go in?"

The actress and the film director are gone, and my mom's standing there, waiting on me.

"Yeah, sure."

I look around, and the red carpet is emptying out. Pat Graves has gone inside. The fans in the bleachers are comparing trophies. A couple of publicity people from the movie are walking up the carpet, making shooing motions and yelling, "Carpet's closing! Please head into the movie! Carpet's closing!" We obey them and walk toward the theater. At the end of the carpet, there's only one person still posing, and that's Jazz Billingham. She looks so small when you see her out in the world. I mean, she looks like the preteen that she is.

Also, the skirt on her dress is gigantic, nearly antebellum, and it makes her look like these dolls that my grandma used to keep in the bathroom to cover up the extra toilet paper rolls.

We step around the front of the carpet to pass by her without ruining her photos. Jazz says to the photographers, "You have your pictures, yes? I'll be going, then." And then she takes a step and falls.

She falls hard. She's tripped on one of the under layers of her dress. I gasp. The press is still taking photos of her. She lifts her face and it's panicky, hurt. You can see the deeper horror of her embarrassment. There's this fear that she's just shown something to the crowd that they're never supposed to see.

"I want my mom," she says quietly, maybe even so quietly that I'm one of the few people who knows what she's said because I'm looking right into her eyes and I'm standing right in front of her. Her parents are never with her. From what I hear, they live somewhere back east. Jazz's lawyer is the one who acts as her guardian. He always stands off to the side in his charcoal suit, taking calls, and occasionally they speak a couple of words to each other.

And then something kind of bizarre happens. My mom runs to Jazz and scoops her up from the ground, taking her into her arms. She hugs her like she's her mom. I think Jazz is going to fling off my mom's affection and say something like, *Hugs are for people who don't have their own art to embrace them.* But Jazz just holds on to her really tight.

My mom protectively blocks Jazz from the press and then guides her off the carpet and behind the step-and-repeat backdrop. I don't think Jazz and my mom have ever interacted before this moment, apart from maybe shaking hands during a backstage introduction.

One of the movie's publicists touches my arm and says, "We need you in your seat."

I can see my mom still comforting Jazz, who seems to need her. So I figure I should just leave them alone. "Coming," I say.

I enter the lobby and another studio person hustles me toward the theater door, saying I'm going to miss the start of the movie. So I head in, but as soon as I'm through the door, someone else grabs my hand and pulls me into an ushers' supply closet underneath the stadium seating.

"Maggie," Ford says. He's standing there in dim light, in a suit without a tie. The way he says my name is both urgent and hopeful.

"No," I say. I start to back out, pulling away my hand.

He doesn't let it go. "Maggie," he says more urgently this time.

"I adored you." This isn't meant as something nice. It's supposed to be a punch to the face. I pull away my hand, hard. I leave him.

Shaken, I walk down the hallway to the stairs for the seats. I watch my step because of this insane jumpsuit. At the front of the theater Mike is saying, "And I just hope you all really dig it!" The room breaks into applause. Pat Graves stands and claps over his head like he's at SeaWorld. I spot Mila near the aisle, and Ricky's taken the seat next to her. I duck down at their row.

"Hey, Ricky," I whisper. "Can I have that seat?"

"There's more near the front," he whispers, confused.

"I just really want to be with my friend right now."

Mila nudges him. "Your eyes are bad, Rick. You should get up as close as you can."

He sighs and indulges me. I take his seat with all my sequins crunching underneath me.

"You look paler than usual," Mila whispers.

"Ford tried to talk to me."

"You're allowed to be disappointed in him. Don't let him get that twisted." She picks up a sequin that's fallen from my jumpsuit to my shoulder and flicks it away for me.

The lights start to go down.

I can't help but be aware when Ford appears in the aisle as the theater is almost dark. I stare ahead. He takes a seat somewhere in the back.

I concentrate on the movie. The Universal logo spins. There aren't any opening credits. It just starts. Pat jumps from the second story of a mall to the first. He tackles a bad guy (who just looks bad) that works in the mall pet shop. The guy produces a scorpion from his pocket. Mila laughs. Nobody else does. Pat expertly takes hold of the creature, and he gets it to clamp a claw down on the bad guy's nuts. I laugh too.

FORD

35

It's Saturday morning, and I'm helping Dillon lug his stuff outside to the waiting town car. He's been pretty quiet toward me since Wednesday's performance show. Even more so after the results came in last night. He thinks I'm nothing but a liar. Last week he couldn't stop projecting his voice to his imaginary Madison Square Garden—now, total silence. We walk down the driveway without saying a word.

The driver takes Dillon's KISS computer bag from me and drops it in the trunk. KISS was vomiting fake blood onstage back when computers were the size of living rooms, so I'm not sure what they're doing selling laptop bags.

"This sucks," I finally say. What I mean to say is, *This sucks that you're going home, and this sucks that our friendship dies here.* And it's also me trying to own up that I know it should have been me, even though I didn't want it to be.

Dillon takes a deep breath and gives me a look full of hurt. "Yeah, well, too bad I didn't have a secret family to pull up and hug onstage."

"Dill, I—" I start.

He doesn't want to hear it. "Yeah, welp, that's show biz, man." He says this like he's a fifty-year-old road dog at the end of an exhausting world tour. He makes a depressed set of rock horns with his fingers. "Friends are strangers, and strangers are friends. Being a straight shooter won't get you anywhere." He looks off down the street. "But don't worry about me. I'm sure you'll get over your guilt. I'm sure people at home will forget about my last performance, eventually. I'll live it down."

That performance is why Dillon's going home instead of me. For obvious reasons, I was in the bottom two with him. What started out as a pretty good version of "Baba O'Riley" turned bad when Dillon climbed onto a giant human pyramid of actual teenagers and it collapsed. He finished the song mumbling "teenage wasteland" from the bottom of a dog pile.

When you make a mistake on live TV, people get to enjoy watching you blow it over and over. Dillon's pyramid collapse has already gotten millions of views online. It's as if that version of him has been pinned up like a butterfly, and he'll be stuck like that forever. How are you supposed to get any better if you can't screw up when you're starting out?

As Dillon ducks into the car without saying bye, I know something has gone bad between us. I guess losing out to someone who killed off his own family isn't sitting well with him. The car pulls away.

I drift back into the mansion.

Everybody's on different schedules with fittings and coaching, so I search the place until I find Mila upstairs doing what I think is yoga in the music room. She watches me walk in behind her, her head hanging upside down between her shins. She doesn't seem any happier with me than Dillon was. But I don't need her to be my best friend—I just need her to help me get to Magnolia.

"Dillon gone?" she asks coldly.

"Yeah, he's gone."

She moves into a kind of side lunge with one arm up in the air. "He's a good person, so hopefully good things will happen for him," she says pointedly. "You know. Karma."

I take a deep breath. "Do you know where Magnolia went?" I ask.

"Hair consult, fitting, story meeting with Lucien."

Magnolia has gotten really good at not being wherever I am. She's been away a lot for coaching, and she disappears somewhere in the house when we get home at night. We've been near each other only when everyone else is around. At the premiere she wouldn't talk to me. This morning she was gone somewhere before I got up.

An hour ago I tried texting her, but she still hasn't responded. I guess that not answering is her answer: *I hate you, go away.* I can't blame her.

But I also don't know what to do with all these feelings now that their reason for existing wishes I didn't exist.

"She hasn't said anything about me, has she?" I know it's a stupid question as soon as I've asked it, but it comes out anyway. I already miss Magnolia so much that even hearing something painful she's said seems better than nothing.

But Mila doesn't answer and just twists her body into something that looks like the letter *D*. I think that's *D* for *Done with this conversation*. I slip out and head back up to my room.

I take a minute to stare at Dillon's empty side. His bed has already been stripped of its sheets. The bareness reminds me of those war movies where your bunkmate goes out on a dangerous mission and never comes back. Another man down. Who's next?

Out of the corner of my eye I sense a shape in my bed, like there's someone in it, and I whip around. But it's just a big USPS box of letters. Hell, it's the biggest one yet. Before I came on this show, I think the last time I got a personal letter in the mail was from my grandmother on my eighth birthday. It was a card with a two-dollar bill inside and instructions to use it to jumpstart a savings account. I spent it on Milk Duds.

I head over to the box and start going through the mail inside. The return addresses are a list of places I've never been but always wanted to go: New York City, San Francisco, New Orleans, one from England. I picture it being written from a castle tower with one of those feather pens. Do they even get the show in England?

But what really surprises me is how many letters are from Arkansas and the feeling these postmarks from my state give me: now that I've left home, I feel closer to it.

My phone rings from the windowsill. It's got to be Magnolia.

I pick it up and see Catherine's name. I eat the barreling disappointment and answer.

Catherine doesn't bother to say hello. "So I was up half the night dealing with your *interesting* family."

I already know what's coming next. Like I'm a psychic.

"They had some kind of trash-tastic party at their hotel and wrecked the place. I kept it out of the press and paid for the damage, but they've been kicked out. I told them they'll have to foot the bill at their next lodging because I'm not taking another penny away from the show to replace shitty motel carpet."

I drop my forehead onto the cool wall. "So where are they going now?"

"I gave them the info for a cheap dive by the airport. But that's not what I'm really calling about."

"What else could go wrong?"

Catherine puts on a sunshiny voice. "Not wrong, right. You get to go to a party tonight for Rocket Fuel energy drink—they're our biggest sponsor, so I don't want you moping around. This is important for rebuilding your image and making people forget we fed them your shady shit. Go. Distract people from your fib. Have fun. Got it?"

"That's nice of you to do this for me, but I'm not really in a mood to go to a party . . . " I start to tell Catherine. I feel small, and low, and I want to find a big rock to crawl under.

"Hmm, yeah. But are you in the mood to be in the bottom two again?" she asks, and hangs up.

A second later a car horn blares outside. Followed by people shouting. Gears grinding. It sounds like a bunch of chaos, so I just know, without having to look, that it's the Buckleys.

36

Again, maybe I am psychic. Because somehow I sensed they weren't going to shell out their own money for a motel. Or maybe I just know them too well.

I drag myself down to the front door, and sure enough there's Aunt Rose's RV, and it's squeezing its way through the front gate. Jesse the PA is running down the driveway, waving his arms.

Here come the four horsemen of my personal apocalypse: Mom, Dad, Sissy, Cody.

Jesse is trying real hard to stop the rusty RV, now splattered with mud from six different states, from parking on the fancy landscaping of the front lawn. He doesn't know this, but there's no way his pantomiming is going to get my family to comprehend that a lawn isn't for parking on.

It's a game of chicken that Jesse's bound to lose. He has to jump aside as the RV tears through the front flower garden that's worth more than the RV is. Black exhaust fumes fill the air as the RV rolls to a stop. Its front bumper breaks the graceful necks of a bunch of what I now know are called birds-of-paradise.

Sissy jumps out of the driver's side, tossing her golden hair, a black sweatshirt hanging off her shoulder. She's yelling at Jesse the second her feet hit the ground. "What's y'all's problem? You looking to get run over?" Her eyes have that fighting gleam in them.

Jesse looks pretty surprised, probably not expecting the driver to be this savage blonde girl. "You can't park that here," he says, all sheepish.

"You want me to park it in your ass instead?"

"Sissy, leave him alone," I call from the front steps. "He's just doing his job."

"Ford!" She runs over and wraps her arms around my neck. "My famous brother. Tell this dipshit what's up."

"Jesse, I'm sorry. I'll get them to move it."

Cody appears from the side door of the RV carrying two garbage bags full of clothes. He tosses his golden hair too. Honestly, it's only a few inches off from him getting mistaken for Sissy from the back. "Hey, bro!"

I'm already bracing myself for a battle. "You gotta move this thing."

Jesse, who's been talking on his headset, holds up a hand. "It's all right, Ford. Catherine says to leave it here for now to avoid any more commotion."

"No worries for the trouble you gave us," Cody says, and throws his garbage bags at Jesse, who awkwardly catches them. "Just take my bags up to my room, will you?"

"Cody, he doesn't work for you," I say.

But Jesse actually takes the garbage bags into the house. Probably because it's the fastest way to get out of this situation. As he heads in, I'm just now realizing that no one else is getting out of the van.

"Where are Mom and Dad?" I ask Sissy.

"Well, they've never seen the ocean before—except the Gulf, but that don't really count—so we left them down on the beach. They're probably pretty drunk, I imagine. Do you think the show could send a car down to pick them up?"

I roll my eyes at their total predictability. Before I can answer, Cody's giving me a handshake that turns into a one-armed hug. He steps back to look up at the mansion. I can see his mind working, trying to find some overlap from the world we come from with the one in front of him. Trying to match up something familiar. But you can't because the gap between the two things is so huge.

Once you really understand how huge it is, it seems indecent, and you wish you could forget it. You can't.

"We had a little trouble down at the hotel. But really, should family be staying at a hotel when you've got a house like this?" Cody shakes his head at me in holier-than-thou judgment.

I say, "It ain't my house," but Cody and Sissy are already stepping around me and going in. I follow like a sleepwalker. Immediately, Cody's patting the walls like he's checking the construction or something, and he's also whistling in admiration at the building details. Cody the architectural expert. Maybe he'll accidentally make himself useful, stumble on the Superstar; but then he'd probably charge me 50 percent of my prize money for it. If I know him, I imagine he's trying to add up what everything costs.

He jogs up the stairs and we end up in the media room, where McKinley's watching a playback of his last performance. He makes notes on places he can improve, writing in a spiral notepad. I swear, the kid runs his life like it's already an international business.

"Hey, it's that little guy from the show!" Sissy claps her hands. McKinley looks up from his notes, alarmed.

Cody steps close to the TV, watching McKinley's playback with his hands on his hips. "You're all right for a little kid. I mean, you can really sing. Problem is, you might be too good, y'know? Too perfect.

You got a voice that sounds like it was made by a machine. You got to put the soul in there."

There's some truth in what Cody's saying, but McKinley is sort of like a robot in that he just can't process it. He stares at my brother.

"He doesn't need your advice," I say. "He knows what he's doing."

"If you say so." Cody pulls a can of beer out of his jacket pocket. Just like that. He cracks it open.

My head starts to swim. I start pleading. "C'mon, man, settle down. You just got here five minutes ago—you want to get kicked out of here, too?"

Cody looks real confused for a second. Getting day drunk is not something he would usually give much thought to because to him, it's as basic as putting on your shoes.

"*You* settle down," he says. "It's a free country." Then he holds out the can to McKinley. "Mc-Coo-Coo, you want one? Might be good for you, get you out of your head."

"I'm only fourteen," McKinley says.

"Hell, when Ford was thirteen, he could outdrink a grown man! Of course, that was back when he was fun. Before he became a monk." Cody takes a swig.

"I'm not a monk." Stress already has my head sloshing like one of those wave tanks at a water park. I don't know why this can't ever just be easy.

"Whatever," Sissy says, and moves the tension elsewhere as she sits down next to McKinley and messes up his perfectly groomed hair like he's a puppy. "What I want to know is, does this little heart-breaker have a girlfriend?"

McKinley stiffens. As cool as this kid is onstage in front of millions of people, he's still been pretty sheltered, so he doesn't have the know-how to deal with someone like Sissy.

"I'm not dating yet. Not until I release my first album. I've got to stay focused."

"Does that mean you're a virgin? Like Tim Tebow? Wink, wink about his virginity, am I right? Well, it's a good thing we met. I promise I'll be gentle." This is just Sissy joking, but McKinley jumps up from his seat like he's been cornered by a wild animal. He darts out of the room, mumbling something about a five-year plan.

"Must be losing my looks." Sissy laughs and then says she wants to see the pool.

When we go out back, Rebecca is sunbathing on a lounge chair. I'm surprised to see a big tribal tattoo in the middle of her back because it's in better condition than the rest of her. She shades her eyes with her hand and squints up at us.

"Sissy and Cody," I say, "this is Nikki's girlfriend, Rebecca."

"Nikki like Nikki on the show?" Cody asks. "The hot island chick with all those flowers behind her ear?"

"Is that a problem?" Rebecca lifts herself up on her elbows, ready to be challenged.

"Dang, girl, you're a lesbian?" Sissy sits down on the chair right next to Rebecca. She's never had much respect for personal space. "We don't get too many lesbians back home, except for Traci Greene. But you don't mess with Traci, now—she will tie a knot in your tail."

Rebecca peers at Sissy for a second like she's going to put out a cigarette on her, but then she kind of just looks interested. "She'll 'tie a knot in your tail'?"

Cody weighs in. "Hope you don't mind me asking this, but what is it gays like about Los Angeles so much? Is it the palm trees?" He looks up at the trees above us, sipping his beer, like he's really trying to come up with a workable theory.

I tense again, but Rebecca's expression is entertained. The likes of Sissy and Cody seem just as new to her as she is to them. "Yeah, that's it. We just love palm trees."

Cody nods like he's made a major discovery.

"So there's the backyard pretty much," I say, trying to move things along before they get weirder. "And now I'll show you guys my room."

"I'm gonna hang with Becky," Sissy says, and slaps Rebecca's thigh with the back of her hand like they're old friends. "Get some sun and talk about lesbian stuff."

I look at Rebecca to see if she wants rescuing, but she can hold her own. With Sissy, you're either instant friends or instant enemies—that's just her way. Rebecca points to a pack of cigarettes at the foot of the chair and says, "Grab me one of those, and I'll tell you the secrets of the sisterhood." Cody and I leave the two of them chatting. I'm just thankful nothing has turned into tragedy so far.

But once we're up in my room, I spot Cody's garbage bags sitting on Dillon's empty bed and a renewed panic goes through my body. Does Cody really think he's staying here with me?

Last time Cody and I shared a room, I was ten years old and I had to build a fort of pillows around myself to survive the nights. Darts. Chinese throwing stars. A bike chain. Whatever was within reach, he flung it at me when the notion took him. I still have a scar on my forehead from a particularly well-aimed G.I. Joe jet plane.

I turn to Cody, trying to figure out how to broach the subject of the family leaving, but he's already diving onto my bed. He starts digging through the fan letters.

"Oh, man, look at this. You got girls writing you from all the way out to space." He tears one open, dumping out the letter and peering into the envelope with an eye closed. "I bet there are some topless photos in here."

I pull the letter out of his hand. "Don't tear those up. Those people took the time to write me."

Cody grins tightly, but his eyes are flashing anger. "Oh, I see how it is now. Don't like to share the glory, do ya, little brother? But you don't wanna forget: If it wasn't for me, you wouldn't even be here. I taught you everything you know."

"Yeah, you taught me how to play guitar. But Leander taught me more about music than you ever could. And then this, being here"—I throw my arm out at the room—"it's something I did on my own." Still, I can't seem to meet his eyes as I say this. He continues to have some older brother power over me.

"You always did think you were better than the rest of us. You didn't think we were gonna see you make us out to be a bunch of sad dead hicks on TV?"

Now I look him in the eyes, and I find out he's not smiling anymore.

"Well, we are a bunch of hicks," I say. "And I don't think I'm better than anybody. I just maybe think different about things than you do."

Cody pretends to be respectfully taking off a hat he's not wearing, meaning that I'm putting on airs. "Oh, you think different, all right. You think family don't mean nothing. But you can't change the blood in your veins. Don't forget: family sticks together."

Family sticks together. Granddad's unbreakable code. I remember a fight I lost the summer I was eleven. I was crying on the hot asphalt street with one eye swollen shut, curled in a tight ball to blunt the stomping feet of the Nolen brothers. I'd tried to stand up to them for calling Sissy a whore. Defending her honor was a full-time job.

When I was no longer able to catch my breath, Cody appeared, wading into the Nolens like an avenging angel, leaving one of them with a broken nose that's still crooked to this day.

"No one messes with my brother," he told me. That day I was just about in awe of him. But the next week he was back to terrorizing me, like nothing had ever happened.

I believe that Cody would die for me, but letting me live the way I want? That he can't do.

"Why don't you cut out all the guilt trip stuff and just tell me what you want?" I say. "Just be straight. Y'all are messing this up for me, out here tearing up hotels, acting stupid. How am I am supposed to focus on winning this thing with you here? I want you to go home, so really, what is it that *you* want?"

Cody drops the hurt act and nods like he's ready to do business. "I think it's fair that the whole family should benefit from your situation here. That's all. You want us out of your hair? I can make that happen. You tell that producer lady that we'll leave"—I wait for it—"after she pays our per diems."

"What do you know about a per diem?" I know from Jesse that a per diem is daily spending cash some crews get when they travel with a show, to buy food and things. I don't know where Cody heard the word.

"Internet research. Per diem, travel expenses, whatever you want to call it. Just tell them to pay us whatever they'd spend for us to stay in a four-star hotel for the rest of the show. In cash, tonight. Then we'll make ourselves scarce." He shrugs. "Otherwise we've got no choice but to stick around. And we might have to talk to the press too. I might have to tell them how terrible you've treated your family, how you had a drug problem . . . whatever will help them sell their gossip magazines. I'll come up with something."

The back of my neck goes as hot as if I have a fever. "Did you come all the way out here just to blackmail me?"

"Not you—you're broker than I am! These Hollywood people, man. It's not like they need the money. And I've got a good little deal set up. I'll even let you in on it, 'cause I'm fair."

I won't lie, it's painful to watch how people here will spend a regular human's yearly salary in one night just on finger foods for their party. Where I grew up, you'd be ashamed of wasting money like that when other people don't have a thing. But it's just like Cody to only see what he can get from other people, not giving a damn if he burns every bridge this show might build for me. Being rich can make you mean, and being poor can make you ugly. It seems like there's a lot of problems in those circumstances that nobody ever solves.

There's a knock. I look over my shoulder, and Robyn's standing against the doorframe, holding up some shirts. The one in the front has a holographic pocket. She says, "Hey, Catherine asked me to come bring you some things for the party tonight."

I can hear Cody sitting up on the bed. "There's a party?"

"Robyn, this is my brother Cody." She waves. "Cody, this is Robyn, the show's stylist. And it's not really a party. It's work. Just a promotional thing."

"Sounds like a party to me, man," Cody says. "Sounds like a party where you get some free things."

"Try this on." Robyn hands me a shirt with the sleeves cut off. It looks like a real ragged, cheap shirt you might make yourself, which means it probably costs five hundred bucks.

"So I'm coming to this party, right?" Cody asks.

I stop in the middle of taking off my T-shirt. "I don't think that's really possible."

Cody gets up from the bed and comes and stands real close to me. Like I said, Sissy invades your space accidentally, but Cody's definitely trying to remind me about something. "Yeah, brother, I do believe I'm including that as the last part of our deal."

37

The final deal we make is this: if I take Cody to this party and get my family the per diem, then they will leave town tomorrow morning.

Before the party, I try to calm down. I try to stop looking at my phone, waiting for a text. I try to get in a good frame of mind. So I kick Cody and Sissy out to the RV, and I return to reading the fan letters.

Some of them are crazy. A teen girl in Florida sends a photo of my name tattooed on her shoulder; I cringe when I see she spelled *Buckley* wrong. A woman in Michigan says she thinks we should be married, and wants me to help explain this to her husband.

The letter that bothers me most is from a ten-year-old in Arkansas named Mason, who wants to know how he can be like me when he grows up. But it doesn't make sense for a kid to want to be like me. He just has some kind of idea about me that's not really me at all.

Reading about this kid's belief in this Ford person, I can't help it. I start feeling real lonely, even though you can always find someone in this mansion if you want company.

I can't help but wonder if Magnolia's no different from this kid. She had an idea about me that she liked, but then she saw the real me, she saw my family, and that was it. I mean, who did I think I was fooling anyway?

The sun goes down, and I pull on the shirt with the missing sleeves. It's dark soon enough. Mila comes into the bathroom while I'm shaving, and we don't speak. I hear Cody yelling from out the window that there's a "huge honkin' limo" in the driveway, but still, there's nothing on my phone from *her*. Jesse comes in and says it's time to go. So I do.

The party's in full swing when Cody and I get to the Aviary, which is some swanky private club in West Hollywood. On the way in they make us walk a photo line with paparazzi taking a hundred photos of us in front of a background with advertisements for Rocket Fuel: "One small drink for man, one giant shot of caffeine for mankind." Cody strikes every big-shot pose he knows, yelling, "What magazine's this going to be in?"

The Aviary is not a dance club, really, even though a lot of people inside are dancing. To me it feels more like Sherlock Holmes's living room, if Sherlock also collected stuffed birds.

Cody hits me in the arm and yells into my ear, "Hey, isn't that the guy from that commercial where he rides a Jet Ski in the bathtub? I gotta meet that guy." Then he's making a beeline toward the free bar without any hesitation, like this is just a roomful of his oldest pals.

I glance over, and it *is* the guy from that commercial. Actually, the whole place is full of people I sort of recognize. People from that show where you live together in a submarine for three months, *Sub-Humans*. And the one where sorority girls have to live like pioneers from the 1800s called *Little Sorority House on the Prairie*. And from that hit MTV show *The High Life* about kids working in a Colorado ski town who spend all day snowboarding and making out.

Everyone here has that reality show kind of fame, the kind you get not because you did something cool, but just because your face has been on enough TVs.

"Hey, Ford Buckley, right? Love this guy!" Some dude puts his arm around me while his friend takes a photo. "Thanks, bro!" He slaps my back as they move away. I nod a good-bye, trying to be friendly.

And then I get it. I *am* one of those reality show famous people. I spot people pointing me out as I move through the crowd. Hear my name being mentioned by strangers. This is something I always thought would be cool, but the truth is that I'm feeling a little embarrassed. Because I haven't really done anything good enough for people to be singling me out like this. And I don't know how they don't know that.

I see Cody and the Jet Ski guy doing shots together like they're longtime buds, and Cody tries to wave me over, but I don't trust myself around a bar tonight. I only feel that deep nagging to drink when I'm in the presence of my family. To save myself, I find a door to the balcony and step outside. Away from the crowd, into the night air.

I lean out over the balcony. Cars wind bumper-to-bumper down below on Sunset. A group of girls in tight dresses dodges between them, laughing and holding hands as they cross the street. Across from me there's a huge billboard of Pat Graves riding a zip line with explosions going off behind him.

Pat Graves's giant head reminds me of the movie premiere, and of Magnolia. I check my phone. There's a text from Catherine telling me about an after-party. That's it.

"I totally thought I was going to scream when you walked in tonight." I glance over, and a really good-looking athletic blonde props an elbow onto the banister next to me. She seems familiar.

"Huh?"

"I was, like, no way, that's Ford Buckley, my future boyfriend. Oh God, aaaaaaand now I'm embarrassed."

A different person might be annoying talking like this, but she has this real playful high-energy way about her. Her hands never stop moving. So she seems like a real person, like she can't help but show you what's going on inside her head.

"You watch the show?" I ask.

"Uh . . . yeah."

"I'm probably more embarrassed than you are. Still not used to the attention. You look real familiar, though. Are you on a show too?"

"Maybe you'll recognize this." She busts out a funny little break-dance move and then laughs at herself.

"You're a dancer," I say, snapping my fingers. "You were on that dance show." I remember her now. My ex-girlfriend the Mattress Princess used to love those dance shows.

"I'm Rey." She shakes my hand. "*So You Think You Can Dance.* I came in second. This close." She holds her thumb and forefinger an inch away from each other.

"You're really good at dancing. As much as I can tell."

"What about you?"

"One of those things I just don't do."

"Then you need to learn how."

She takes my hand and literally drags me back inside and into the crowd of people dancing to some dance track I've never heard before. I kind of nod to the rhythm, but Rey's dancing has this whole kind of vocabulary to it. Like one second she's sexy; the next, funny. Dancing with her is like having a conversation without saying a word.

The music feels good. Dance music isn't usually my thing, but its heavy beats overwhelm my brain. It's too loud to hear thoughts about Magnolia, my family, alcohol, myself—all of it. I think I might be having fun.

Then within a minute Cody is dancing near us with a girl from the sorority pioneer show, waving a drink in the air. His eyes meet mine with a look of drunken camaraderie, and I see him yell, "Whoo!" but I can't even really hear it over the music.

I give him a full-blown "whoo!" back.

A new song comes on without me even realizing when it started, and a sharp ball of light appears right to our left. It's a news camera crew. The reporter holds up her mic and starts talking about the party right in front of where we are.

Still dancing, Rey leans in my ear and says, "This is so great. We're in the shot."

That gets me thinking about what Catherine said. I guess this is the sort of scene she wanted. I try to look comfortable, like a guy you'd vote for.

Rey leans forward again. "You know what wouldn't hurt?" she shouts over the beat.

"What?"

"Drawing some attention to ourselves. You have to make people care about you! Because they stop."

She pulls back, and she's giving me this look like we're in on something together, but it's also a look that says I should kiss her.

We're right behind the reporter and right in the path of that ball of light. I cup Rey's head and lean down.

Magnolia

38

Lucien and I are sitting in a sports bar slash restaurant in Burbank. There are a bunch of guys and a few girls yelling at TV screens so huge that the players are the actual size of seventh graders. Normally, I'm not allowed to leave the mansion except for show stuff, but Lucien told Catherine maybe it would be easier to get me to open up in a more relaxed setting. She bought it. We ran out the gate and to his car like two kids ditching school.

"Get yourself together, you lump! You piece of garbage!" a guy in a beanie violently yells as he brings his fist down in a bowl of peanuts. He's upset at a football player on the screen. It makes me glad that people don't get *so* invested in us on the show. Well, I guess sometimes they do, but mostly in a gentler way.

"That's a lump calling the kettle lumpy," mutters Lucien, briefly looking up from poring through the notebooks and pads of paper I've brought him.

I try to eat my fries, despite all the space the butterflies in my stomach are taking up.

It's Tuesday, and I've successfully spent the day out of the house in wardrobe fittings and voice-over recording and vocal coaching. Lucien and I were supposed to meet back at the mansion, but I called him and asked if we could have our meeting somewhere, anywhere else.

Today Ford tried a new tactic; he started texting me. I've turned off my phone. For me, there's no conversation. Because there is nothing that I want to hear him say. I don't have imaginary moments going through my head where I fantasize about him coming to me and begging, "Please forgive me. I'm so sorry." I'm not walking around inventing monologues that a mental hologram of him delivers when I lie down at night. When I think about Ford, I see a blank space. I don't know him. So there's nothing for him to say now that can reverse and change how he represented himself to me.

It wasn't just a lie. It was a real death, taken from my life, that he dredged up and pretended to understand and, more than anything, let me believe he'd experienced too. But the whole time there was a nauseating gap between us.

He was acting pained, and I was in pain. It sounds like a simpler difference than it is. But I guess that's how people can watch shows or movies and believe that the character on-screen is the same as an actual person who has to live with those feelings. How actors and actresses can meet with people who've undergone the heartbreak they're pretending at, and believe that they got a reasonable glimpse of it. A handle on it.

Even if they just believe that temporarily. Even if Ford got confused and for a second was doing such a good job of acting that he thought he was feeling what I was feeling, having lost a good dad.

No matter what, it wasn't the same. And he didn't.

When Lucien suggested that we go out into the real world

to grab dinner, I asked, "But how are we going to do that without making a whole scene?"

"Context," he said.

He told me that all we had to do was go somewhere a *Spotlight* contestant wasn't expected. "If you don't make sense in that context, you won't get recognized." He brought me an Anaheim Angels baseball cap, and I borrowed a blonde clip-on ponytail Mila had, because the fuchsia really stands out.

We walked in, took a corner booth, and no one has looked at me twice. And now Lucien has barely glanced at me since he started going through my *Ships in the Night* notes. I don't have everything on hand to give him, but there's enough from the past few weeks.

He's flipping through pages while I'm nervously waiting. Nobody has seen any of my imaginary TV show except for Mrs. Corinthos, and she mostly cared that I was using the vocab right.

I look around the restaurant. Even though I'm not a sports fan, I have to admit it's kind of giddy and festive. I think it's because all the different-colored lights on the beer signs make it feel like we're inside a Christmas tree. Some of them are blinking.

Finally Lucien looks up, a piece of the hotel pad in each hand. His eyes are big and lit up. "Well, hell, you really have something here!"

The butterflies go faster. "What, you like it?"

"I didn't think you were going to have something here."

"Thanks a lot!"

Lucien manically spreads out the pages across the table, moving our drinks. "Don't get all pouty yet. You've got the formatting all wrong. This is nothing like how a TV show is written. But you've just got the feeling of this world *down*.

There's a real voice here, and believe me, I hate precious, shitty terms like—" He pauses. "I shouldn't be cussing."

"I don't care if you cuss!" I shout, just wanting him to continue what he was saying. I have to hear what he thinks makes the pages *something*.

"No, I really shouldn't. Ever since I had my kid, I've been intending to watch my mouth. I look at you, and I think, *Lucien, this could be your daughter.* Not just meaning that if I'd knocked up my high school hookup, I would literally have a daughter your age by now. But would I want a mentor figure taking my daughter out to dinner and saying *shitty* this and *shitty* that? No. I wouldn't." He seems to be getting sentimental, just thinking about his daughter.

I'm thinking, *But what about the voice? What about the voice?* but I don't want to interrupt his moment.

He's not done. "It's strange to feel so fatherly all the time. When Jay-Z announced he wasn't going to use the word *bitch* anymore now that he has a baby daughter, I thought that was a dumb reason. But I get his frame of mind now." Lucien takes a sip from his gigantic glass of Coke. "I feel a little fatherly toward you, especially reading your writing."

I can only wait a second, and then I have to ask, "But what about the voice?" It's like the butterflies could fly up and out of the top of my head.

Lucien goes back to leaning over the papers spread out before him.

"I hate the term, but it just means that the world you've created here has a distinctive feel. There's something under and between the words that's all yours." He rubs his thumb and forefinger together like he's trying to test the thickness of the air. "It's nearly impossible to talk about. But you have that here."

"Here?" I say, tapping on my scrawled notes. I want to make sure I'm really hearing this. Sometimes, on the show, the judges tell you something positive just to keep you from wanting to kill yourself before they flip it around.

"Let me tell you, this Warren Gettysburg character? Teenage rebel without a cause, except that his parents are tragically unreachable? I love him."

"I love him too!" I say. Hearing Lucien's appraisal, I feel like a human exclamation point.

"What I like so much about your characters is that nobody's all good, or all bad. Warren does some shitty"—Lucien stops to correct himself—"messed-up things, but he's not a hopeless person. You understand gray."

I'm feeling so extremely exuberant, like I'm made up of the blinking bar lights. "Yeah, I think I actually do. I mean, I've never thought about it like that before. But you just really simply explained what I want him to be. Gray."

"And like I said, this isn't formatted right. But I think you could do something with this. I think I should teach you how to write a script, and then we should show it to people."

"People?"

"Well you're only seventeen, so it's a long shot that anyone in entertainment would hire you to work. Yet. Besides a singing show. But that doesn't mean you can't get an agent." He taps on the table. "We should also start talking to film schools."

I lean back in the booth, blown away by the turn in my life that Lucien is suggesting to me. "Are you being for real?"

"I am."

Suddenly the restaurant erupts in a wall of cheering because something amazing has just happened in one of the games on the TVs. At least fifty people are throwing both of their arms up for victory and yelling some version of "YEAAAAAHHHHHHH!"

Then the same kind of excitement tears through me, and I throw both up my arms up in the air and yell, "YEAAAAAAHHHHH!" too.

Lucien punches the air like he's an action hero in a freeze-frame at the end of a movie. "YEAAHHHHH!" he yells.

I stand up on the booth seat and do a kick, which really kills Lucien.

"YEAHHH!"

"And I format a montage using all caps: BEGIN MONTAGE and END MONTAGE," Lucien says, "but some people just change the slug lines."

He's got a bunch of napkins laid out on the table and he's written all over them. He's giving me a lesson in professional screenwriting. We've been at the sports restaurant so long that the first big game ended, and there's a whole new wave of fans at the bar. I only notice because they're wearing a new color. There's a ton of red.

"Got it," I say.

"Some people also like to do all caps on sound cues for emphasis"—he scribbles, *As Magnolia walks into the house, a telephone RINGS*—"but that's kind of a personal style thing."

I nod and make myself a note on my own napkin. I borrowed a pen from the bartender, and it has a tiny plastic guy who slides up and does a dunk when you turn it upside down. I feel like I'm psychologically dunking, if that makes sense. That's how happy I am, sitting here. Inside my head, it's like *swoosh brungwungwungwungwung* (that's the best I can do for a ball going through the net and the rim shaking afterward).

"And I think that about covers it in terms of what you need to know to get started."

"I wish I could get started as soon as I get back to the house," I say. We're not allowed to have computers in the mansion. While we're on the show, they want the house to be our whole world.

Lucien checks the time on his cell. "Speaking of the house, I've got to take you back. So we'd better switch gears and talk show. Have you given more thought to how you want to come off this week?"

I take a minute and think about how I want to seem. I could yell at Ford on camera and look tough and strong. Lucien could write me a few brutal insults to throw at him. I could write some. It could be like a movie. It could be this opportunity to say the perfect devastating thing at the perfect moment. And everybody watching at home would be able to see how perfectly I'd reacted to Ford having hurt me.

Or I could do a water-off-a-duck's-back kind of portrayal. Lucien would help me. I could just seem like the most happy and carefree spirit to ever walk the TV screen. This could be the culmination of everything I came onto this show to be. I could be the girl with the open face and the unstoppable heart and the sunshine in her soul! I could be her. And she would be the type who could actually, really win this thing. Because she would be all full of light and forgiveness. And everyone would just have this feeling like, obviously, they want to turn toward her.

Except sitting here with Lucien, looking at the writing in front of us, there's a new picture of what a future could mean. I look at him. Here's a person who doesn't want to be the center of attention—who isn't generally all that great with people, in fact. He's "rough around the social edges," says my mom. At this moment in his life he's not doing *exactly* what he wants to be doing, but he's on his way. He's not, like, tap dancing on a cruise ship when actually he wants to be alone with a piece of paper.

"What? Why are you looking at me like that?" asks Lucien.

He has someone who loves him. He's not trying to be someone else. He has a well-rounded life.

Maybe this is so obvious to everyone else, and I'm coming to it late because I get so sidetracked by the small stuff, but here's what just now occurs to me:

It's not my job to make everybody else comfortable.

Not that I'm discovering that you should go through life being a huge asshole for the sake of it. More that it's dawning on me that the future isn't where you've finally trained yourself into being someone else. The future could just be me, older. Me following my own inclinations instead of looking at myself from the outside in. Instead of trying to scramble myself into what basically amounts to a pageant contestant.

How I want to come off is:

I just want to be myself.

I can finally answer Lucien. "I want to go home," I say.

Just like that, I've said it out loud. The thing I knew in my gut from the second my mom told me we were coming on the show, the thing I've been working overtime to ignore. I wouldn't even admit it to myself. But hey, there it is.

This show is just not who I am. It's as simple as that.

It's what I wanted to want. Not what I really want.

Lucien sighs. "I know you hate talking about how we're going to depict you, but we have to have this conversation before I drop you off."

"I mean that I want to go home *from the show*."

The giddiness that has been swelling in me all night is now so big that it's almost too much. I've failed to reinvent myself. But being a failure is totally fine! I thought my problem was how hard it was going to be to change myself. But that wasn't it.

My problem was that I didn't understand what had to change. I needed to get out from under this idea that I wasn't doing life right. This idea that you're only whole if you can feel at home at a party. Only whole if you can go out into the world with a smile and get more charged up the more contact you make. (In bio, our teacher told us that in studies, healthy monkeys thrive on group interactions while the damaged ones go off by themselves.) Only whole if you're famous, even on the smallest scale. I get up on my knees in the booth and slap the table with both palms.

"Maybe I'm not disappointed in myself!" I say. "Maybe I just felt other people's disappointment in me and I thought it was mine too. But it's not!"

Lucien is giving me his crazy grin that says he thinks I've gone nuts, and he's just soaking it in. "I've always thought sports bars can cause psychic breaks. I'm sorry I brought you here."

I just laugh, I'm so happy. "You think I'm being kooky. But I'm not, Lucien. I'm not."

He slides out of the booth, still holding the grin. "I'm going to run to the bathroom and splash some water on my face before humoring you."

I watch him head toward the glowing neon sign that says BLOKES. Some of the sports fans good-naturedly hit him on the back as he passes, even though he's not in red. Everybody assumes everybody else is for the same team.

I relax against the wall of the booth, feeling a calm wash

over me. It's the calm of being at peace with myself. It's better than being on a beach.

I glance over at the TV that's hung from the ceiling across the room. The late local news is on, and there's a reporter standing in front of some kind of party. I can't hear the sound over the music pumping through the bar and all the people talking. The reporter smiles and waves her arm at the room. There are shots of people who look like they might be famous, except they're not famous enough for me to know who they are. They just seem like they're in show business somehow.

Then the story cuts back to the reporter, and I watch her expressions for a moment before I'm distracted by two people who are kissing behind her. One of them looks like Ford in profile. There's the same bruised quality about this guy's eye, which is open as he kisses this girl. He even carries himself like Ford. It's in the bend of his neck and the way his chest goes concave in lowering his face to hers.

It is Ford.

I sit there, watching him on TV. The giddiness drops straight out of me. The only thing I can do is sit and stare at the TV and feel it all.

39

I stop by the guesthouse to say good night to my mom before going into the mansion. When I open the door, she's lying on the couch, and I think I hear her say, "Jazz," as though that's who she's talking to. It surprises me to think they've stayed in tight contact since my mom helped Jazz up from the red carpet, since I imagine Jazz's walls don't stay down for long. But maybe she wants a surrogate mom? Or maybe my mom is just saying she's jazzed about something.

My mom sits up like she's going to get off the phone, but I put up my hand to mean *Don't*. I make the sign with my hands for going to sleep. She says, "Absolutely, yes," to whomever she's talking to and blows me a kiss. If she notices that I'm sad, she pretends not to.

I walk across the rose garden, along the pool, and into the mansion. It's late and the house is quiet.

I pass the downstairs powder room where I saw Dillon last night, sitting on the closed toilet with swollen eyes. We'd just come home from the elimination show.

"I'm sorry," I said.

"Back to the minor leagues," he said. "Back to Temple

Bat Yahm. Before you know it, I'm going to end up being the annoying grandpa making the kids listen to him play guitar and sing at the holidays."

"At least you'll have your grandchildren?" I hadn't known what else to say because I was already having feelings, even if I wouldn't admit them out loud, that the show didn't mean as much to me as it did to everyone else. And so I'd already started to feel like an imposter for making it through.

Now I run up the staircase. I make a left at the hallway, away from the bedrooms that the show is using. I go into the maid's room and flip on the overhead track lights. I shut the door behind me. There's no furniture, and it's partially the bareness of this room that makes it feel like such a relief to be in here.

I go to my favorite closet and open the sliding door. I shut it behind me. I let myself think about Ford. I think about meeting him on the rooftop at the hotel. I think about standing with him at the window at Stacy's house, how I felt weirdly close to him, fast. About the time we looked at each other when he was leaving the elevator, me telling him I'd heard his parents were dead. What I thought we were saying as we looked at each other then, the transparency I believed in. About our first kiss, about being underwater together, about every other single time his mouth was on mine and his body was against mine and I was so happy to feel like I was myself, even as I was his. And he was mine, even as I had no idea who he was. About his family walking up to the stage. About him kissing that girl tonight on TV, about him projected up there on the TV like a stranger—but if he was a stranger, then why did his image feel like it was wringing my heart?

I let it all tear through me. The feeling wells up, and I kick into the wall of the closet, the part where you're supposed to store your shoes. My foot goes through the wall. I'm kind of surprised that the wall is that thin, but I don't care about the hole. It feels good to have made it.

I lower my foot and notice there's something catching the light down in the hole. A glinting tiny head. I bend down and reach in and pull out a silver figurine holding something that looks like a comet.

I guess my mom was right to be examining the wall. I've found the hidden Superstar.

FORD

40

It's after two a.m. when I finally get home. The party *was* fun: an escape from the show, from thinking about Magnolia. But things went downhill pretty fast.

Cody must have taken something, because he started getting weird and crazy. Shirtless on the bar, tossed a drink in a guy's face, started a fight, the usual. When the bouncers threw us out, I managed to wrestle him into our town car before anyone called the police.

"Don't take us home. I want to party!" Cody yelled at the driver from the backseat. He had his arm slung around my shoulders, and it felt so heavy. "This is my brother. *My* baby brother!"

We had to stop twice on the way up the hill to let him puke. He hung his head out the open door until he had nothing left but the dry heaves. I apologized to our driver about twenty times, trying my best to keep Cody from getting vomit in his nice car.

It's been a long night, I'm thinking as the driver drops us off at the front gate, which is still all lit up. The mansion's always lit.

I have to help Cody stumble over to the RV because he can barely walk. It seems quiet inside the vehicle at first, but as we're coming up the pathway, my mom opens the trailer door. She's wearing a crisp-looking Venice Beach T-shirt and a brand-new sunburn.

"You're late," she says to Cody. "You just almost screwed things up." Then, to me, "Hi, baby boy."

It's rare to see Mom so engaged in life. Her usual state is zoned out, not seeing or caring much about anything that's happening around her. I guess the change of scenery has been good for her. Woke her up, at least.

"Late for what?" I ask. "It's, like, a quarter after two in the morning."

Cody drunkenly mumbles, "Chill, chill, it's all gonna work out." He splays out on the lawn.

I sigh. "Are Sissy and John sleeping?"

My mom holds a finger to her lips, even though she's not keeping her voice down. "Sissy's sleeping in the back. Dad just went out to take a leak. The toilet's broke."

"Take a leak—where?"

She nods, and I step around the RV to see into the yard.

My dad is pissing into the swimming pool like one of those little-boy-peeing fountains.

"John! Dad!" I snap. "You can't be doing that!"

He stops, but just because he's finished. He walks back to the RV, and when he reaches me, slaps me on the shoulder. "That's what the chlorine's for." He looks at Cody all collapsed on the grass. "Cody, about damn time. You got the funds on you?"

"What funds?" I ask. A nervous feeling is settling in now. They've got something going on. They're up and waiting for a reason.

"Perrrrrr diem. That beautiful olllllll' perrrrr diem," Cody slurs.

Catherine reluctantly agreed to the amount just to stave off more trouble, and she had Jesse deliver it in cash to Cody as we were leaving the party. My brother has an envelope with thousands of dollars wadded up in his back pocket.

"He's got the money. That was the deal," I say.

"We've got money for the deal," Cody says.

"That them?" my mom asks, looking past me. I turn and see a pair of headlights at the front gate. The car turns off, and two very questionable (believe me, I'm well acquainted with questionable) dudes get out and just stand there. My hands start to tingle immediately. I already know what's happening.

"Jesus Christ, you guys!" I turn to my family with a terrible ringing going through my body. "You're doing a drug deal? At the place where I'm being put up by the show?"

My dad rolls his eyes at me as he goes to get the money off Cody. "Stop being melodramatic. It's a good deal. We're gonna clean up back home."

"Do you know how much cheaper weed is in California?" My mom is practically in awe.

One of the guys calls through the gate with a Spanish accent, "I leave in thirty seconds!"

"Look, amigo, it's all here, but I don't speak Mexican," Cody answers.

"Jesus Christ," I say again, and then I start backing away from my family. "I'm not staying around for this. I don't care what you do as long as I wake up tomorrow morning, look out the window, and see a big empty space where this RV now stands." I spit on the ground— that's how angry I am. "I want you gone by sunrise."

You can actually see the insult ripple through my mom's eyes. "I guess we're just big disappointments to you," she says. "Look who's giving his own mother orders. You know, you should be a whole lot sweeter to me because . . ."

I don't wait to hear the rest. I turn and run up to the house. I slam the front door behind me, pretending it's some kind of magic portal that erases what's outside. I jog up the staircase just to feel like I'm getting even farther away from my family as quickly as possible.

When I look up, there on the top step is Magnolia, sitting. She stares at me as if I've gone fuzzy, like there's nothing solid she can make of me.

"I don't even know who you are," she says. Then her eyes get real sharp. "Are you *so* desperate for attention?"

It takes me a second to come back to the planet that doesn't revolve around my family. Then I remember the kiss, and I know that she knows.

41

How is it that you can spend hours trying to get someone who's giving you the silent treatment to respond, yet somehow, right when you forget to obsess about them for one goddamn minute, *then* they want to talk?

"I saw you on TMZ tonight, kissing that girl. I just want to let you know how desperate that looked," Magnolia snaps. We've ducked into the upstairs game room so we can raise our voices.

I knew that the kiss with Rey would get back to Magnolia—and maybe that's partly why I did it—but they don't keep cable or computers in the house, so I thought it would at least take a day.

It's been a long night. I want to say something hurtful. Even though, at the same time, all I want is to hit rewind. "You're the one who's avoiding me—what am I supposed to think? I saw you that night sneaking around with your surfer boyfriend—Keanu or Kahuna or whatever the hell his name is. So don't get all holier-than-thou."

I know it's not the same thing, but right now I don't care.

"How could I be so wrong about someone?" She yells this, almost like she's angry with herself. She's now sitting slumped on the air hockey table, rubbing her eyes, obviously crazy tired. Her makeup blurs underneath her lashes.

In my head I'm racing through all the smart points to make. In my head I ask her, *How was I supposed to know you would care what I do? You've been avoiding me like I had rabies ever since you found out about my family. I've tried talk to you, text you, but you don't respond. Do you expect me to read your mind?*

But all I say accusingly is, "You didn't answer my texts."

She looks up. "I've been trying to sort out my feelings."

"Oh, I see."

"And I didn't want to get into it over text."

"Didn't want to get into what? That you think I'm trash? That's pretty easy to type." I act out texting with my fingers, *I THINK UR TRASH*. I don't know why, but I'm angrier toward her than I thought I'd be if I could get her to talk to me. Maybe it's just my family. But I feel like I want to get under her skin. Make this her fault for ignoring me. Make her say words I want to hear.

She brushes aside my blame with a wave of her hand. "I'm sorry if I wasn't on your unbelievably fast timeline for getting over things! One day you're telling me your family's dead, and the next they're running up onstage. That's no big deal, right? That's how you act! So I shouldn't think it's a big deal either? And then seeing you tonight on TV with that girl . . . I mean, is it all an act with you? Is that it?"

She's making me into a husk of a person.

"Look, I don't know how to say or explain things right. We never talk like this in my family. I've always been better at doing than I am at talking." I stare at her, hoping she can just understand what I'm going to say. "That girl tonight, that wasn't real."

Magnolia gets up from the hockey table. And she laughs. But it's a sad laugh. It's full of disappointment.

"It wasn't real," she repeats. "It was special effects. It was an optical illusion. I know—it was a performance."

"Partly." I stand up too. "Partly it was a performance. It was about something Catherine said. I know you think it's stupid, but

she told me I had to do something to, like, save my brand." I'm basically watching myself talk at this point, wondering why I think this
is going to make things better.

"Your 'brand'? Are you a breakfast cereal?"

"I can't go home. If I go home, it's all over for me." I want her to
understand this so badly.

But she bends forward and crosses her arms on the edge of the
hockey table, sinking her head down into them. Muffled, she says, "I
don't get how someone can do that. Lie about who they used to be,
who they are, be someone different from one second to the next.
Believe me, I tried. That was my whole goal coming on here! I was
going to try to lie about myself and couldn't pull it off. But you're
totally fine with making the whole world into an extension of this
stupid show."

"If you think I'm such a fake," I tell her, "then I guess there's nothing I can say. But if you think I wasn't being real with you, you're
wrong. I meant every bit of it."

She turns her head to the side so she's looking at me, and we're
just staring at each other quietly for this instant. It's like a crack in
the wall, like I can see a little light coming through. Maybe the girl
who felt like my girl is still in there—if I can only reach through and
go back to where we were before. I walk toward the table. I'm gonna
get to her. Her dark eyes look up at me from under her hair. I can still
make this right.

"Maggie," I say.

We both jump a little when the door to the room creaks open and
a bleary Mila, hair up in a pillowcase, walks in. "Late game of foos-
ball?" she asks.

"We're kind of in the middle of something," I say.

"It's hard for me to believe you're not at the end of something. I
can't believe she's even talking to you."

Magnolia curls up. "We're just finishing. I'm going to bed soon."

"This is between us," I throw in.

Mila just shrugs and says, "It's kinda between you and every-one with an Internet connection, buddy." Then she gives Magnolia a look, and leaves.

When we're alone again, I discover that Magnolia's expression has gone distant. She's rested her head on her shoulder like she's made up her mind. "I think the problem underneath it all is you're not true to yourself," she says flatly. "It makes me doubt what I feel about you."

This girl operates from a kind of pure place. Not pure like some of the churchy types back home, who put on their own kind of perfor-mance. It's not like some set of rules she's following for a gold star. It's a thing that's born out of her own self. It reminds me of when Leander told me about that Greek god who holds the Earth on his shoulders, and I was like, *Okay, but what the hell is* he *standing on?* With her, she's standing on some immovable ground inside herself. If I push against it, I'm going to collapse like a thin cardboard person.

I start to feel angry, really angry that she can't see what it's like for us regular humans, who never found a place like that to stand.

I say, "You think you know everything when all you know is your own situation."

"And you think you don't deserve anything," she says, "so you're afraid if people see the real you, they'll think that too. You're great; you just don't really believe it. If you did, you wouldn't need this show. Winning this show isn't *that* important."

It's the snobby way she says this that riles me. It's like she's talking about whether I'm going to make the school soccer team. Like the fact that I *need* to win is a personal flaw. This is one judg-ment of my shortcomings too many. All I can see now is the giant gulf between us.

I pace the room. "Your whole life, your biggest worry has been whether you'll grow up to make the best, most perfect choice from your millions of options. You grew up in a nice house. In a nice place. You were comfortable. You were safe. You had parents who wanted the best for you, even if you had to lose one of them too soon. People thought you were smart. Your mom's a bit much, but she'd obviously do anything for you. It's all good for you to float above it all because there's no real risk for you, is there? So which one of us is really the fake here?"

From the look on her face, I can tell she's not sure if I'm wrong.

I keep going. "The consequences for me are real. When I fail, there isn't going to be a net to catch me." I have so much anger, I want to hurt her, get to that part of her she thinks is so superior and untouchable.

"Everybody has other options," she says, but yeah, she isn't sure.

"The minute they vote me off, what do you think my chances are? I don't have anything. All I'm good at is music. I was ten when I started drinking. I've got a juvy record instead of a diploma. Nobody ever expected anything more from me until the night Leander caught me breaking into his music shop. Guess what? His store might not make it past the year, but I suppose you would also tell him that his talent will take him as far as he needs to go."

Magnolia looks upset. It doesn't feel like winning. But still, I keep talking.

"People at home live just to get through the day. I've never known anything else. Until I got on this show, then it was like someone showed me a kind of map of the world I never saw before, directions I never even imagined. The difference between you and me is that you were born with the whole atlas." It's like I can't stop talking until I know I've torn everything all the way down. "You don't know anything about me. It's like I said that first night I met you—someone like you will never understand."

Magnolia takes off the Pat Graves sweatshirt we all got at the premiere, like she's starting to undress for the night. The motion feels defeated. I think she's accepted what I've said and now she's packing it in.

"You're right," she says. "All the nervousness I feel about this show was this luxurious paranoia about staying true to myself. And yes, yes, I'm sheltered. I know I am. But I swear, Ford, I get that you've had a hard time, and I see how you could think the world's against you. I'd make it all go away if I could. But then who would you be?"

I don't have an answer for her.

It seems like there's nothing more to say.

We just kind of squint at each other in the halogen light of this room. It's like we're a couple of vampires up too late, who can't stand to look at each other in such a clear bright light.

Magnolia

42

Over the past two weeks, I've been brainstorming how I can get America to turn on me.

Ten minutes ago Jesse delivered a gigantic bouquet of magnolias to my dressing room. It's from a group of girls who say they are my biggest fans, the Magentas. They've only seen me sing three times. At last week's elimination Lance surprised us by announcing that no one was going home because we were "going out on a yacht! Right now!" They taped our group performance on the boat and made a Saturday special out of it for more money. Catherine says she's keeping the show fresh.

But I know it's more fun to watch a game if you take a side, and this is definitely a game.

I run my fingers along the petals. Some of the flowers have a little bit of pink in them, and some have a little bit of purple in them, and I genuinely hate disappointing these girls when they've decided to emotionally invest in me.

Still, I have to remind myself that I never had it in me to be a person who wants to be turned outward all the time. I'm an introvert. Happiness is keeping a small world for myself.

This morning I was watching Felicia rehearse her song, "Losing My Religion." She's doing the Tori Amos version from the movie *Higher Learning* because it's soundtrack week. She was singing about being in the spotlight, losing her religion. I took my mom's phone and Googled interviews with Michael Stipe, and I read an interview where he said the lyrics are about pining for someone. But when I was listening to those lyrics today, I felt like religion was a stand-in for the sense you make of yourself. You can lose it to a person; you can lose it to a show.

In my case, though, me in a corner is just me. It feels so good to accept that. And now I have to do what I want. Not what my mom wants, not what Stacy wants, not what Robyn wants, not what Catherine wants, not what the Magentas want.

Most of all, this means giving up romanticizing what I was convinced people in general want out of another person. There are a lot of ways to live.

I want to go home, open a blank page, and write my own show.

You'd think it would be as easy as giving a bad performance, but even that can be risky. The week before last McKinley sang "Purple Rain" by Prince for the song that best represented him, who knows why. He did such a shaky job that Jazz Billingham told him he seemed washed-up. Chris James said that it was more like "purple migraine." DJ Davey Dave said (as usual when he doesn't like something) that it had depressed him.

The girls in the audience made really furious animalistic sounds at the judges, and then a lot of them started yelling that they loved McKinley anyway. The ones at home must have had the same reaction in their bedrooms because the next night, he was safe. There's always the danger of America feeling bad for you.

So I've really been brainstorming. A bad song, a bad vocal, a bad performance are only maybes. Somebody else could always do worse than you. America might like how bad you were for reasons you couldn't have predicted.

I'm contractually obligated to perform when I hit the stage, so I can't just stand there, or else I think I get sued. But also, America is fickle, and I don't think it's that crazy to think that viewers might get behind a person for resisting authority because really, that's the very thing that America's founded on, when it comes down to it.

I know I could just half-ass it for a couple more weeks and eventually get voted off, but I want out. There's a frenzy in me to leave. It's like if I were a bull with some asshole on my back and you said to me, *Hey, Magnolia, you don't have to buck him off. Just give him a ride to the mall.*

So I've been through a lot of options in my head. There's only one I've come up with that I believe is pretty close to a guarantee. Because there's one thing that America hates all the time, without ever budging, and that thing is when you disrespect America.

There's a knock at my dressing room door.

I stiffen, wanting it to be Ford, even after everything that's happened. I can't help it, and I don't like it. But I'm admitting to it.

"Come in," I say.

The door opens, and it's my mom. I'm instantly nervous to see her. In less than an hour she's going to be so confused, pissed, and let down.

"Hey," she says, leaning in with the door, draped across it. She's totally at home around the set. Her body language reminds me of how she'll swing in with my bedroom door at our real house, interrupting me in the middle of studying because she's bored and wants to go to the beach.

"Hey," I say.

She tips her head and stares at me sideways. She looks like an innocent kid in high heels. The pair she has on is too big for her, and they gap at the back like the ones Disney puts on Minnie Mouse. "I'm proud of you."

Oh, Jesus, I think. That's what she would have to go and say while I'm doing my best not to think about her looming disappointment. I feel like the parent who knows the one present her kid wants isn't in front of the fireplace (that's where we put our presents at Hanukkah).

But I don't want to be the parent.

So I try to just let myself be the kid with the proud mom for a moment.

"Thanks, Mom."

"Your dad would be proud too," she says.

Now my head goes, *Oh, Jeeeeesus.* I'm almost panicky with needing her to leave if she's just shown up to tell me about her pride and to start suddenly saying warm things about my dad. I avert my eyes and stare at the magnolias on the dressing table. If my dad hadn't died, I would have a vase of carnations.

I tug on the belt of my robe. "Well, I'd better get dressed for the show."

"Yeah, why aren't you in wardrobe already? It's, like, ten minutes until show time, Mag."

"I've already been to wardrobe. I got out of the outfit because I was uncomfortable sitting in it." I gesture over at the wardrobe bag lying on the couch.

It's true. The outfit was uncomfortable because it's pretty

much a chain mail dress. And it is in that bag. But it's not what I'm going to wear onstage.

"You need help?" my mom asks.

"I'm good."

"I have a feeling that you're going to be especially off the hooooook tonight." She laughs at her bad hip-hop inflection and starts to shut the door while lounged across it. "And I've been hearing everyone thinks it's Nikki's night to go home, so don't worry."

I'm alert. "Why? Why does everyone think that? We haven't even performed."

"You didn't hear? Some old girlfriend sold e-mails between her and Nikki to the tabloids, and all of a sudden it's, like, *Duh, she's gay.* Fans are saying she misled them. There are groups out there being hateful, like they get off on being."

It's all so petty, so stupid and exasperating and shitty. "That's horrible."

The other day in the bathroom I asked Nikki if Rebecca cared that the audience just automatically assumed she was Nikki's aunt.

"No, uh-uh," Nikki said.

"Because she thinks it's better for you in the competition?"

Nikki began taking off her blush with a baby wipe. "We just both think it's funny. Because the chemistry between us is so obvious, and people want to say she's my aunt?" She laughed. "People are lolo."

"Lolo?"

"Crazy," translated Nikki.

"I know," my mom says now. "Bad people come out of the woodwork when you get famous. Mo' money, mo' problems." She does a momentary kind of raising-the-roof thing. "I'm going to grab my seat. I can't wait to watch you up there. It seriously makes my heart sing." She clasps her hands over her heart, mimes a fist bump, then is gone.

Now it's not only that I want to go. I want Nikki to stay. I have to give a performance that, if Nikki were to pull Rebecca onstage and sing into her mouth for four minutes, would still leave the worst people out there angrier with me. I go over to the duffel bag I've stashed beside the couch and unzip it.

There's another knock. I don't want to, but I think about the last time Ford walked in and almost undressed me, in here, on this couch, with his palm pressing on my hipbone.

"Yeah?" I say.

The door opens, and Catherine steps in. It's for the best. She's holding a spiky plant. "I saw Jesse back on his way to bring this over." She puts the pot down on the tabletop next to the magnolias. "Why aren't you dressed yet?"

I get up from crouching on the floor and go over to the dressing table. I pull the card from between two big thick leaves. "The dress they gave me is *really* heavy," I say, opening the envelope.

Catherine says something, but I don't hear well while I'm reading.

It says, *Tiny: I figured you're probably getting a lot of flowers. But probably not as much aloe. Laugh now, but you'll be thanking me later when we go to the beach and you get a sunburn on your shoulders. Like you always do. No matter how much sunscreen you wear. Love, Scott.*

Scott now? Scott wants to reappear for no reason I can understand just to throw himself into the mix of my anxiety? The last time I saw him, I yelled at him, and he seemed to grasp that I wasn't joking. I was sick of him, sick of us. Not looking to go to the beach. But there's Scott for you, and it's just like him to send a card that completely ignores reality. Maybe my dismissal of him got him down for a couple of weeks, but he has this bizarre resiliency. He pops back up. He creates an alternate universe and has weird faith that you'll just accept it too. That's how incredible he is at playing dumb.

"So is that all right with you?" Catherine asks.

I look up. "Is what all right?"

She shakes her head, and her earrings, which are circles inside of circles inside of circles, spin in circles themselves.

"The candles."

"Sorry, what candles?"

Catherine makes a gesture of wanting to take me by the neck and throttle me. "You kill me!" she suddenly yells, looking me straight in the eyes. I'm surprised because she's never been direct with me before. I mean, of course we've had conversations and she's talked directly to me, but you can always feel that there are wheels turning in her mind, and she's actually watching those instead.

Now she's staring straight into me. "You don't understand how great this is, do you? If we didn't have such dumb stringent laws for the workplace, I would slap you upside the head. And I'm not saying that in an aggressive way. This is sensitive personal frustration."

"You're mad at me?" I ask.

"I have worked *so* hard, harder than anyone knows, to make a name for myself in this business. But you think the people at home watch the credits? They don't."

"Maybe someone who wants to be a produce—" I start, and she says, "Can it."

Then she says, "Then here's you. Oi-ta-doi-ta-doi, skipping into this world"—Catherine mimics a kind of yokel type skipping—"except, no, you don't skip. It's more like this. Muawah-wah-wah . . ." She switches over to a Goth kid shuffle with her head and arms hanging, legs limp. "The very next day, millions of people know your name. The show pulls a miracle and does better than anyone expected coming from me and a tired format on its last legs. You're a *direct* recipient of that glow. And you don't even understand how meaningful that is. I could go out onto any street in this town and give your name, ask who you are, and right now I can find a person who can tell me within two minutes."

I understand it, I think, but that doesn't mean I want it. Is it such a crazy thing to not want? Is it a given that everybody wants to be famous almost more than they want to be anything else because this is just the bigger version of being really popular at school? Because fame is just the smaller version of leaving something behind when you die? Did my dad wish he'd left more, been more noticed somehow? Why am I thinking about death right now? Why am I such a bummer? This is exactly what Catherine is talking about.

I throw my arms up in the air in bewilderment. These things don't make any sense, why one person wants one thing, why another wants another. "I'm sorry!" I tell her.

"There are a million girls who would give their left pinkies to be you. No joke. They would go to Claire's in the mall and instead of getting their ears pierced, they would let the salesgirl use a pinky-removing gun. Okay, Magnolia?"

"Okay." I nod, feeling both worse now that I have a deeper understanding of how disappointed Catherine will be in me after tonight, and also feeling more positive that I'm not supposed to be here.

Catherine pinches the bridge of her nose and reigns in her emotions. She says, "I was telling you that they were putting out rows of votive candles for your performance, but I thought you deserved more drama, so I had Jesse go and pull you a truckload of pillars."

"Thank you. For everything."

"Get dressed." She walks out the door. I wait for it to click closed, and then I go back over to my stashed duffel bag to get my outfit for the show.

I'm singing "In Your Eyes" by Peter Gabriel, which is from the movie *Say Anything*. I've always liked that movie because the characters feel honest. And, Jesus Christ, the scene where Lloyd stands outside and holds the stereo above his head and plays "In Your Eyes" to Diane, who's in bed, because he knows that he doesn't have any better words? Right there, that's what I love about music, what I love so much more than performing it.

Yesterday morning I took a cab down to Hollywood Boulevard, wearing a big pair of sunglasses and my hair tucked in the Angels cap. I was there to shop in the older, trashier stores, the ones that were there before the new hotels and Hollywood and Highland Center came in. Back in the days when I was pretending to be a social butterfly, my mom drove me up to the trashy stores so I could get a Julia-Roberts-in-the-beginning-of-*Pretty-Woman* costume for an eighth-grade Halloween party.

I take the outfit I bought out of my duffel and put it on. The shorts feel a little bit up my ass, but this is all going to be uncomfortable anyway, so who am I kidding?

I take a deep breath. I put the robe back on and tie it up so I can make it to the stage without anyone stopping me. I'll just say I'm cold.

Mila's waiting for me out in the hallway. She's wearing her show clothes, which are a yellow neoprene crop top and bronze harem pants. Shiny white eye shadow too. I'm looking at one of the few people in the world who can pull this off. Tonight she's going to be singing M.I.A.'s "Paper Planes" from the *Slumdog Millionaire* soundtrack.

"You're really going to do this?" she asks. She's the only person I've told about my winning idea. It came to me in a dream, and I woke up and told her because I knew she would laugh.

"Yeah."

"I'm not going to stop you."

"Thanks. I wouldn't want you to."

The stage manager, Patty, is coming down the hallway for me. I'm up first tonight.

This look comes over Mila's eyes and it feels older than she is. Not that I'm getting all kooky with old soul and past life shit. I just mean that it's like I can actually see the show biz in her irises. "You can't want this as much as I want this"—and I know she means fame; she means something bigger than the show—"without also getting what's wrong about it. So I get you. I don't want to be you. But I get you."

"I mean, also," I say, "you'll have the room to yourself."

Mila shuts her eyes. "I have an early memory that I don't know is true. I look in the crib next to me. My sister's lying there. I think to myself, *I wish I had my own room.*"

Patty reaches us and folds her arms over the top of her big headset. "What's this?" she asks me. "Why are you still in a robe? I had to get you in the wings a minute ago."

"Brrrr." I shiver. "I'm not wearing much under here. Trying to keep warm so I don't pull something."

"Come on," Patty says, and Mila makes the gesture of pretending to wave a tiny flag. I smile at her and go. Patty and I walk down the hallway and through the dimmed backstage, which is its usual crowded chaos. The show's audio comes over the backstage speakers. It's starting. The theme song kicks in, and the audience claps and whistles, and Lance comes on the mic and says, "Gooooood evening out there! It's time to turn on the spotlight!"

Liz from makeup puts more last-minute lipstick on me, and then Zara is behind me, sticking in one more bobby pin. Patty makes me hold her hand for support on the way to the wings because I'm wearing high heels and there are cables and wires all over the floor.

She gets me into position, and I can see Lance from the back, the lights over the stage, just the shapes of heads filling the audience.

He says, "Let's see what's been going on with Magnolia Anderson. . . ."

My video package launches on the screens in back of Lance. Ever since Lucien found out that I wanted to go home, he said I could do whatever the hell I wanted. He wasn't going to drag me through a performance.

When Skip came over to the mansion with his crew, I got into an inflatable tube in the pool. I brought a lemonade with me and floated around and drank my drink.

From the edge of the pool, Lucien asked questions so he could at least say he'd tried to do his job.

"How are you feeling this week, Magnolia?"

"That's personal," I said.

"Anything on your mind?"

"This is good lemonade."

"Anything upsetting you?"

"It's a little bright out. I wish it were raining. I really love the rain."

While the video plays, a couple of stagehands wheel out low platforms loaded with the pillar candles that Catherine got me. They're in a race to light them.

The producers have cut together the footage to tell a story about how I've been pampering myself after the shock of Ford's reveal and betrayal. They've turned my wishing for rain into a melancholy moment, like it's a sign of my inner turmoil. But tonight I don't care if people see me as melancholy or moody or gloomy. Or tomorrow. I mean, every single one of the seven dwarves didn't need to be bouncing off the walls. There's a downbeat Care Bear. Why isn't there the same understanding of actual people?

"And here she is, singing 'In Your Eyes!'" throws Lance as he exits left. The stage lights drop. The stagehands are gone. The hundred candles flicker. Patty says, "Go," and I pull off the robe and hand it to her.

I walk to the middle of the stage. I can hear the floor creaking a little under my feet, but no one in the audience will.

The mic is waiting in the middle of the candles. I step behind it. The first notes of the song kick in. The house piano player and the drummer are somewhere below the stage. The lights lift, and the stage is cast in a kind of romantic, quivering blue green.

I'm wearing a red-white-and-blue stars-and-stripes bra bustier with red-white-and-blue stars-and-stripes jean shorts. I've cut some holes in the shorts. Around my shoulders I've tied on an American flag, making myself a shawl.

I take the mic off the stand and hold it so close that my lips just touch the metal. With one hand, I untie the knot in the flag.

I start singing. "Love."

I take the flag from around my shoulders and let it drift

down to the floor like I'm dropping an old silk scarf for drama. There's an audible gasp from someone in the wings, probably Patty since she's aware this wasn't in rehearsals. I sing that I want to run away.

I lower myself onto my knees until I can sit myself down on the American flag. And then I just repeat the line that I want to run away instead of moving on to the part about coming back to the place you are. I just sing it and sing it until I get to the chorus. Then I sing about being complete in their eyes. I'm being sarcastic and it's pretty obvious, but that's okay.

43

After my song, I walk down the hallway toward my dressing room as fast as I can. My heart feels like it's part of my pounding headache. It's a headache from the tension.

Gardener's gone up onstage; I can hear him over the sound system. He's singing Nine Inch Nails "The Perfect Drug" from the *Lost Highway* soundtrack. When Trent Reznor talk-sings, it's sexy, but Gardener doesn't have that kind of ache in his voice. He sounds like some guy from my high school reading a book report. He's singing the part that goes, "And I want you!" and it basically sounds like he might as well be singing, "By Herman Melville!"

"What did you do?" my mom cries out. I turn around.

She's standing there in her quilted stovepipes and her top that hangs off a shoulder. Both of her hands are up on her collarbone. She has multiple rings on every finger, even her thumbs. I know she's loved every moment of this show. It sounds dramatic to say that it's given her a reason to get dressed in the mornings, because it's not like she was hanging around the house in a robe, but it's given her that reason to do herself up the way she always wanted to.

"I don't want to be here, Mom," I say, and the thing is, I mean it as an apology. I know from her perspective, this is coming out of nowhere. I never told her that this was only her dream because she never would have believed it.

Tears form in her eyes. I'm watching in horror as I make her cry. That's one of the major reasons she thought the *Real Housewives* wouldn't have her: because it's so hard to make her cry.

"What did you do?" my mom says again, but with a choke in her voice. "I don't get it at all. I don't get why you would do this to me. You have ruined *everything*." She gives me a look that slices at my heart. "What's wrong with you?"

Something about that question flips a switch. I agreed to be on the show because I thought there was something wrong with me, because I thought I had to change myself. I didn't have a mom who told me that there was nothing that needed fixing. I had a mom who couldn't see me beyond herself.

Now, instead of asking why when I tell her I want to go home, she asks me what's wrong with me. Something has to be wrong because I don't want what she wants. So this question instantaneously binds my heart and makes it go faster than before, like it's anger that's pushing my blood around.

"Nothing's wrong with me!" I yell. "What's wrong with *you*?"

"Me?" She wipes her tears away with one hand, anger taking her over too. "What have I done to you except support you this whole way? What have I done except make this all possible?"

"You've made this all possible for yourself!" I shout. I can't stop myself now. "Who said I ever wanted this kind of stress? This level of attention? Do you even have any idea what I'm like? Have you *seen* me, Mom? Have you ever actually seen how I act in a roomful of people? Or have you just created some imaginary version of me in your head like you did for Dad after he disappointed you? In your head you just turned me into an extension of yourself. And turned Dad into someone who never existed after the divorce. You just totally wrote him off. Even when he was dying. And now, even after he's dead. And you've totally ignored how I might not want what you want, because I guess that's also been unpleasant for you to think about." It must be a commercial break now because no one's singing, and people are starting to stream backstage.

"I have some questions for you too," I go on. "I want to know if you've had any awareness of how shitty it's been for me to have you refuse to speak about Dad after he died, considering he was my parent? And considering whatever went down between the two of you didn't go down between him and me? And do you know how hard it is for a kid to feel responsible for her mom's feelings all the time? Like, to feel that she's got her mom's happiness in her hands, but also to feel that her mom is kind of clueless about how that might work in the other direction?"

Stagehands are looking around the corner to see what the fight in the hallway is about. I'm sure Catherine is on her way to rip me a new asshole any second.

"So please, Mom," I say, "don't act like it's my problem here. Nothing's wrong with me because I'm not eating up being out there in front of millions of people every week. It's you who has the problem. Your problem is that this shit is more meaningful to you than your real life. Your problem is that you only see what you insist on seeing. I'm okay."

While I've been confessing everything about how I feel, my mom's tears have stopped. I'm shaking. I've never come close to saying any of this out loud. I could never do it before, but the same thing that's churning in me to get off this show is making me feel incapable of being anything but confrontational and stark about it all. I don't know if she's going to rail back at me or cave or what. It seems like she's going to say something.

Her hands drop down to her sides. "You want to be miserable?" she asks, her face tightening into an unrecognizable mask. "You be miserable. But I'm not going to let you force me to be miserable with you. You're on your own." She turns her back on me and walks away.

44

I'm given my own town car for the elimination show on Friday because Catherine held me back for a meeting with legal. I didn't realize it at the time, but when I left the stage after Wednesday's performance, I accidentally left my American flag cape too close to a pillar. It briefly caught on fire before the stagehands brought out extinguishers. Burning the flag was absolutely unintentional. But I'm hearing it wasn't really interpreted that way, considering I'd already used the flag as a rug.

Two of the show's lawyers came to the mansion to impress upon me the financial trouble I could be in if I disrupt the show tonight. The numbers sound unreal. I used to think seventy-five dollars for a night of babysitting was amazing.

These past two days Catherine has bounced back and forth between being personally furious at me for being ungrateful (and almost burning down the set), and then professionally happy about the media attention my performance brought the show. I've supposedly angered a lot of people out there and confused a lot of others, but the worst part is that I've also inspired this casually anarchist online group to start a campaign for keeping me. I heard they've been using computers to dial in and vote for me repeatedly.

I was right to worry that you can't reliably predict what will make an audience abandon or get behind you.

Now I'm nervous, sitting in the backseat of the Lincoln, being driven down Ventura to the studio lot. My mom, not speaking to me, is in another car with McKinley's mom. The fortysomething driver has been making eye contact with me in the rearview mirror every so often like there's something he wants to say.

"You hear any of that, my friend?" he finally says.

"Of what?"

He gestures to the dashboard radio. He's had it on low volume on the front speakers. I can hear DJ types talking, but I haven't locked on to anything they say.

"Story about Ford."

From the way he says Ford's name, I can tell he watches the show. His pronunciation sort of has an eye roll in it.

Around the house I've tried not to pay attention to things having to do with Ford, and Mila is great at never mentioning news of him. I hang out with her, and it's like she's this editor who effortlessly chops him out of our lives. But now curiosity gets the best of me.

"What are they saying?"

The driver adjusts the mirror so we can see each other more fully. "You want the gossip? Look, I can't get enough of gossip, but I have enough self-control to be respectful if you're not into it."

"Let's hear it."

I see a happy flash in the driver's eyes. "Okay, so here's the deal. His mom gave a phone interview to KIIS FM Wednesday night after your performances. Told them Ford didn't hide his family because he was protecting them—she said he did it because he was an ungrateful kid and, quote, a bad seed, unquote. Said the family was just pretending like that was the story because they'd wanted to help him, but now she'd decided that Ford didn't deserve it because he was so awful to them. He wouldn't even let his family come stay with him when they ran out of money for their hotel. Did you know that? He turned them away like they were nothing. Said that's the kind of son he is. So she's finally had to come out with the truth."

I'm not planning on having kids any time soon, but I'm sure that if/when I do have a kid, even if that kid were to majorly disappoint me, even if that kid were to crush my feelings, I still wouldn't want to destroy his chances at realizing his dream. I think only a bad mom would throw her kid under the bus like that, and that's even if he was the person she said he was.

"Why would she do that?" I wonder.

"She was sloshed. Slurring. What, you don't have embarrassing drunks in your family?"

"Not that I know of. I mean, obviously, I'm sure somewhere out there I have a third cousin who's at the bar every night. But my parents never really kept in touch with their extended families."

"Well, if you had a loose cannon drunk in your family, you'd know there doesn't have to be rhyme or reason. Sometimes they just get crazy mean. You don't always see it coming. My sister did AA and it worked out for her, but let me tell you something. Before that she would pick fights with me that were ten years old. High school stuff, my friend. For some people, booze just magnifies feelings they buried when they weren't wasted."

We pull up to Gate 2 of the lot, and the driver rolls down

the window to show the security guard his credentials. "Good evening," he says, suddenly professional.

"If she was obviously drunk, then people probably won't put that much weight on what she's saying about him."

"Well," the driver says, being waved through, "then there was also the town car driver—I actually know the guy—who told E!Online that Ford and his brother puked all over his car. My friend had to scrub the chunks out! So that's probably not going to help either."

I lean my head against the window, and it's not that I want to be thinking about Ford right now, but I can't deny a gut feeling that this kind of thing was the reason that Ford tried to pretend like his family didn't exist.

The driver pulls to a stop in front of the studio.

"So many chunks," he reiterates.

"Magnolia," Lance says, and I get down from my stool. I walk across the stage to electronic music that's both sad and pulsing, however that works. I take my place next to Lance and face out toward the judges and audience. I've made it into the bottom two. Here we go.

"I wonder who's going to join her?" Lance ponders into the microphone. The anxiety of waiting for this to be over is undoing my nerves. I'm close to shaking him to just get it out.

After what seems like a whole minute, he says, "Gardener."

Wonderful! Gardener! I think. I can beat Gardener for worst in show. I know I can. He's had his own problems with approachability because he's got the vibe of a long-haired magician, except he can't do any illusions. And his song was really bad this week. But I think I have the upper hand because I actually pissed people off.

Still, if America wants him out, I've got my backup plan. I can feel the silver Superstar where I've tucked it in the back waistband of my silvery pants.

Gardener walks over to the music and stands next to me. The PVC of his trench coat smells like wet paint.

I look to Lance, his bronzer visible up close; I'm jittery and waiting for him to make the announcement about which one of us is going home. But he says to the audience, "You thought I was done calling names? Well, I'm not done. Because . . . this is a double elimination week! We have a bottom *three*, ladies and gents!"

The music switches to something more ominous than sad, the beat still pounding, though. There are surprised reactions across the board onstage. The judges swivel in their chairs like the shock in the audience has created some weird quaking field of energy.

I'm telling myself, *Great, two eliminations. You've got this.*

"Who's the third contestant in danger of leaving tonight?" Lance asks, twisting to look at the contestants on the stools. He pauses. Of course he pauses.

He says, "Ford, man, I'm sorry, but come on down here."

The look on Ford's face when his name is called is so raw that I don't know how they can put it up there on the projection screen behind us. Who wants to have to stare into his eyes, which are blown up times fifty, and linger on how hard he's taking this? You can see what going home would do to him. I mean, you can see this moment threatening to break him. Even if we're still not talking, that doesn't make me want to see him like this as he's walking across the stage to take his place.

"Here's your bottom three, America. Two of these singers will be going home!" Lance moves so he's standing behind the three of us. A spotlight whips around the stage to create suspense.

I can't believe Ford is in this line. Gardener separates us. Ford's votes stumbled a little after his family reveal, but the producers have done a pretty good job of smoothing that situation over. He sang well on Wednesday. So it has to be the stuff that his mom said about him, that the driver said about him.

I can't look at Ford anymore. I'm only going to worry about myself. My mom is the only mom I'm going to be angry with. I give my attention back to Lance, who is pressing his tie against his chest. He's looking sort of gaunt in the cheeks. I think he's been trying to lose weight even though he shouldn't.

"Our first contestant going home tonight is . . ." Lance waits for the lights shining down on the stage to turn white then green then blue.

"Gardener," he says.

I take a breath. One spot left for elimination. Gardener flips up his coat collar and hangs his head, then Lance puts his hand on Gardener's back and gestures for him to leave the stage. Gardener does, to audience applause and the good-bye song of the show. It has a chorus that goes, "Got to find another light, if I can just make it through the night." In my opinion, it's a little melodramatic and bleak.

Ford and I are now standing together in the middle of the stage. We're not looking at each other.

"Ford and Magnolia, Ford and Magnolia," says Lance, shaking his head. "Former show lovebirds, and now one of them is the next contestant eliminated from this show." A clip package of us kissing starts running on the screen behind us.

I thought I would be up against Gardener or Nikki, because of what my mom had said. And I was totally enthusiastic about giving the Superstar over to either one of them. I tried to give it to Mila last night in our room, but she wouldn't take it.

"Why don't you hold on to it, just in case? Just keep it wrapped up in a sweatshirt," I told her.

"Don't want it." Mila shrugged.

"What do you mean, don't want it? I'm the one who doesn't want it. But you want to win. So take it." I was packing my bags, and I shoved the statue across our floor toward Mila like it was something gross or a hot potato or a gun.

"I went on this show to beat my sister for once. It has to be real. So if America votes me out before her, I screwed up. That's the only competition I care about." She shoved the statue back at me.

I threw the statue onto her bed. "But what about if Felicia's already gone and America tries to vote you out? Don't you want to use it then?"

Mila went to her bed and picked up the Superstar, tossing it back at me. "I would respect the decision. This isn't between me and America. This is between me and my twin."

When she wouldn't take it, I decided that I'd take it onstage with me just in case something weird happened. I felt confident that I'd done enough to lose, but just in case.

I didn't think through whether I would want to hand it over to Ford.

The screen goes dark. "For one of you, this is the end," Lance says.

Magnolia, I think, like I can actually plant an idea into Lance's mind. *Magnolia. Magnolia. Magnolia. Magnolia. Magnolia. Magnolia. Magnolia. Magnolia. Magnolia.*

"Ford," Lance says.

I glance over at Ford. I'm still angry with him for not letting me know I was the only one of us with a dead parent.

But as I'm looking at him, I can't ignore the haunted expression on his face. I don't see a fake. In fact, as we're standing here, I think I see him even more clearly than I ever have.

Oh, Jesus Christ.

"Uh, hold on a second, hold on," I say, leaning over so I can be heard in Lance's mic as I pull the statue from behind my back.

Three
Weeks
Later

FORD

45

I feel like I'm forgetting something. Bags are packed. Voices echo in the mansion as production people shout about cleaning it out and shutting it down. Every few minutes I'm hearing the beep of a walkie-talkie bouncing off the hallway. In the two hours since elimination, this place has already gone from home to the county fair on its last night in town.

"Car to the airport will be here in five." I look over my shoulder, and Jesse is in the doorway wearing his usual stressed-out expression, but tonight he's even more wound up. He doesn't wait for a response before he splits.

I look around my room one last time.

Don't know what I feel like I'm forgetting since I brought almost nothing with me, and I'm leaving with the same. The sheets with the high thread count aren't mine. The big terry cloth robe in the closet isn't mine. The spa slippers at the foot of the bed were there when I showed up, and I've decided they're staying. I'm just not a spa or a slipper kind of guy.

My lone new item is the expensive leather jacket I'm wearing that Robyn gave me to travel home in for good luck. She said it was for luck, anyway—I realize that mostly it's so I look less like a hobo if anybody takes a photo of me.

Somebody should shake me, I think, turning around in this room that's been mine for the past couple of months. I'm not getting it. I mean, look, I know what's happened, I'm not a total idiot. I understand that tonight I've made it to the final three. I, Ford, am in the final three. Ford Buckley is included in the final three. That's me. Ford Buckley, finalist.

I know I'm supposed to be packing up, getting on a plane within the hour.

But I only ever pictured leaving in defeat. I never really thought about how I'd feel if I made it through.

Just three weeks ago I thought I was done for. When my mom called the radio station to talk about me being an awful son, and America wanted me out during double elimination week, I was sure that was it. Without Magnolia, it would have been over.

I expected my parents to keep talking and dragging me down. I fully expected to be booted the following week. But then things went quiet on that front. Mysteriously quiet. And a few days after they left town, I found out that my mom, dad, and Cody were in a Texas jail. Sissy called me to break the news.

They had been chugging down the highway in that RV loaded with weed, living their version of the old American dream of striking gold in California, when two officers pulled them over for speeding. It was a drug corridor. The officers got suspicious. They smelled something, did a search. Fortunately for Sissy, she'd hopped out at a truck stop near Vegas because she wanted to do some gambling. She took a Greyhound home, and on the way she received a collect call from an inmate in Amarillo.

So that was that. They were back inside. You can expect to be disappointed by certain people, and you can tell yourself they're always going to do what they're going to do and it's time to learn to accept that you can't do a damn thing about any of it. But it's just not so easy.

Family has a weird power over you. They implant something way down inside while you still have that wide-open little kid heart. They're in there somewhere, chiming in with their opinions all through your life, whether you like it or not. They can hurt you worse than anyone, and then make you feel guilty about it.

Yet here I am, still standing in this contest.

So I'm just a little bit stunned.

You're going to go to the airport and get on the plane, I tell myself, thinking maybe the way around being stunned is to take baby steps. Mental baby steps. Forget figuring out what it all means and just do the next thing on the list.

But the next baby step goes to hell because next on the list is *fly to Calumet.* You can't even fly right into Calumet, though. The only airstrip we have is for dusting crops. So now I'm attempting to picture the production crew driving a long line of white rental vans all the way from Memphis and past that airstrip, with its sad orange wind sock flapping over the cotton fields. And then picturing them whipping onto Main Street, turning sleepy Calumet into the crazy beehive that is a Hollywood production. All with me at the center of it.

My brain just can't fit those two worlds together.

I wonder if the production crew understands how small Calumet is. If they're expecting a big crowd, they're going to be disappointed. They could probably rouse, like, thirty people to stand with their arms crossed in a half circle, hanging back as far from the stage as possible. That's how things at home usually go. Maybe the producers could pay some extras to show up and look alive.

I check under the bed just to make sure that the nagging feeling isn't due to something I've left there, and I spot a squashed trash bag between the bed frame and the wall. It's one of Cody's "luggage" pieces. He left it here that afternoon before we went to the party and never came back for it.

I guess he doesn't need any of this stuff now that he's back in a jumpsuit. I consider dragging his stinky clothes onto the plane with me. But then I think, *Why would I do that?* Why would I want to go out of my way to watch out for his stuff when he didn't even give a second thought to destroying mine?

I'm reminded of my pile of dirty laundry waiting in the corner of my bedroom back in Calumet and all the other little things I left unfinished. Bills in the mailbox, dishes in the sink, the stray cat I always feed (I've got Leander refilling a huge butter tub with kibble, just in case the little guy's still coming around): that's my real life. There's no way people back home are going to buy into me as some kind of wannabe celebrity. Although they might line up just to laugh in my face.

Back when I used to get dragged to Sunday school by my grandma, they told this story about Jesus returning to his hometown and preaching. Everybody there was like, "Isn't that Mary's kid? Who does think he is, coming back here and acting like a big shot?"

I'm pretty sure it's going to be worse for me. I haven't even performed any miracles.

I lean against the windowsill, looking out. It's not like I'm cocky about my chances of winning this thing—I know it could all still amount to nothing. I know singers come and go all the time. They get forgotten. I know I haven't won anything I can take to the bank. But I suppose I'm the kind of happy you get when you feel like you proved something to yourself, something you can always keep with you. Even if I turn out to be the only one who remembers it.

Even so, something is bothering me. I always thought if I could just win this thing, my life would line up straight and make sense for once. Instead I feel like there's a missing component.

In this momentary stillness, I know what it is. I can't stop thinking about Magnolia. This whole spectacle feels borderline empty without her.

I remember how hard it is to find someone in this world who really understands you. And how hard it is not to be afraid once you realize that means they can see right through you.

Catherine yells from the hallway, "Ford, I swear to God if you don't get in the car right now, I'm giving you 'Wind Beneath My Wings' in the finale!"

"Coming," I say, and head out of the room.

There are lots of people on the first floor already working on getting the mansion back to its original state. The recessed lights are on their brightest setting, like a bar that's turned up its lights at closing time. A production assistant is removing some giant neon letters from the wall they brought in for filming to make the house look younger and cooler. Another girl is tagging the furniture for storage.

"Don't forget to empty the fridge!" Catherine calls to the staff, her voice vaulting off the high ceiling.

Mila and McKinley, the other two finalists, have already left in their limos, headed back to their hometowns. I'm the last one out. It's odd, the mansion coming undone like this, like seeing something you're not supposed to. Or seeing something that never really existed.

Catherine continues out to the front, but I stop for a second in the entryway and just look back at the house. I was here. This is where I first really kissed *her*, just the two of us alone. I make myself walk out, leaving the big doors open behind me.

Whatever happens now, I went into this house one person, and I'm leaving a different one.

Urgent honking blares from the limo. Catherine is over there, holding the back door open. She gestures like she wants to strangle me. "Chop, chop, let's go!"

As I walk toward her, the headlights of the limo wink off metal in the open garage. It's the chrome of my motorcycle propped against the wall. I hadn't stopped to consider how I would get it back home. I think, *Maybe that's what I felt like I was missing.*

But it isn't that, I know it.

"What about my bike?" I ask.

"Don't worry, it'll get to you." Catherine's a woman of her word, so I don't doubt it. I head over to the limo, and she gives me the rundown. "I thought I was going to die before I got you off this property. Anyway, Tiffany will be accompanying you to Arkansas—"

I look in the limo and Tiffany, who's a junior producer, is already sitting in there, typing on her iPad. She gives me a tired smile.

"And I'm staying here to set up the LA performance, but I'm reachable. Do you have everything you need?"

Catherine's asking that as a joke because I've taken so long to get out of the mansion, not really expecting that I'm going to pause and consider if I do have everything I need.

Her face starts to go from impatient to alarmed when she sees the look on mine. "Ford, no."

"But I don't," I say, and I start to back away from the limo.

"Ford!" she calls.

"It's true! I really don't."

Her increasingly loud threats turn into background noise as I turn and walk toward my motorcycle.

Magnolia

46

I've been back in school for three weeks now. At first I kept going through the same three interactions. The first was that someone I'd never talked to before would pass by my locker and say, "You seem to be glowing. . . . Is there a *spotlight* on you?" And I'd say, "Hey, good one," even after I'd heard it for the hundredth time.

The second one was specific to Mrs. Corinthos. When she'd see me in the English building hallway, she'd say something along the lines of, "That Superstar was *yours*. Not his! You didn't have to give up your power!" And I'd say, "Got to run, late for class!"

The third was that every time I passed near one of the American flags on campus, another fellow student I'd never talked to would stick a thumb out at me and make theatrically nervous eyes, or tell the teacher that she should take it down before I made the flag a picnic blanket. I would also say, "Good one," to that. So in the beginning, it was basically "Good one, got to run, good one" for a few days straight.

It's always people I didn't really know making the comments.

Acquaintances and former friends just watch me carefully, like I've come back from TV as something else, like I'm only in disguise as myself. It's been very weird.

In the midst of this heightened scrutiny, there have been three saving graces. The first has been the Xanax that my new psychiatrist, Dr. Turnbull, prescribed me after I came home from the show and had my first panic attack. My mom still isn't especially speaking to me, so I had to find him myself.

But the thing I've learned about modern psychiatrists is that they only want to give you medication, and they don't actually want to talk to you beyond checking that your dosage is effective. So my second saving grace has been Lucien. We video-chat a few times a week about how my script is coming along, but there's always time for him to go into his mode of fatherly analysis.

The second week home I had another panic attack while I was alone one night, writing up in my room. I wasn't feeling panicked about anything in particular, I didn't think. I Skyped Lucien once I didn't feel like my chest was going to crack in half, and he answered with Scottie sitting on his lap.

I told him, "It's weird because I actually felt more consciously anxious when I was on the show, but I didn't have panic attacks then."

When Lucien is about to help me toward a realization, he looks like he's biting on an invisible pipe.

"What's today?" he asked me.

"Wednesday."

"What time did you have the panic attack?"

"It was probably . . . a little bit after eight," I said, understanding what he was getting at. "Oh. Okay. Right."

That would have been show time. I haven't been watching the show because I'm trying to separate myself from it. But I talk to both Mila and Lucien, so I always know who's gone home. I hear it around school too. After me, it was Nikki. After Nikki, it was Ricky.

"I'm thinking these attacks might be a delayed response," Lucien said in a baby voice to Scottie.

"Like maybe now I'm feeling the weight of performing because I have the time and space?"

"Maybe something about the experience hasn't been worked through."

"Like what?" I asked.

"Oh, man, this kid just took a shit that came out the sides of her diaper," Lucien said, and then he had to hang up abruptly.

The third saving grace has been the rediscovery of Jenny Irving. Jenny used to be in the group of thirty that grew from my group of fifteen in middle school that grew from my group of five in elementary school. In the group of thirty, there was always so much going on that it was easy to not actually know some of your friends. I never had a real sense of what Jenny was like.

But the second week back, I saw Jenny rolling her eyes at Sebastien Rodriguez when he jumped on the flagpole during our run in PE and yelled over at me, "I see you eyeing your new gym towel!" I rolled my eyes too, and it was like when you're a little girl and you hold hands with a new friend, this tandem rolling of Jenny's and my eyes.

Jenny and I started running together during PE. It was so easy to start doing this, it was almost—almost—hard for to me to remember how stuck within myself I'd felt. There was this role I was assigned, and I just couldn't leave it, until I could.

After a fourth panic attack, Lucien had suggested I try

dyeing my hair back as further separation from the show, to see how it felt. I thought that was a decent idea. Jenny's hair is bleached platinum, and all I had to do was ask, "Do you dye your own hair?" She did, so I asked if she would help me go back to brunette. That night she came over with a box of Garnier Nutrisse in Sweet Cola. Yesterday Jenny and I had lunch together at the wall across from the lockers.

This morning when Lucien and I were Skyping before school, he had me virtually babysit Scottie for a few minutes so Amy, his wife, could take a shower and he could make himself breakfast. This just meant that I watched Scottie gum her teddy bear in her playpen via Lucien's laptop. If there was a freak accident with the bear, I was supposed to scream at the top of my lungs so Lucien could hear me in the kitchen, and dial 911.

Scottie was still happily gumming the bear when Lucien sat back down with his waffles in front of the computer.

"So tell me how things are going with Jenny Irving," he said, chewing. "Sounds like you two are simpatico."

"Seems like it," I agreed.

"I saw promise when you told me about the dual eye rolling. You know, lasting bonds are often built out of mutual antipathy for something. Does it surprise you that you're going to end up being friends with her?"

"It just seems weird that that we weren't friends before." I was sitting at my bedroom desk and put my head down on my arm. "I guess I feel kind of stupid that all these hurdles I felt weren't real."

"They were real."

"They probably didn't exist outside my head."

"There's a distinction. I know you had a shitty—" He

looked at Scottie. "Sorry," he said to her. "Sorry," he said to me. "I know you had a bad time on the show, but maybe you could make your peace with it by thinking about it as the place that started transforming your inner reality, right? It's where you became friends with Mila."

"True."

"And where you profoundly bonded with me."

"Yes, yes. I mean, what do you want to hear, that you've changed my life?"

"And Ford."

I was quiet.

"And Ford," Lucien said again.

I was still quiet.

"Should I go for a third?"

"I heard you."

Lucien made the look like he was biting on an invisible pipe, and I thought, *Here it comes.*

He said, "Remember what I first responded to in your writing, what I said about your understanding of characters?"

"Uh-huh."

"That when it comes to motivation and personality, you don't see the world in black and white. You're able to see . . ."

He paused. He wanted me to fill it in.

"Really?" I asked.

"Tell Scottie. She hasn't heard it." Scottie was lying face-down on top of the bear.

I sighed. "Gray."

"There is it. You're able to see gray. In people that don't exist. You can't do that in real life? You have to keep Ford in the black cowboy hat?"

"But I think I *can* do it in real life," I say. "I don't hate my mom, right? I still can see the gray in her, even though she's ignoring me. I would never say she has only terrible qualities even if things are terrible between us right now. And, hey, Scott's supposed to come over tonight and we're actually going to try being real friends. When I came back home and I was able to say to myself, maybe there's something worth preserving—that's gray, right? I haven't made him all bad in my head, or I wouldn't be giving this a shot."

"But Ford's still not gray? How long do you want to carry that around with you?"

I lifted my head up and shook my backpack in front of my computer's camera. "Well, conversation has to end here for today," I said. "Got to get to school."

47

I'd barely set foot on campus when Mrs. Corinthos spotted
me. I was drinking a smoothie I'd picked up at McDonald's on
the way over to school. She was holding a travel mug in both
hands and walking out of the main office.

"Magnolia, I want to talk to you!" she called. The first bell
had already rung.

I pointed, trying to look busy. "I was just going to English."

"As am I."

So we started walking together because there really wasn't
much choice. Mrs. Corinthos's stilettos echoed dimly on the
concrete. She started shaking her head, curls bouncing on her
shoulders. She said, "Honey, it's really been bothering me that
your dream was derailed."

"Well, honestly, it wasn't my dream—"

"Sweetheart, don't do that 'I don't care about anything'
teenager move. I've been doing this long enough that that
doesn't work on me."

"Okay."

"But maybe it's good you got away from that boy. I got the

sense that he was distracting you. Maybe now you can pursue your dream without him keeping you—"

I looked at her. "Mrs. Corinthos, when you watch a movie and it has a love story in it, do you root for the two people to not end up together at the end of it?"

She gave me a confused glance. "Which movie?"

"I don't know, any movie that has two people in it who fall for each other."

"What? Why?"

"Because even if I hate a movie, I'll root for the two people to end up together. I don't think it's me buying into a message about life being about getting the guy. It's just what's uplifting about romance. You know? Romance fulfilling itself. Like it's supposed to, if everything goes right."

Mrs. Corinthos returned to shaking her head at me like I was making some kind of big mistake. "That's what you *think* you think."

"But isn't that actually just what you think?"

"Huh?"

"Huh?"

"I like a good adult love story as much as anyone else." When Mrs. Corinthos said *adult*, I was pretty sure she meant that a good story is about grown-ups and not that she was admitting to watching porn. She was telling me that your romance doesn't really matter until you hit a certain age. Maybe it's the age that she got married. Maybe it's older than that, and she thinks she gave into romance too soon. I didn't know, but I also didn't want to know because life through her eyes was just kind of getting me down.

So I said, "Never mind."

My cell phone rang from my backpack. I suddenly had

the fantasy that Ford must have seen my mom on set with Jazz and managed to get her to give up my private number. I had to return the cell the show gave me an hour after I was eliminated.

Jazz was shaken by my elimination only because she thought my mom was going to drop out of her life, and that night she asked her to be her manager. My mom has been going back and forth between LA and Orange County since then, but she's up in LA much more than she's not. I have mixed feelings. On one hand, it's honestly a relief to transfer my mom's happiness over to Jazz. On the other, my mom's absence has probably just made me angrier that being closer to fame is more important than being closer to me.

"Sorry, I have to take this," I told Mrs. Corinthos, and fell back for some privacy.

What I hadn't told Lucien this morning was that I had watched the show last night. Or, I'd watched Ford's performance. It had been "love song" night. He stepped onto the stage. He looked directly into the camera, and I could see how that kind of stare becomes confusing when you're on the other side of the screen. You forget there's a screen. It's easier than you think to feel a real connection, even if you don't believe in it at the same time. Because you tell yourself, *No, that's silly. He's on TV.* But still you feel that you know him somehow.

Ford sang the song "First Day of My Life" by Bright Eyes. I knew the song and the words. He kept his eyes straight on the camera in front of him, and he sang about being blind before he met you—the "you" on the other side of the screen. He sang about how he wanted to let you know that it had taken forever. That he was especially slow. But he had a realization that he needed you, and he wanted to know about coming home.

I hit the answer button on my phone. It was the pharmacy's automated machine telling me that my Xanax was ready.

48

Scott is standing under the hanging lantern on my porch, holding a bottle of champagne. He's wearing the same blue poncho from when he visited me at the mansion.

"Hey," I say.

"Heyyyy," he says, more drawn out. He smiles. His face has that talented way of convincing itself that nothing has ever gone wrong.

This is the first time Scott's been over to my house since the night he broke up with me at the beginning of summer. You could look at his presence on my doorstep as the result of a moment of weakness, but I don't feel like that's necessarily the whole truth. Yes, I was taken aback to run into him at Del Taco two days ago. Yes, that surprise might have given him the opportunity to say, "Please hold on, please don't blow me off," and just start talking.

Some of the things he said were "It was totally unfair of me to say I was jealous. I know now"; "It bums me out that we were so important to each other but I went and ruined that and turned it into nothing"; and "What do you think about trying to be friends, Tiny? I mean like *real* friends?"

While I was standing there listening to Scott, I was also thinking about change. About how the last time I saw him, I considered that change wasn't a tumbler that just finally clicked into place. That it was more likely small movements that added up with you barely noticing. So change could be almost invisible, unknowable.

In Del Taco I watched Scott trying to bring me over to this friendship idea, tucking his hair behind his ears in agitation. I kind of zoned out, trying to pay attention to what I was feeling. The discovery was that I wasn't feeling horrible about this friend idea. Bad feelings had changed into tolerable ones. I'm sure that falling for someone else had helped that along. Also, maybe I only had so many bad feelings to go around, and they had collected over in the parts of my brain responsible for caring about Ford and my mom.

Anyway, that's why it was okay to invite him over to my house. Tonight we're going to start our attempt at a friendship.

"Come on in," I say.

He steps in and shuts the door behind him. He seems to be waiting for my mom to come out and wrap him in a bear hug, but it's just us, and the house is quiet. "Your mom isn't home?"

"She's at *Spotlight*."

As I said, my mom has been spending a lot of time up in LA ever since I got off the show. It's not like she hasn't been taking care of basic things—there's food in the fridge and take-out money on the kitchen counter when she's going to be gone past dinner—but she's definitely been absent.

Mila tells me that Jazz disappears from the judge's table during commercial breaks and huddles in the green room, whispering with my mom. I don't know how they spend their time together during the day. Maybe they shop.

A couple of nights ago I asked my mom, "What do you and Jazz talk about?" and at first she looked surprised that I was asking her a conversational question. From my end it's been a lot of "Do you mind if I turn on the heater, getting kind of cold," and "Is there any more detergent in the garage?"

My mom looked like she was wrestling with herself about whether to give a normal answer or keep up the cold shoulder. Finally she said, "Stuff you wouldn't care about." But her tone was more sad than icy. Before there had been a distance between us because I wasn't being completely honest with her about how I felt. Now we're actually separate.

"Well, let's celebrate that you're not there anymore," Scott says. He starts unpeeling the foil from the champagne bottle.

"None for me. I'm going to try to write later tonight. The writer who's helping me wants to show some of my pages to some Hollywood executive this week."

"Always thinking things through, Tiny."

He disappears to go get my mom's champagne flutes from the glass cabinet in the dining room. He knows where everything is in our house, down to the first-aid kit. I drop into the reproduction eighteenth-century France chair my mom moved from her bedroom down to the foyer. It has always made me feel like I'm sitting in a linen version of the buggy from the Haunted Mansion ride.

I hear clinking. Scott calls back, "When did your mom buy all this new fancy china? It looks like royal kind of shit."

I say, "Her most recent attempt to get on *Real Housewives*."

Soon he reappears holding a couple of her new flutes by their stems in one hand and a can of Diet Coke in the other (also my mom's; he's been to the fridge). "We're going to have a toast, yes we are," he says.

Scott pours Diet Coke into one flute and champagne into the other. Then, before he hands me the Diet Coke flute, he pours a little champagne into it. "Ceremonial splash."

"I give in," I say.

We tap our flutes together, and I take a sip of my champagne Diet Coke. The champagne just makes it taste even more diet.

"Where'd you get the champagne from?" I ask.

"Someone rang my doorbell and when I went outside, the bottle was just there in a bassinet with a note that said, *Please take care of me.*" Scott laughs. Everything feels so familiar. I could have almost predicted that answer from him.

We take our glasses and the can and the bottle and sit in the backyard with our feet up on my mom's iron patio table. It has so much scrollwork, it's actually uncomfortable to get your legs under it. The air is crisp.

The first time we kissed, two winters ago, it was out here. We sat in my yard while my mom was at Sundance (for fun) and drank wine coolers, pretending like we were just going to be friends. I wanted him to understand that I was tipsy so that if there was a pause, and I looked at him, and the moment became awkwardly but also perfectly charged, we could write it off the next day if we had to. But we didn't write it off.

Now I tell Scott a little bit about being friends again with Jenny, how she's decided she's going to be Buddhist now, just to piss off her parents. "I think I remember seeing that girl with you when you were a freshman," he says.

"You noticed me before that day behind auto shop?"

Scott just jokingly gasps and covers his mouth with his

hand, like he accidentally let that slip. I didn't know this. My cell rings.

"One sec," I say.

I get up from the table and walk around the side of my house. It's an LA number on the screen, but I don't recognize it. My chest tightens.

"Hello?" I answer.

"I did it!" yells Mila. "I finally did it!"

I look through the window at the time on the microwave. The elimination show has just ended. "Oh my God. Oh my God!" I say.

"They picked me over Felicia. The people watching." She sounds like she's maybe teary.

"Is it better now because you waited all these years for it to happen? How does it feel?"

"It feels totally magical. Better than I thought. I'd dreamed of it too. But it's better."

"You could easily win this whole thing. Oh my God, what are you going to do right now?" The final three give their finale performances in their hometowns this weekend. Lucien told me the network is giving the show a two-hour special on Sunday because they're choosing to make a big deal out of it. There's more money in the commercial time. But Mila's from Sherman Oaks, so she won't have anywhere to travel.

"Uh, I'm going to go take care of Fel," Mila says in this almost insulted way. Her tone says it should be obvious where her priorities lie now. "She's wrecked. I'm getting everyone out of my face and being there for her."

Gray, I think.

She hates her sister and she loves her sister. She always

wanted to beat Felicia, but she never wanted to see her hurt. I remember how before our first performance, Mila warned me that I was going to see a different person up there on the stage. There's gray there too, in the way a person can be one thing in public, but that can also not be who they really are.

Through the phone, I hear a door shut and then soft crying. "Got to go, talk to you later," Mila says, and hangs up.

I walk back over to the table, where Scott is working on carving the champagne cork with a Swiss Army knife he keeps on his key chain. He holds it out to me.

"I made you a little microphone."

I take the cork. It's pretty good. I talk into it. "That was my friend Mila from the show. She made it to final three."

Scott says, "What about the guy who kissed you?"

I realize if Felicia was the one eliminated, Ford went through. He must be out of his mind with happiness. "Yeah, him too."

"I'm glad you got out of all this bullshit, Tiny."

I put my feet up on the table and look at Scott. "Why didn't you leave for college when you were supposed to?" I ask.

Scott tries to act like the question doesn't bother him by messing around with the knife. Then he laughs. "I didn't know who I wanted to be." He's playing it off like a joke, but I don't think it is.

"Like on the inside?"

"In life."

"But isn't that the point of college? I don't think you have to go there knowing everything."

Scott stretches his arms up in the air. "I'm hungry. You wanna go inside?"

I humor him because I guess that's the courtesy you can give to your friends: more humor and more patience. And that's why friendships can last so much longer than romances. Everything's less urgent. We pick up our glasses and go into the kitchen.

We take Dixie cups (Dixie . . . the South) and fill them up with snacks from the pantry. This feels familiar too; we used to do this after school.

"You want some yogurt raisins?" Scott asks, searching on the top shelf that I can't see without a step stool.

"Yeah, definitely."

We take the cups and sit on the floor and look through my mom's cabinets. In one of the cabinets under the island, she's storing a box of all the former tassels that have held back our dining room curtains. She changes them out with her mood.

Scott pulls out a lilac one with pom-poms hanging from it. "These go up when she's feeling old. She thinks they're fun and flirty and girlish." His voice is a little draggy from the champagne, but he's right. He knows these things about us. He takes the tassel and starts wiggling it back and forth on the floor. "You guys totally need a cat. Here, kitty, kitty. Here, kitty, kitty, kitty." I laugh.

I take one of the aqua tassels with beads out of the box. It matches his poncho. I scoot back to tie the cord so he's got a low ponytail with a gigantic tassel hanging out of the bottom. "This one looks like it was made for you."

Scott turns and kisses me.

Our mouths are together for one second before I understand what's happening. The smell of his skin takes me back in time again. I pull back. I say, "I'm not doing this. The whole reason you're over is that we're actually going to be friends."

Scott tries to kiss me again. I get up from the floor.

"We're not just going to fall back into old patterns!" I yell. "That isn't the point of tonight."

I expect Scott to laugh to diffuse the tension, but instead his face is so angry that it's like I'm seeing a new him. "'The point of college,' 'the point of tonight.'" He kicks the cabinet door, which is unexpected. "Does every goddamn thing have to have a *point*? Does everything have to be explained to death? Can't a person just exist? Can't things just be different and we don't have to talk them into the ground?"

I'm taken aback. "Well, things are different. We're trying to be friends."

"I don't need to label everything, Magnolia! I can just be different than I was before! You can too."

"Huh? How do you know I'm *not* different? We've just spent months barely talking."

Scott pops up from the ground to stare me wildly in the eyes. "You think about everything too much—that's why I couldn't be around you over the summer. It was always pressure, you being with me. It was like make sense of this, make sense of that. Why can't you ever just let whatever's going to happen, happen, without thinking it to shreds? Why can't you just go with the flow, huh? Why can't you, why can't you, *why can't you?*"

The way he's asking me this is full of so much desperation, I'm too stunned to begin an answer.

The doorbell rings.

"Who is that?" Scott asks, almost accusingly, as if I've planted someone to get myself out of this exact moment.

"I don't know," I say. I live in a gated community, so no one ever really just stops by.

We stand in silence for a second.

"I'm going to go get that." I leave the kitchen, feeling Scott watching me. I feel dizzy from that interaction, like it physically took me by the shoulders and shook me. I'm not the one who's not ready to be friends. It's Scott. Sadness starts to overpower the dizziness—the sadness is about giving up the idea that we could pull off this new kind of relationship. But it's also clear to me that that's what I have to do.

In the foyer, I stand on my tiptoes so I can see out the beveled diamonds of glass my mom recently had installed in the front doors.

Ford is standing on my doorstep. He looks up, and our eyes meet. He's squinting from the lantern hanging above his head.

My chest tightens again, but along with fear, I'm not going to deny that there's relief and happiness clamping down on it too. A few weeks ago I believed there was nothing Ford could say that would change what he did. But it looks like I'm ready to be a little more open-minded because now I open the door.

Ford is wearing his old white shirt with his old jeans. But a new jacket.

"I never really got to thank you for saving me with the Superstar," he says.

It's like I can feel every molecule of air on my forehead, on my cheeks. Jenny hasn't been seriously adhering to Buddhist beliefs, but she has been talking about looking at anger and transforming it. From what I understand, this doesn't mean you have to ignore it. It just means that you learn how to turn your anger into something less destructive, something new.

"Don't worry about it. How'd you get in the gate?"

"Some kids came out the pedestrian side. I walked my bike

through." I lean forward and see Ford's motorcycle parked against the curb.

There's an awkward pause then, and I watch Ford as he glances around my porch and takes in where I live. He gets this look that communicates everything about how this scenario is so far from what he had. It's kind of the face you'd make if you were going to give one of those low, sinking whistles at being shocked by a price.

That look tells me exactly how much he wanted his life to change. And why he pretended to be someone else in the hopes that it could happen. And how it's possible that he was just trying to play a different part and got caught up in it to the point where it wasn't as much lying as it was wishing.

Ford goes from looking at the chandelier hanging in the foyer behind me to looking into my eyes. I stare at his face, and I find out that I am easily able to see the gray.

He says, "Look, I need to be with you." My chest feels like it could crack at that admission. "I need you, okay."

"Well, here's the thing," I say. "I love you."

His whole face changes like he's been lit from within. "Well, here's my thing—I love you." We break into what I can only describe as dumb smiles at each other. "Will you come with me?"

"Like, right now?"

Ford thumbs in the direction over his shoulder. "I have to get to Calumet. I want to show it to you. The only problem is that I just missed my flight, and two of us aren't going to work on my bike."

Out of the corner of my eye I see Scott appear in the dining room threshold, waiting to see what I'm going to do. I'm sure he's heard the end of our conversation. I disagree with what he said at Del Taco, that we're just ending up as nothing. I don't think you ever get over people you loved. It's just one day you get the strength not to go back there because you finally know what's bad for you.

Before, Scott told me that I think too much, but now I don't even have to put a second of thought into what I want to do.

I say to Ford, "I have a car."

FORD

49

It's after sunset the next day when we take the worn-out steel bridge over the Saint Francis River. The familiar rhythm of the bridge's warped roadway feels like an old friend waving me home.

"Take it all in." I motion like royalty at the not very exciting landscape out the windshield. "As far as the eye can see, this is all my domain."

"It's breathtaking," Magnolia says in an exaggerated way that might be her attempting to pull off a Southern accent. "My, my, my."

"Is it? I guess I was too distracted by your beauty to notice." I reach over and awkwardly stroke her cheek with the back of my hand, doing my impression of a creep who does things like that. "You see, before you, Bella, my life was like a moonless night. And then you shot across my sky like a meteor. My eyes were blinded by the light."

"I've already had enough." She laughs, grabbing my hand, intertwining her fingers in mine. "How do you even know *Twilight*?"

"A lot of the girls who sent me fan letters kept mentioning it. They said I was like Edward, except with normal skin."

"Whatever, you know you read it."

I'll admit, the Arkansas Delta isn't the most exciting landscape on earth, but to me it has a sort of muddy charm. Maybe it's just because I grew up here. I may not legally own a single acre of land, but this is all still mine: my turf, my hood, the land of my fathers. All that stuff. It's weird how much confidence can come out of something as simple as knowing your surroundings.

Magnolia's watched the delta pass by her window for hours. The slow-moving brown rivers. The endless fields, harvested and bare now. The one-stoplight towns. The mobile homes that sit out in front of, and replace, the rotting wood farmhouses from better days. She watches them all go by like an astronaut getting her first look at the surface of the moon.

"Right here, past Dead Man's Curve, people race their cars sometimes. One night Will Portis flipped his Chevy over in that ditch. Thought he was going to drown before we could get him out."

Magnolia tips her head against the window and stares into me. "We have ditches at home too, you know. I want to see some real South."

I give her the sternest look I can pull, and I put on my heaviest drawl. "Listen, li'l darlin', you're just lucky I brought you to these parts at all after I had to come save you from that surfer boy, from havin' to listen to his stories about getting spiritual with them dolphins."

She keeps her face serious too. "I think it's just that there's nothing I love more than long, flowing blond hair."

"All right, that's it. Get out." I reach over and tip her toward the door. "Just open that door and jump. I'll be nice and slow the car down. Remember to roll when you hit the pavement, and you'll be fine."

"*You* get out! I'll show myself around," she says, and tips me back. We end up in a fierce battle of arms and elbows, which she wins by leaning over the armrest and suddenly kissing me. I try to keep an eye on the yellow line as she pulls my face toward hers. It's hard to drive straight with her lips and the smell of her hair, but luckily, the road's all ours.

Except for a couple of power naps, we've pretty much driven fifteen hundred miles straight through. To sum up those fifteen hundred miles, you've basically got: city, mountain, desert, desert, desert, desert, Great Plains, Great Plains (getting less Great and more Boring at this point). Things turn green again, and you're in Arkansas.

Back in Arizona, we passed cool rock formations that looked like old castles, but Magnolia doesn't have any love for the desert.

"Maybe it's because I grew up in one," she said.

I argued that Southern California isn't really a desert, that there are lots of trees and green things. But she said modern people did that, and all the palm trees and sprinklers are just Los Angeles pretending to be something it's not. I told her that sounded just like something she'd say.

If it were up to me, I would've stopped to check out every single point of interest on the road. I want to see all the petrified forests, the meteor craters, the Grand Canyon, the average-size canyons, ancient Indian ruins, and especially Billy the Kid's grave. But this last performance ahead of me tomorrow (and Magnolia's complete lack of patience) has kept us on a tight schedule.

So instead of grand canyons and dead underage outlaws, we've settled for cheeseburgers in Flagstaff and tacos in Albuquerque. In New Mexico I finally called the production office and told them not to worry. I'd be there. We haven't bothered with a hotel because we're only stopping for power naps. In the car last night, parked underneath a faded neon cowboy on the sign of the long-abandoned Six-Shooter Motel, the temperature dropped until our breath covered the windows with white frost.

Curled up in the backseat, we held each other for warmth like a couple of stranded Antarctic explorers. And inside the icy car, surrounded by nothing but desert night and empty highway for a hundred miles, it felt like we couldn't have been more alone. Finally, truly alone. We woke up stiff and half-frozen.

We've taken turns DJing with Magnolia's MP3 player. A sample of this past afternoon's playlist:

1. Alicia Keys—"Try Sleeping With a Broken Heart" (Magnolia's pick)
2. Bob Dylan—"Blood on the Tracks" (mine)

Magnolia took exception to my insisting the entire Dylan album be listened to all the way through, so she paid me back with:

3. Britney Spears—"Till the World Ends"

When I asked if it was some kind of punishment, Magnolia launched into a long lecture on the artistic value of pop music. She said, "Some things that just sound simple really have complex things going on underneath."

I said, "I hope that goes for me too."

4. Spoon—"The Underdog" (my choice)

A sing-along because Maggie also knew this one.

5. Fleetwood Mac—"Gypsy" (hers)

Magnolia got sad talking about the sadness of Stevie Nicks's voice. I told her that Fleetwood Mac was always what I'd pictured in my head when I imagined the beaches of California. Like somehow that sound translated perfectly into the place. She said, "Yeah, I know exactly what you're talking about."

6. Led Zeppelin—"When the Levee Breaks" (all me)

Guess we got into a kind of seventies groove here.

7. Haim—"The Wire" (all her)
8. Iggy Pop—"The Passenger" (mine, but Magnolia loves the song too)
9. Prince—"I Would Die 4 U" (Magnolia's)

Come on now—everyone likes Prince.

10. The Rolling Stones—"Exile on Main St." (back to me)

Once again Magnolia was skeptical when I told her *Exile* is an album you have to listen to in its entirety, straight through. But this time, I won. Look, I don't make the rules.

So we crossed the country to our own soundtrack. Sometimes neither of us could shut up, and we talked over each other about how she wants to write and how I want to make music, and the future in general.

"God, I hope we'll know each other years from now," she said while driving.

I looked at her. "It'll be our own faults if we don't."

Sometimes we just sat quietly, staring out the windshield or nodding along to the music. Sometimes Magnolia would wake up from a nap and start bouncing her shoulders in her seat to whatever song was playing, and suddenly we'd have crazy energy and roll down the windows and sing along really loud to our audience of bored cows and lonely windmills.

But when I start getting really close to home, recognizing town names and roads I know, I realize that before this drive, I saw my hometown as a separate piece of the world, tossed off by itself. Now I spot the rusting silver water tower of Calumet, and my mind slides it into its proper place, right in the middle of the big old American puzzle.

Then there are flashing blue lights in my rearview mirror.

50

Magnolia looks over her shoulder, surprised. Only people who don't get pulled over very often look that way.

"Were you speeding?" she wonders.

I keep a wary eye on the cruiser behind us. "I don't think so."

"Oh God, but we're so close," she says, pointing at the town visible a few miles ahead.

"Maybe they just want to give me a hero's welcome," I say, not believing this at all, but not wanting to scare Magnolia.

I pull off onto the shoulder, watching in the mirrors as the cop does the same. He steps out and adjusts his clothes in the reflection of his cruiser window. He tugs at his uniform, trying to make it stretch over his big belly. That's when I realize who he is.

"Oh, shit," I say.

It's Steve Greggs, Cody's nemesis. And just like that, all the confidence and good feeling of the past day is flat gone, and I start to feel that trapped animal feeling coming on.

"What?" Magnolia is concerned.

"It's just—I know this guy. He doesn't like me."

Steve walks up to my window, and I roll it down. He shines his flashlight directly into my eyes, half blinding me.

I squint in the direction of the glaring light. "Hello, Officer . . . Steve," I say, trying to sound as friendly as I can manage.

He lets out a disturbing laugh when he realizes it's me he's pulled over. "Well, well, well, if it isn't our local celebrity! I saw that California plate and figured it had to be someone with the circus coming to town. But I didn't know that I was pulling over the *main attraction*."

"I don't think I was speeding."

"I didn't say you were speeding." Steve nods toward the back of the car. "You've got a brake light out."

"Oh, sorry, I didn't even know. Swear. We've just driven all the way from California."

Magnolia leans over so she can talk to him. "It's my car, officer. It's not his fault."

"Uh-huh." Steve rolls his eyes at her and holds up a hand. "You just sit your butt down and shut your mouth, hon. You're not in California anymore."

I know he's a born asshole and it's in his very fiber, but I'm not going to let him be an asshole to her. "That's unnecessary, man. Just write me the ticket, and I'll get it fixed. I'm kind of in a hurry."

"Naw, doesn't work like that, big shot. I'll decide what's necessary. Ford, why don't you step on out of the car?"

Now I'm beginning to get real nervous, the way this feels like it's going. "Why?"

"Don't make me say it twice, or I might have to cite you for being disorderly too."

I sigh and get out as Steve stands back, one hand resting defensively on his sidearm. "Go ahead and put your hands on top of the car," he says.

"What does this have to do with the brake light?" He's enjoying embarrassing me. The smug look on his face sets loose a righteous anger inside me. If America had pageants for being a dickhead like they have pageants for beauty, Steve would run away with the crown.

"Do it now."

"This is bullshit," I say, and turn slowly, putting my hands on the car. I look down through the passenger window and can see Magnolia looking back at me, confused and worried. Steve frisks me.

"What are you looking for, Steve? I don't have a weapon, I don't have drugs—you *know* I'm here to sing in the show. You *know* that."

"We'll see about that, Buckley." He says my last name like just pronouncing it puts a bad taste in his mouth. He throws everything in my pockets on top of the car and pulls my driver's license out of my wallet. "Now you just sit still. Don't you move a goddamn inch. I'm going to run you."

Steve returns to his cruiser. I'm so angry, I can barely breathe. Magnolia climbs into the driver's side seat to talk to me through the open window. "Why is he being such an asshole?"

"It's my family. He wants to embarrass me. Something isn't right. If he takes me—"

She looks astonished. This possibility had never occurred to her. "But why would he take you?"

"Whatever happens, don't get involved."

There's chatter on the police radio as Steve steps out of the cruiser. In the dark I can only see him walking as a silhouette against the bright headlights from his car. He steps behind me and says, "Well, Ford, here's your license back."

I turn to face him and immediately I'm hit in the face with a blast of liquid. My skin feels like it's on fire. I reach for my face as my eyes close tight against the pain. Pepper spray. Military grade. I don't even realize I'm yelling until Steve sprays my mouth and I feel it burning my throat. Within seconds I'm on my knees vomiting, then dry heaving. Mucus starts pouring out my nose, and I really can't inhale. I'm sure that's Magnolia yelling, but I can't hear much of anything besides roaring in my ears. Can't get my breath.

Then, suddenly, my arm's twisted behind my back, and I'm pushed facedown on the asphalt, a knee between my shoulder blades. I feel the handcuffs going on behind my back, biting into my wrist joints. When I catch my first breath, I use it to curse him.

"You bastard," I say, wheezing.

Calmly he says, "I told you to keep your hands on the car."

Now I can definitely hear Magnolia shouting at Steve—I think she's out of the car. "What are you doing?" she yells. "What's wrong with you? He didn't do anything!"

"Get back in the car, miss. This man has a warrant for public intoxication and disturbing the peace over in Ouida County. I'm taking him in. You're just lucky I'm not impounding the car."

Steve pulls me up by my arms, sending a pain through my shoulder blades. I try to open my eyes, but it's like they're full of gritty sand. Magnolia is still yelling, "This is police brutality. I'm a witness! Police brutality, asshole!"

Then Steve's shoving me into the backseat of the police car. I blink over and over, trying to clear my eyes. Tears pour down my cheeks, but everything is a dark blur. My feelings are a blur too. They're a hot red blur of anger, humiliation, and worry about Magnolia, all from this one guy doing something just because he can. I hear her yell something indistinguishable to him, and he says something about "scoops" back.

Then the car shifts with Steve's weight as he gets in. I lie back in the seat and kick the metal cage that separates us as hard as I can. "Do you feel like a big man now with your pepper spray?" I ask him. "My brother was right: you're just a fat coward. That Ouida County thing is four years old."

I hear the leather of Steve's seat creak as he twists to face me. "In my car you're nobody. In this town, you and your family don't count for shit. Shame you're going to miss your big show, being locked up in jail and all, but at least you'll be with your own kind. Maybe I can get the guards to turn on a TV so you can watch yourself lose."

He starts the cruiser, and we pull away. Blinking my eyes frantically so I can see out the window, I can barely make out Magnolia in the flashing blue lights, standing in the road next to her car.

Magnolia

51

I thought *I* was bad at putting on a public face, but this girl at the police desk is impressive. When I walk up to her and ask, "How can I talk to Ford Buckley?" she reads another page of her novel before slowly, slooooooowly, putting it down on top of her printer and looking up at me.

Then she doesn't say anything.

So I give her the same eyeballs back. I'm no amateur when it comes to bitchface. I'm free to be me.

"Ford Buckley," I repeat.

She tips her head forward like my voice is making her skull go heavy. "That kid on the TV?" she says. I don't think her ponytail is supposed to be a side one, but the rubber band is so loose that it's migrating to the far left.

"You guys have him in custody. And I think you should know that one of your officers pepper sprayed him, which was truly excessive force." She looks unmoved. "Can I talk to Ford for just a second? Even through glass? Is that how it's done? I've never had a conversation in jail, so I have no idea how this works."

The receptionist suddenly looks 1 percent more interested

in me. "Oh, right, you're that girl from TV too. I didn't recognize you because your hair's that dirty brown now. Looked better pink. More special."

"Thank you."

"You should change it back."

"I'm good, thanks."

She looks me up and down. "Some people don't know how to help themselves."

I stare at her. "But you could help me."

It's hard to tell if she's more annoyed with her job or with me, but she shoves her rolling chair back from the desk. "One sec," she says, and goes through a door.

I look out the front window of the lobby. I've got this weird, displaced feeling of being on vacation (even the night air outside somehow looks strange and new and different from what I'm used to) except I'm at a jail. And jail is pretty much the opposite of vacation.

"Well, here's Arkansas," I think, admiring a couple of full trees outside because if I dwell on what's really happened, I'm going to panic.

52

When Ford got thrown in the back of the cruiser, his eyes all swollen shut, I yelled to the officer, "But where are you taking him?"

The officer said, "To go get triple scoops in a waffle cone at Baskin Robbins."

And I said, "Yes, thank you for the sarcasm, but I meant—" and this probably wasn't the best thing to say to this cop because he just got in his car and started to drive away. Calling him an asshole before that probably wasn't the best move either.

I climbed back in my car to follow them, and I swear this officer was trying to lose me because he took off faster than the speed limit. I got paranoid that if I matched him, he'd call me in for speeding because he was obviously that kind of guy. So I just tried to keep the cruiser's lights in my sight line as it headed through Ford's town.

I'd pictured that when we got to Calumet, Ford and I would be sightseeing together, and he'd be telling me stories about what happened where, and who Bruce of Bruce's Country Mart and Gas is. But I was just whipping by shingled houses with lit porches and then what looked like a small diner on a corner. A sign above it read, RON AND JUDY's, except the RON had been struck through with a line of paint, so I figured that their relationship hadn't ended very amicably.

I lost the cruiser shortly after Judy's. So I parked at the nearest grocery store I could find, and I ran in to get some directions. The woman at the register said, "Hi, hon," and that calmed me down a little. It's honestly pretty nice to get called hon when someone doesn't mean it condescendingly.

I asked, "Do you know how to get to the nearest jail?"

She pulled off some receipt paper and started to draw a map.

On the way out of the store, I spotted a pay phone, an actual living pay phone, which was exciting because my cell had lost its charge on our trip. I wanted to call Catherine, who seemed like the person who would definitely know how to get Ford out of jail. But I didn't have her number.

I thought about calling Lucien, whose number I do know by heart now. But it was also the middle of the night on the West Coast, and I know how important sleep is to him with the baby.

So I called my mom.

She picked up on the first ring. "Mag?" I was calling from an unknown number, so I knew she just was hoping it would be me.

"Mom. I'm so sorry." And I meant it both for leaving without telling her and for making her feel so badly about the wall she'd put up around herself when it came to my dad. I started to feel so emotional, standing with that strange, cold receiver to my ear. I thought about how I had no idea what it was like to be her.

"Tell me you're okay."

"I'm okay."

I could hear her breathe out. "Oh my God, I was so worried. Mag, I almost sent the police after you when I found your note! And there's a motorcycle just sitting in my driveway."

"I know, I know, I should have told you before I left town, but there was just this moment, you know? A true moment where everything felt like it made sense." It was weird to remember that feeling while talking on a pay phone in the parking lot of a regional grocery store after seeing my boyfriend get pepper sprayed and carted off to jail. *I'm in Arkansas.* "And now Ford's in trouble, and I really need you to do something for me, if we can just put all our other stuff behind us for tonight."

I could hear my mom's rings clicking against each other. She must have been running her fingers through her hair. "Sure, we can do that. You're my kid," she said. "You're all that matters. I'm here for you."

I was stopped for a second to hear her say that. I felt taken care of. I felt like we were in our right places: me, the kid; her, the mom.

Then I explained to her as quickly as I could about my brake light and the bad cop and the pepper spray and how much Ford really didn't deserve to miss his chance at winning *Spotlight*— no one ever really deserves anything like that. Because it's partly about talent, but it's mostly about something you can only describe as luck.

In the background I heard Jazz say, "So true. It is a lot of luck." My mom had me on speaker with her. But I didn't feel put out about it.

I pictured the two of them sitting up together in Jazz's huge condominium (I'd seen pictures in my mom's celebrity magazines before), and it struck me that they must need each other a lot. I realized that my mom's job in regard to Jazz was to keep her from getting too lonely. And that Jazz was doing something back for my mom, who has always just wanted to feel like she's in the middle of things.

My mom wasn't going to change her longing to be noticed. But Jazz could help provide that for her. I thought she could slow the accumulation of my mom's regrets. And for that, the part of me that still can't avoid mothering my mom was glad.

"Jazz, thank you," I said. And then, "Mom, will you please call Catherine for me and tell her everything so she can do something to get Ford out?"

And my mom agreed to help because you can count on her to come through like that, when you really need her to.

"Mag? Before you go—I'm sorry. I'm sorry for pushing you like that."

I felt the same. "Let's really talk when I get back. I'll be me, and you be you, and we'll just try our hardest to respect that."

She sang a couple bars of Aretha Franklin's "Respect" to me before I heard her send a kiss and hang up the phone.

There are ways in which my mom and I will always misunderstand each other. No matter what we go through together. No matter how many times I disappoint her or she disappoints me. And that awareness is actually comforting because it means that I can't mess up some perfect bond by being myself.

So as my mom was presumably getting ahold of Catherine, I followed the grocery store woman's extremely clear directions to the jail, where I am now standing, waiting for the receptionist to come back through the door.

Fifteen minutes go by, and I start to wonder if she just up and went home out the back. I've read the poster on the wall warning about the dangers of being irresponsible with firecrackers thirty times, and I don't think there's anything more I can learn from it. A twentysomething guy comes in and asks if they arrested Bill again tonight. I say, honestly, "I don't know."

"She been gone for long?" he asks, nodding toward the desk.

"Really long. What should I do?"

"Make the phone ring. She'll want to get it in case it's her boyfriend, Tyler."

The guy has a cell on him, so I find the station number on the front desk and call it. The girl literally comes running out from the back. She doesn't even glance at us before she answers the phone.

"Hello?" she says breathlessly.

"Hi. I was wondering if you found out anything about Ford Buckley," I say, and once she hears that my voice is coming to her in stereo, she makes eye contact. She puts down the phone.

"He's being held, but you can't talk to him because he hasn't been booked."

"When will he be booked?"

"They've got to come up from Ouida first and get him to take him to their county. That's where his old warrant's from."

"Bill in here tonight?" asks the twentysomething guy.

The girl tightens her ponytail. "Does a frog bump its ass when it hops?"

The guy takes that as his answer. He waves and walks out the front door.

"Hold on," I say to her, "how long is that going to take?"

She shrugs and picks up her novel again. "Depends when they can get one of their guys to come up here. Sometimes it's fast, like a couple of hours. And sometimes it's a day."

"But it can't be a day! He's got his finale performance tomorrow!" I'm wishing that I'd paid better attention during political science because I have no clue what the law actually says about holding someone for a whole day without booking him. I'm feeling very helpless.

"Well, I'm not in charge of anything here but this phone. But you can wait if you want," the girl says, and I think this is her actually trying to be nice.

I look at the chairs in the lobby, which all have armrests so you can't lie down across them. I'm just realizing how tired I am. There's nothing to do but wait until either Catherine shows up or some guy from Ouida comes to take Ford.

"Listen, from what Bill's friend said, it sounds like you have very strong feelings for Tyler." The receptionist doesn't disagree with me. "And I have very strong feelings for Ford, so I think you might understand this kind of thing. I plan to stay here until I know what's happening with him. But I'm also completely exhausted, so I'm going to go lie down in my car out front." I point to it through the glass front door so she can see which one it is. "And the only favor I'm asking of you is that if the officer comes from Ouida to take Ford to the other station, will you come knock on the window?"

Her love for Tyler is strong. She shrugs, meaning, *What the hell.*

"Thank you," I say. "And I didn't ask before because I thought we were just going to take turns being bitches to each other, but what's your name?"

The girl considers me. Then she answers, "Portia."

"Thanks, Portia," I say, and then I head outside. Luckily, the weather is still pretty fall-like, and it's not going to be too bad. After I grab a sweatshirt from the trunk, I settle into the backseat with my head on Ford's balled-up shirts and my feet on the inside of the other door. I tell myself that someday, this will be good material for a script I'm going to write. Someday. Then I hit the lock button with my shoe and try to relax.

The night is so still except for the crickets. I say, "Ford" out loud like he can hear me from the inside of the station.

I'm a bad sleeper in even the nicest bed, so I wake up only a handful of hours later. Out the back window I can see the sky is lighter now, but the sun's not exactly rising yet. My right hip feels bruised because I fell asleep with it pressed against the seat belt latch.

My hair's all teased from the upholstery, so I twist it into a sloppy, high bun. I figure I might as well go into the station and see if Portia has heard anything from Ouida. I get out of the car and stretch, then walk toward the reception door.

Through the glass, I see Catherine working the Calumet station like she's been there before. I open the door and she turns toward me, mid-speech, as she's saying, "We don't have time for games, Portia! I just got off the world's worst flight in the *history of flight*, and I don't have the stomach for any additional stress!"

I can tell Catherine left in a hurry because she's wearing a velour tracksuit with just the word *DON'T* embroidered across the chest. She's also not wearing makeup.

"Catherine!" I say. I couldn't be happier to see her.

She gives me a look. She still thinks I'm a brat. "Your mom got me the message."

"Porsh—Porsh," she says, turning to Portia. "Let's get whatever paperwork going, and I'll send Magnolia over to the bail bondsman so we can get this wrapped up before I lose my mind."

"The problem is, we can't bail him out because there's no bail," I tell her.

"What do you mean, 'there's no bail'?"

"He's not processed," says Portia.

We explain the whole trouble to Catherine, about how we need a guy to come up from Ouida, and after she's heard the problem, Catherine shuts her eyes for a couple of seconds.

When she opens them, she says, "Magnolia, you're coming with me to Ouida, but only because you're young and you're cute, and God knows what will win them over."

53

Catherine hits the tuner on the car radio. "Preaching!" She hits it again. "Songs about being on a pontoon—what the hell is a pontoon? Songs that were popular when I got my first period! Is that all there is?" she yells.

It's still early morning, and the peacefulness of the outside world is a weird contrast to Catherine's manic energy.

She hits the tuner on the radio once again, and it lands on a station playing classical. "This is supposed to make babies smarter if they listen to it in your womb," she says, finally taking the rental car out of park and backing it out of the station lot.

"Are you pregnant?" I ask.

She laughs. "Okay, okay, I can appreciate a black sense of humor."

We pull onto the road, and Catherine sighs as she makes the turn. "All right, let's go try to get your lover boy hayseed out of the pokey so he can have his shot." We drive in silence for a few minutes before she glances over at me. "Why couldn't you do it?"

"Do what?"

"It," she says, like I should know what she means. Then I understand she means the show, its world, all that.

I reply, "I've noticed you wear this same perfume all the time—it's maybe oranges . . . and something metal?"

She gives me a look. "The top notes are mandarin and red clay."

"Okay. Well, you seem to have it on every day. Have you ever thought of switching up perfumes?"

"Are you avoiding my question to insult my signature fragrance? This perfume is me. When I've tested others in Sephora, they've given me a full-blown headache."

"See, the same reason you can't live with other perfumes is the same reason I couldn't do the show. It gave me a headache, but, like, in my soul." I turn up my hands. "I know *soul* is a very dramatic word to use here. But I don't have a better one for it."

At this, Catherine half rolls her eyes, but not in a hostile way. It's more like, *Well, what are you going to do.* I can sense a truce settling between us. She leans forward and takes in Ron and Judy's diner, which I passed the night before, looking thoughtful. "In a Podunk like this, things are even more out of our control because we're not from here. You need the help of a local to get a favor like we need. Back in Hollywood, I would know somebody who knows somebody. Now, if we knew somebody . . ."

I look out the window and see a car ahead of us with a Graceland bumper sticker. I stare at the illustrated guitar on it. A second later I lean forward, slap the dashboard, and say, "I think I know somebody!" And the great thing about a small town is that he can't be far away.

FORD

54

When I wake in a stiff orange jumpsuit that smells like a chemical spill, I'm more than confused. My face feels sunburned, and I'm sore right down to my bones. I stretch my neck both ways until it pops.

How long have I been asleep? There are no clocks, no windows, just the always-on overhead fluorescents of the jail's holding tank. Did I nod off for minutes or hours? Hard to tell when nothing here changes. You've got your blank cinder block walls, a row of gray steel cell doors, and hard molded plastic benches with ridges so you can't lie down. It's been a couple of years since I was last in this room, when they picked me up for public intox. It's not a room I ever thought I'd see again, and to find myself here now fills me with exhaustion. I want to pull Mom's move and just sleep through all the trouble.

I meet eyes with a bearded dude on the bench across from me. I guess something did change in this room—he wasn't there when I fell asleep.

His gap-toothed grin is kind of a mess, but at least it breaks me out of the Twilight Zone, unfreezes time.

"Have a good nap, sleeping beauty?" He chuckles. "I never could sleep sitting up. Have to stretch out."

The prisoner next to him, Parker, who was here when they brought me in, leans over. "Kid got pepper sprayed, Dale. I'll give you one guess who did it."

"Greggs." Bearded dude, aka Dale, nods sagely. "That boy is a pepper-spraying fool. Does not miss a chance. He's got mental issues . . . and that's coming from me." He lifts his eyebrows to mean that's really something.

The first few hours here, I tried to get answers from the guards about how long they would keep me. But no one seemed to be able to tell me anything. In here, you're not a person. When that door closes, you're basically subhuman, even if you only ran a stop sign.

Earlier I tried to make my one phone call. They gave me the special number to dial out on a pay phone with a hilariously short cord, but I couldn't get a dial tone. I tried to explain this to a guard, but he just shrugged.

"Do you know what time it is?" My voice comes out raspy, and my throat feels like a coal chute. Even if I do get out, I don't know that I can sing.

"Midmorning sometime? Not sure. I think I came in 'round two," Dale says.

"Shit, Dale," says Parker, a sentimental look crossing his face. "You just got out two days ago, and I got out last month. Here we are, together again."

Dale pretends to raise a toast with an invisible mug in his hand. "They should give us our own key!"

They do seem at home here, but I don't know how they can stand it, living like this. After a few hours, I already feel like I'm going crazy.

The only available entertainment is a poem blown up and posted on the wall, written by an eighth-grade girl who won a contest. (By the way, worst prize *ever*.)

The poem's entitled "I Am Meth" or "Yo Soy Meth," if you want to read the Spanish version beside it. I became familiar with both about a hundred times before I fell asleep.

> *I am the thief who steals your dreams.*
> *I am the end of your plans and schemes,*
> *the life of the party turns out to be death.*
> *I'm not your friend.*
> *Yo soy meth.*

I guess it's better than the poems I was writing in eighth grade, but her message doesn't seem to be getting through all that clear to Dale and Parker.

Parker gestures to me. "Get this: Ford here is Cody Buckley's brother."

"Is that right?" Now Dale is staring incredulously, making me feel even worse. I tip my head back and take in the ceiling. Because if Dale thinks you messed up, then you probably really, really, really messed up. "Aren't you supposed to be playing some show today for a million dollars or something? Or is Cody full of shit as usual?"

"No, it was true," I mumble.

I think of Mom, Dad, and Cody in Texas. Here I was trying to do something right for a change, and I find myself locked up just like them. Maybe there is such a thing as fate. Maybe family does stick together after all.

Dale shakes his head, genuinely disturbed. "Now this ain't right! We finally get our own celebrity, and what do we do? Lock him up with a bunch of drug addicts. That's a damn embarrassment, is what it is. I don't know what this town is coming to."

The outer door buzzes, and a well-rested Steve saunters in, sipping coffee from a Styrofoam cup. He ignores us, turning to the female guard working the counter. "Morning, Janet." She doesn't appear all that thrilled to see him. "You're looking real nice this morning.

Looking like that, I wouldn't mind if you locked me up, y'know?" He winks, and if I didn't hate him so much, I'd feel bad for him. The guy has got worse than no game.

"It's too early in the day to start this harassment nonsense," says Janet.

"C'mon now, I'm messing with you. I just came by to see my prisoner." Now Steve decides to make eye contact, and he puts his foot up on my bench. "How was your night, Ford? I know it's not the four-star accommodations you've grown accustomed to. So if you have any complaints, I want you to feel free to write them down . . . and shove them up your ass."

I don't reply. The reality of it is the show is in a few hours, and I have no idea how I'm going to get out of here.

Then it dawns on me. I'm not getting out.

It's pretty simple: I didn't build up enough speed to escape the gravity of my old life.

"What? Don't want to talk anymore, Buckley? Where are your Hollywood friends? Or maybe the truth is, they don't give a shit about a piece of trailer trash like you. You know they laugh at you behind your back, at your dumb accent, your cluelessness. And now that your fifteen minutes are over, you can kiss that little groupie you brought with you good-bye."

"You don't talk about her." I know he's baiting me, but hearing him talk about Magnolia with that gross look on his face, I just don't care anymore. What else do I have to lose? I start to get up. Without permission, that's a big no-no in here.

Steve snaps into a combat stance with a look on his face like I gave him a present.

"Hey, Steve!" Dale yells, sternly signaling for me to sit. "Why don't you tell Ford about how you moved to New Jersey to play for the minor leagues after high school—remember that? I do. Oh yeah, you made a real big deal how you weren't gonna waste your life in this town like the rest of us losers. How long were you gone again? Three weeks?"

"I think it was two." Parker laughs.

Steve stiffens; his eyes dart away from mine. "You think I care what a couple of tweaker burnouts think?"

Dale adds, "Or maybe tell him about when Kelly Dawes left you for Cody Buckley. Not such a great year for you, huh? What happened there? You two were always the big couple. Some girls just don't like poseurs."

"Shut your mouth." Steve pushes Dale down on the bench, putting his elbow into his throat. Janet and another guard rush over to separate them.

"Why you down here, Greggs?" asks Janet. She pulls him aside. "You just get all my prisoners riled up. Don't you have someplace to—"

The phone rings behind the counter. She makes sure that Steve is done with his Hulk routine, and then she goes to answer it.

"I've got a town full of West Coast queers that need to be sent on their way," Steve says. "Looks like I need to make it clear to them that there isn't going to be a show here today." He's still doing the superior thing, but I can tell his confidence is shaken.

Janet is saying, "Okay, got it. Yes, got it," into the phone while looking at me. She hangs up the phone. "I wouldn't do that just yet," she tells Steve. "That was Sheriff Dawson. Mr. Buckley's warrants have been dropped."

"What?" I say.

"Looks like you're free to go."

Is she saying I can leave, like, now? "I can go?" I say, pointing at myself like a goon. The other guard motions for me to stand up, nodding toward the metal door leading to the outer booking room. They mean me.

Steve is in disbelief. "No. No way. I have him on multiple charges."

"He'll pay a fine for the brake light. You can take the rest of it up with the sheriff—he says he wants to talk to you anyway." Janet smiles to stick in the knife. "Didn't say why."

I stand up, feeling like I'm coming out of a dense fog. I say, "You guys take care," to Dale and Parker, meaning it, hoping they can. Then I walk to the outer door. Janet hits the buzzer.

As a guard pushes the inner door open for me, I look back at Steve. "I really hope you can make the show. I'd be happy to sign autographs for your girlfriend or whoever you have that's special in your life."

"You'll blow it, Buckley." Steve almost spits at me. "You're a born loser."

"Yeah, I was, but maybe I grew out of it."

Dale starts clapping, and a startled Parker wakes from a nap (I didn't even realize he'd fallen asleep) to join in. "Whoo! Win this one for the losers, bro!" Dale yells before he seems to throw up a little bit.

Minutes later I'm back in my clothes. I step through another door into the morning sunshine of reception, and just like that, I'm a human again. First I see the girl at the front desk, not looking up from her book. And then I see a tired-looking Leander in one of the chairs.

I'm so happy to see him, I don't know what to say.

He grins, standing, shaking his head, and letting out a deep breath of relief. "Boy, I swear this is the *last* time I'm coming to get you out of this joint. Who do you think you are? John Dillinger?"

He walks forward and puts his arms around me, even though we've never been the hugging types.

"Last time, I promise," I say. I think he's going to release me, but he holds the embrace, and I realize I'm choking back tears, but I don't know why. "I thought I was going to let you down."

"You wouldn't do that." He pats my back, and we separate. He nods, looking away awkwardly because it's not natural for him to show emotion.

"How'd you get me out?" I wipe my eye with the back of my hand.

"Called in a favor. I used to give guitar lessons to one of the policemen over in Ouida when he was a kid. Also, it turns out the mayor here wasn't too thrilled about having Calumet's big moment screwed up because of an overenthusiastic cop." He nods again, this time toward the door. "Your girl was ready to break you out. With dynamite if she had to." His eyes crinkle. "She's just outside."

That's all I need to hear. I'm out the door.

Magnolia's sitting on the front of her car while Catherine paces, barking orders into her phone. But as soon as Magnolia realizes it's me coming out, she runs and throws her arms and legs around me, almost knocking me over.

"I'm sorry, baby," I say, kissing her. "And thank you."

She holds my hair back with her hands to take a look at me. "Are you on any other wanted lists? Just so I can mentally prepare."

I smile. The happiness of being out and her being here for me is almost too much. "I don't think so. I think that's it."

"Because if I'm being honest, I don't think I'm cut out to be an inmate's girlfriend. It's too stressful."

Catherine hangs up her call and comes over to us, also checking out my face. "I always thought your just-rolled-out-of-bed look weirdly worked, but this spent-the-night-in-a-Dumpster look—we're going to have to fix that."

"I'll powder my nose," I say, my voice still sounding so scratchy and thin.

"Oh God, that voice." Catherine gawks at me in horror. "Can you sing? Tell me you can sing."

"I guess we'll find out."

"Oh, you're going to sing. We're going to get you prettied up with more makeup than Jared Leto, and we're going to get some honey, lemon, and ginger down your throat, and they're going to be sorry they messed with my guy. Because for the next twenty-four hours, I am the emperor of this town, and if anyone even looks at you funny, I will have their head *on a spike* on top of that water tower."

She walks toward a production van. "Now I've got to deal with this ancient ruin they're calling a stage. Get everyone to sign something saying it's not our fault if they die under a collapsed pile of rubble." She puts her hand over her heart, seeming moved by herself. "Riding over with your girlfriend is my finale-day gift to you. But don't make any stops. Don't do anything moronic. Just get there." She hops in the van, slams the door, and is already back on the phone as they drive off.

Leander has come outside. He sticks out his hand and says, "I'm gonna go close up the shop, but you know I'll see you at the show." We shake, and then he's off.

Magnolia and I have to let go of each other's hands to get in on separate sides of her car.

"I need to make a stop," I tell her.

55

One of the funny things about Magnolia is that she's a real straight
arrow, but she also tends to bristle at authority telling her what to
do. You just wouldn't know it unless you'd seen her around a dom-
ineering police officer. So now she doesn't balk at ignoring Catherine's instructions to get me directly to the stage.

I guide her across town and over the railroad crossing. We pull
into the gravel driveway of my shotgun shack. They say it's called a
shotgun because you can fire a shotgun at one end, and the pellets
will pass thorough every room and out the back door without hitting a wall. I've never tried it, but my place is real skinny and all the
rooms are in one straight line.

"Home sweet home," I say. "You want to come in?"

"Yeah," Maggie says.

We get out and walk across the overgrown lot with the blackened
fire barrel out front. The place is just like I left it: paint peeling, rusty
tin roof, sun-bleached sofa on the tilting front porch.

But with Magnolia next to me, I'm uncomfortably aware of how
unlivable it looks. Second thoughts about bringing her here start
to creep in. I have to remind myself that I wanted her to see how I
lived. And she wanted to know who I really am. I was so proud when

I moved in, on my own for the first time. I'd say that before *Spotlight*, this place was probably my biggest accomplishment.

I grab my hidden key from under the couch cushions and unlock the padlock on the front door. "I'll give you the grand tour, if you have, like, five seconds."

"Great," she says.

We begin in the living room, which I explain is "furnished with fashionably modern lawn chairs" and a television. I don't have cable, but I like to watch DVDs. I keep a collection on a bookcase I inherited from Leander.

"Please watch your step," I say as we move around the hole where my foot broke through the floorboards when I was dancing alone, and maybe too enthusiastically, to Kings of Leon one night. Then into my bedroom, which I explain should "technically be called the mattress room," since it only contains a mattress on the floor and piles of folded clothes.

Magnolia doesn't try to bullshit that any of it is nice. I love her for it.

I change my shirt and jeans as she watches. Being here, it feels more intimate than anything I've ever done with anybody before.

"It's so quiet," she says.

"Wait sixty more seconds."

Like clockwork, the two p.m. train rumbles past the house, its cars taking up the whole view out the east windows. It lays on the horn at the crossing. *Whaaa-whaaaaaaaaaaahhhh.* Magnolia winces, squinting one eye against the noise.

"It's even louder at night!" I shout.

"Ford?" she says.

I wait for the train to pass. "Yeah?"

"I didn't understand." I automatically know she's talking about the first conversation we had by the pool on top of the hotel, when she wanted to know how my life had been different from hers, and

I shut her down because I was too embarrassed to explain. But her saying that lets me know that now she really does.

We kiss. And then it gets more serious, fast. I run my hands up the nape of her neck, digging my fingers into her hair. She reaches around to my lower back and clutches me there. We're about to finish what we started back in her dressing room, but then I realize there's no way I'm going to let this happen on my frameless mattress in my shack.

Holding Maggie's face in my hands, I say, "Tonight, when it's all over, let's stay the night in the most expensive hotel we can find."

"Yes," she says.

I take her hand and lead her out of my house, shutting the door behind us.

The WPA, meaning the Works Progress Administration, built the stage back in the Depression of the thirties. The WPA was this government program that built all kinds of things back then: dams, roads, parks, bridges, so on. The general idea was just to put people back to work. My great-grandfather worked on this stage, so it probably fed my family for at least a few months. It sits on the circle plaza on Main Street, where they also put in a movie theater and this ritzy-looking library with white columns. All boarded up now, since before I was born.

The outdoor stage is just a big concrete platform with a band shell, and it may not look like much, but all sorts of real acts used to play here: Hank Williams, Jerry Lee Lewis, young Elvis, Little Richard. It was the heart of the town until the acts stopped coming in the sixties. The last person to play it was Johnny Cash in '76. He grew up close by. That's probably how they talked him into it.

When Magnolia tries to make the turn onto Main, I get my first look at the crowd. I stare from behind the window. I am thoroughly bewildered by the mass of people. We can hear them, the hum of them talking to each other. I've never seen the street so crowded in all my life.

"This is all for the show?" I say, partly just to comprehend it myself.

Magnolia starts backing up the car. "Don't freak out," she tells me. "Don't freak out."

There are thousands of people. The side streets are all closed off. Not only have I never seen the town so crowded in person, but I've never even seen it like this in the old photographs from its heyday. My great-uncle used to say that on Sundays in downtown Calumet, "a drunk could walk without falling down." I suppose this is the kind of thing he meant.

Times a hundred.

"This is crazy," I say. But I wish I had something better to capture it. I really didn't think more than a few dozen people would come out to see me. But maybe people came out *because* it's a small town, because so many of them have known me my whole life. Because I'm one of their own, and they're taking this ride along with me. I'm realizing now that someone from here could have easily gone on the Internet and revealed my family lie, but no one did. They understood what I was up against, and they protected me.

I feel like I owe it to them to do well. And my stomach feels like it's trying to turn inside out.

Magnolia drives a loop around the crowd to get behind the stage, where there's a barricaded entryway for production.

"Ford Buckley," she says to a security guy in a yellow shirt, and he takes a look at me, then moves the barricade to let us park. It isn't so much a backstage here as it is several trailers set up on the pavement. As soon as we step out of the car, Tiffany and a production coordinator named Huck immediately appear and hurry us to hair and makeup while reporting my whereabouts into their radios. "We've got Ford. Ford is on site."

The makeup girl back in Hollywood usually didn't do much besides powder me up so I wasn't all shiny, but Tasmin, who tells me she's from Nashville, has some work to do once she puts me in her chair.

"Do you always have this bruising under your eyes?" she asks, patting concealer on it.

"It's usually one shade lighter," Magnolia says from where's she's slouched in the director's chair next to me. She's trying to take a nap.

Adrenaline is the only thing keeping me awake at this point. Catherine appears, followed by a guy in a sports jacket. "This is Dr. Bursch," she says, "vocal cord specialist. He's going to fix your throat."

Dr. Bursch makes a face as he looks down my throat with a tongue depressor. "They really shouldn't be spraying people in the mouth with that stuff."

I'm aware.

"Normally, I'd recommend rest, but if you have to sing today, then I should give you a cortisone shot. It's the fastest way to reduce inflammation—but there's the possibility of further damage singing with your throat like this. Ideally, you would rest for a week."

"Who am I gonna have to sing for in a week? Please just give me the shot," I say.

He injects me in the upper arm, then slaps on a Band-Aid. "Gargle this right before you go on," he says, handing me a small bottle of liquid. "And drink lots of water. Good luck." He pats me on the back, and Catherine sees him out. Someone's calling for her on her radio about the fire marshal.

When Tasmin's done, a guy named Wesley comes in to mess with my hair. And when he's done, Tiffany reappears to take me to wardrobe. I kiss Magnolia on the forehead to wake her, and she immediately opens her eyes and says, "I wasn't really sleeping." As we're being hustled over to the next trailer, I hear someone shouting my name by the barricades.

"Ford!"

There's a commotion with the security guys, then I see Sissy hop a barricade and dodge past them. "Ford!" she yells as one of them grabs her by the arm.

"It's okay! It's okay! She's with me!" I shout, jogging over. "She's my sister!"

Tiffany shouts, "It *is* okay!"

The security guard lets Sissy go. She says, "You're lucky my brother showed up. I was about to bust you wide open." The security guard backs up, shaking his head.

"Can you believe *this*?" Sissy asks me, opening her arms like she could fit the world in them.

We hug. "I'm glad you didn't get locked up with them."

"Well, shit, me too."

I pull over Maggie. "This is my girlfriend, Magnolia. Magnolia, this is Sissy." Sissy throws her arms around Magnolia so forcefully, you can almost hear her spine realigning.

"Very nice to meet you," says Magnolia with her chin on Sissy's shoulder.

"You're as cute as a bug's ear," says Sissy.

"Thank you?" Magnolia answers. Sissy releases her.

"Don't you let my brother get a big head. You've got to keep him in his place, girl."

"With a shiv, if I have to," Magnolia jokes, because I've told her about Sissy—and let me tell you, Sissy just loves that response.

This is when I notice the guitar case Sissy has brought and put down on the ground beside her. I didn't see it in all the ruckus. It's the '53 Telecaster. I know it right away.

Sissy notices me looking at it. "Those idiots pawned it, but I got it back. Snuck the last of the per diem off Cody before they dropped me in Vegas."

"I thought it was gone," I say, kneeling down to crack the case open. And there's the chipped but shiny blond paint of the guitar, back home with me. "This is so amazing."

"Well, Grampa gave it to you. I think he'd be pretty pissed if you didn't play it tonight. I don't need that old man haunting me." She looks around at the trailers, the production folks running around, and she smiles. She's got a good smile when she bothers to use it. "You know, it's almost like being in a damn movie."

I'm expecting to meet a local stylist hired just for the finale, but when Maggie, Sissy, and I walk into the wardrobe trailer, there's Robyn, steaming a pair of jeans.

"You came out?" I say.

Robyn looks up and smiles. "I told you from the beginning, I always have a favorite."

I couldn't be happier to see her. I introduce my sister and start taking off my shirt. "So what am I wearing, a jacket made of lasers or something?" Sissy wanders over to the shoes to check them out.

Robyn shakes her head. "No lasers. I don't want anyone to be thinking about the person who dressed you. This is *your* hometown—I'm gonna let you do you. With maybe a little Marlon Brando thrown in. T-shirt and jeans, man." She pulls out a vintage T-shirt for the Pine Mountain Jamboree in Eureka Springs, Arkansas. "I mean, yeah, it's a vintage T-shirt and designer jeans, but still."

I change into Robyn's outfit while Sissy asks her questions about what famous people she's seen naked. "That guy who plays Thor?" she wonders hopefully. Magnolia's lying on an extremely furry fake blue fur coat I guess the show provided just in case the T-shirt didn't fly. It's so furry, she almost disappears into it.

The door to the trailer bangs open. We all look over to see the crazy blank eyes of Spider looking back.

"This is bullshit" is what he enters with. Magnolia sits up. "All they have over in craft service is granola bars. You know what it is? I don't think they have stores here. This place is the asshole of America."

"You're the one who insisted on coming," Robyn says. She doesn't look at him. It seems like they've already been fighting.

I have plenty of terrible things to say about my own town, but I don't like hearing this guy talk bad about it.

"Who's this rude son of a bitch?" asks Sissy, looking kind of nonchalantly at Spider. She's used to this kind of demeanor.

"No, who are *you*?" demands Spider.

"Stop, stop, stop." Robyn puts up a hand. "Enough! Do *not* start."

"Start what?" Spider says with this innocence that also comes off as mean. "I thought one of the things you wanted me to change was for me to be more social, so I'm just trying to get to know everyone."

"Ugh," Robyn says. She turns her back on him to wrap a belt around my waist. "I can't believe I let you convince me that this trip would be good for us."

"Don't turn your back on me," Spider says, and he goes to put a hand on her again. This time it's her neck. I can tell you my thought process in this moment. I immediately wish I could land a punch right between Spider's crazy eyes. I want it to be solid and real and to feel his nose give way under my knuckles.

But instead I open my hands and I place them on his chest, and I apply only the force I need to get him off my friend. Because this time, I'm not going to do the stupid thing. I'm not going to put myself at the mercy of all the disappointment in myself, all the regret. Because I refuse to watch the finale slip away from me like a light that's being dimmed.

Spider stumbles back toward a rack.

After I've pushed him, I learn that his eyes have an even crazier setting. "That was pitifully stupid, man," he says. "I think I might just have to call the police and tell them you assaulted me. Yeah, that was definitely assault."

"No, it wasn't, Spider," Robyn says.

"You have no one to back you up," Maggie says.

But Sissy says, "Go ahead and call them. I'll confess I hit you."

Spider cocks his head. "What?"

"Yeah, I hit you."

Spider looks confused as Sissy punches him right in the nose.

Spider staggers back into a rack of clothes. Nose bleeding. He screams, "What the hell?"

"You had it coming." Sissy shrugs. "You have a face that needs punching."

"Sissy, you still have a record," I say. "You could get in real trouble."

She looks at me with something tender in her eyes. "This is what family's for. And also to win singing contests and buy their older sisters a top-notch lawyer."

I look at her with something tender in my eyes too. So maybe I've changed, or am trying to change, and Sissy probably never will. Maybe she's set firm, like a kid's name carved in the sidewalk. But in her case it just feels like something I can always find my way back to.

Sissy turns to Spider. "But thing is, I'll just tell the police I was defending your woman from you—"

"I'm *not* his woman," Robyn says.

Sissy continues. "And that will get even uglier for you than your nose."

Spider stares at her from atop his cupped hands. "I need to see a doctor."

Robyn's voice is all ice toward him now. "There should be a medic's tent right outside the trailer."

"I'll escort you, bud, since it's the least I can do for hitting you," Sissy says, going over to open the door for him. Spider pauses like he's going to do something else here, but then he just turns and steps out.

Before she leaves, Sissy says to Robyn, "I want you to introduce me to Thor." Once she's outside, we can hear her telling Spider, "Don't worry, could have been worse. Could have been a pair of scissors in your knee."

"I don't know, you would think a guy named Spider would be tougher," Magnolia says. The tough thing for me was not punching him, but I know now I just can't keep having the same reactions over and over.

A girl with a clipboard peers into the trailer, looking freaked out, probably about the guy with the bloody nose who just passed by. "Uh, fifteen minutes to show time. They want you in the wings."

"I hope this incident doesn't cause you more problems," I say to Robyn.

She smooths the collar of my T-shirt and makes a shooing motion toward the door. "It's called a restraining order, and it's so way overdue. Now, there's no point in you looking great if you don't win."

"Thank you for everything," I say.

"Go get it."

Magnolia and I follow the clipboard girl out of the trailer, through some tents, and toward the back of the stage. I can hear a warm-up guy working the crowd, firing *Spotlight* T-shirts out of an air cannon. It's cheesy, but sometimes cheesy is all right. It sounds like an actual concert crowd. I can sense the size of it before I see it.

I feel outside my own body. Crew members ask me questions about staging and placement because there's been no time for a morning rehearsal. I'm saying stuff back, but I'm not sure it makes sense. Catherine appears and passes me the bottle of liquid from the doctor, and I throw it back and gargle before I spit into a plastic cup.

Maggie and I take steps up to the side of the stage. We're concealed, but now we can see the crowd. It stretches back as far as I can see down Main Street in both directions. The sun is gilded. My dying town, exploding with humanity, totally alive.

Magnolia looks out, then silently mouths *Whoa* at me. The backing band is already in place. A crew member starts to hand me the guitar I was using on the show, but Magnolia gives him the case with the Telecaster. She's been watching over it this whole time. I take it out and let the tech guys plug it into the wireless system and tune it up.

"I don't think I've ever been so nervous. What if my voice won't work?" I say, trying to shake the nerves out of my fingers.

"Don't try to figure out what it all means. Just do the next thing." Maggie looks steadily into my eyes, her dark eyes radiating calm steadiness. I take a deep breath.

"I love you," I say.

She kisses me. Then they're doing an introduction over the sound system. I look out at the stage. It seems like someone should go out there and perform. Oh yeah, I guess that would be me.

Someone hands me the Telecaster.

56

I walk onto the stage, pulling the guitar strap over my neck. The noise from the crowd rises up and floods over me. As I take my place at the edge, I see Sissy in the front row, howling and whistling. There are other familiar faces, including Janet from the jail and even my ex-girlfriend, the Mattress Princess, who's found her way up close. She's accompanied by the Mattress King himself, and he's pumping his fist in the air.

"Thank you for coming out, Calumet!" I say into the microphone. "I'm Ford Buckley." The crowd roars, and hearing my amplified voice pulls me back into my own body. I'm in this moment, where I belong. I look behind me to check on the backing band and do a double take because Leander's on the bass, which must be Catherine's doing. He flashes a peace sign, and I smile at him. I wait a few seconds, trying to settle into a feeling for once.

Then I begin strumming the opening E chord of "In the New Year" by the Walkmen.

The first verse the band doesn't play along, so it's just my slightly distorted, steady guitar chords, and my voice. I start singing, my voice subdued, lyrics about living at the same old address, waiting on bad weather to pass.

Now bass and drums drop in (*duh-duh-duh-thump-duh-duh*), and I can feel the force of them in the monitors. I take a deep breath. Dueling emotions of fear and hope start to rise in my voice. The cameramen get closer. The keyboard climbs along with me, sounding like a church pipe organ, soaring higher and higher.

My performance is about clinging to the hope in these lyrics that it's finally going to be a good year. The hope starts to rise above the fear, but it can't seem to erase it. They can't be separated. They're joined together.

The emotion swelling in my chest almost breaks my voice as I sing the lyric about my heart being in such a strange new place. I look over at Magnolia, standing on the side of the stage, eyes shining.

These lyrics paint scenes of great victories over all our troubles, fears, and failures. The song gives me this image of a dark frozen landscape, where nothing ever changes. Then, something new: a flower grows in the snow, a lightning bolt out of the dark sets a dead tree on fire, *something* is finally different than it was, and then you know if something can change, maybe everything can.

The crowd sways, a sea of faces and waving hands in a street that's been empty my whole life.

But I know the song's dark side too. It's foolishly optimistic, only wanting to see the good outcomes, ignore the bad. I know I might lose. I don't know how Magnolia and I are going to stay physically close to each other; win or lose, we'll still have to be in different places. Calumet might slowly sink and disappear into the mud around it; and one day, when I look back, this might have been the high point of an ever-shrinking life.

But today it feels like even something as small as a rock song can set in motion changes that no one can stop.

I sense the vibrations moving specks of air and light around me, pushing between the bodies in the crowd, reverberating through the town, shaking the old brick buildings, echoing across the roof-tops, ringing off the silver water tower, and out over the farmland where my grandparents are buried. I imagine the sound waves roll-ing on until they're rattling the boarded-up windows of dying towns all across the country.

I look again at Magnolia. Here's to hope.

Appendices

To: Hayes.Sarno@UnitedProductions.com
From: Magnoliahere@gmail.com
Subject: ships

hey hayes,

per our discussion, i revised the last scene of ep. 8
of ships--please see attached.

and to answer your question about that "access
hollywood" interview:

sorry, still can't do it.

hope all's well, though!

magnolia

322 ° Andrea Seigel & Brent Bradshaw

To: Lalalucien@gmail.com
From: Hayes.Sarno@UnitedProductions.com
Subject: Help managing Magnolia

Lucien,

We can't get through to Magnolia about this interview. Can you PLEASE tell her it will be great???
They just want to spend an afternoon with her
over at Ford's new house. The conceit is that she's
helping him decorate because he has terrible taste
in furnishing. Cute, right? The exec producer Angie
has sworn to me they'll let Magnolia talk about Ships
for at least a minute of the segment. It's a win-win!

Can you help us out and convince her to do this? I
know she respects your opinion a ton.

Hayes

This email contains information which may be confidential and
privileged. Unless you are the addressee (or authorized to
receive communications on behalf of the addressee), you may
not use, copy, re-transmit, or disclose to anyone this email or any
information contained in or attached to this email. If you have
received this email in error, please advise the sender by reply
email and immediately delete the email, or you may contact us at
security@UnitedProductions.com or call (310) 555-9000.

Sent from my iPad

To: Hayes.Sarno@UnitedProductions.com
From: Lalalucien@gmail.com
Subject: Re: Help managing Magnolia

Hayes man,

That doesn't sound that cute. I'll be honest. I want to get to continue to make money with you in the future, so I say this with peace and love, peace and love:

I can't help you with Magnolia.

She doesn't want to parade her relationship around. She doesn't want to do segments. She just wants to write, and I support her on that.

Good talk!

L

To: Magnoliahere@gmail.com
From: Hayes.Sarno@UnitedProductions.com
Subject: Re: ships

Magnolia, Magnolia, Magnolia,

The people at AH are telling me they'll pay for Ford's furnishings, so how does that sound? I know he probably thinks that money will get him his dream everything, seeing as how he's not from around here. But shit's expensive in LA!

Ha ha ha.

But seriously. U should want to do this interview. Don't you want people to care about Ships? Make them care about you. Something to think about.

You're very young, still. I'm offering guidance. Really think you should take it.

Hayes

Sent from my iPad

To: Hayes.Sarno@UnitedProductions.com
From: Magnoliahere@gmail.com
Subject: Re: re: ships

hayes,

my dad was an investment consultant, and i have to
tell you, i understood next to nothing about what he
did. i'm just not a numbers person. when i was really
little i'd play with his briefcase and pull out papers and
they might as well have been in egyptian. no clue what
any of it meant. once i got to elementary school age,
my dad started bringing me into his office for "take
your daughter to work" day, and this one year i got
to sit in on a big meeting. i was around eight. again, i
had zero clue what they were talking about. zero. but
there came this moment where i could sense that my
dad was fighting for some kind of decision that all his
colleagues at the table were nervous about. they were
saying, "bad idea" and "we can't see the logic in it."
my dad turned on the projector and this page with all
of these calculations and tables came up on the big,
glowing screen at the front of the room. to this day, i
have no idea what any of those calculations or tables
meant. that's not the point. i'm not talking about math.
my dad pointed to his calculations and tables and he
said to the other people in the room, "this is all you
need to know." that's all he said! i was so struck by that

move, even as a little kid. he put his work up there for them to see, and he left it at that. no song and dance. he wasn't trying to hide anything. or trying to tell them to just trust him based on nothing. he was showing them his very best ideas. he was letting them know, "here's what i have to say." they could look as deeply into it as they wanted. because the answers were all in the work.

magnolia

To: Magnoliahere@gmail.com
From: Hayes.Sarno@UnitedProductions.com
Subject: Re: re: re: ships

Magnolia, you're KILLING me here.

I just talked to AH. They're saying they can get you some free furniture too. I know you're still living at your mom's, but what about a new bed set?

Hayes

This email contains information which may be confidential and privileged. Unless you are the addressee (or authorized to receive communications on behalf of the addressee), you may not use, copy, re-transmit, or disclose to anyone this email or any information contained in or attached to this email. If you have received this email in error, please advise the sender by reply email and immediately delete the email, or you may contact us at security@UnitedProductions.com or call (310) 555-9000.

Sent from my iPad

To: Hayes.Sarno@UnitedProductions.com
From: Magnoliahere@gmail.com
Subject: this is all you need to know

i'm good, thanks.

magnolia

SHIPS IN THE NIGHT SHOOTING SCRIPT EP 1.8

INT. AN OLD HOTEL ROOM IN ARGENTINA—NIGHT

Warren Gettysburg picks up the phone on the
desk. Calmly, he dials, watching the snow fall
outside. Despite the weather, he's still only
wearing the rumpled undershirt and flannel
pants he was taken in.

INTERCUT—INT. HOTEL ROOM/BART GETTYSBURG'S
STUDY—CONTINUOUS

Bart, sitting at his desk, looks at newspaper
clippings about Warren's kidnapping. He
answers the phone.

                    BART
          Bart Gettysburg here.

                    WARREN
                  (casually)
          Hey, Dad. Happy birthday to
          me.

Bart instantly sits up straighter, his mind
racing.

SHIPS IN THE NIGHT SHOOTING SCRIPT EP 1.8

                    BART
          But how are you—
               (catches himself)
          Where are you? Thank God
          you're all right.

                   WARREN
          Not as good at acting as
          you were at gymnastics,
          huh, dad?

Bart eyes his collegiate gymnastics trophies
on the shelf, one of which still bears the
cigarette burn that Warren gave it.

                    BART
          I was so distraught about—

                   WARREN
          Well, your acting is bad,
          but turns out what you're
          really bad at is staging
          your own kid's abduction.

Bart has gone white.

SHIPS IN THE NIGHT SHOOTING SCRIPT EP 1.8

> WARREN (CONT'D)
> Just wanted to call to say
> I'll be seeing you soon.
> And don't worry about the
> million dollars you paid
> those goons—I took that off
> their hands too.

Warren presses down the switch hook on the
cradle. Then he dials again.

INTERCUT—INT. HOTEL ROOM/WICKHAM BOARDING
ACADEMY FOR GIRLS—CONTINUOUS

The phone rings at the lobby desk of the
Wickham Boarding Academy for Girls.

Mrs. Cale answers.

> MRS. CALE
> Wickham Boarding Academy
> for Girls.

> WARREN
> I need to speak to Jacinta
> Yarmouth.

SHIPS IN THE NIGHT SHOOTING SCRIPT EP 1.8

Mrs. Cale's face ices over. She knows who it is.

> MRS. CALE
> You are not able to do
> that.

She glances over at Jacinta, who has been reading a book in an armchair by the fire. But now Jacinta watches Mrs. Cale speak on the phone. It's as if she knows who's on the phone too. Her face has a quiet hope.

> WARREN
> Is she reading in that
> chair she likes right across
> the room?

Now Mrs. Cale looks alarmed, as if Warren is somewhere close.

> MRS. CALE
> What game are you—

> WARREN
> Good. Then you can tell her
> that I'm on my way to come
> see her.

SHIPS IN THE NIGHT SHOOTING SCRIPT EP 1.8

He hangs up the phone.

INT. WICKHAM BOARDING ACADEMY FOR GIRLS—VERY
LATE NIGHT

Mrs. Cale sits at the lobby desk after
bedtime, by herself now. The academy is dark
except for her small lamp.

She gets up and checks that the front doors
are locked. She's wary. On edge. Then she
sits again, returning to her watch.

INT. WICKHAM DORMITORY—SIMULTANEOUS

Jacinta, coat over her nightgown, picks a
lock on the dormitory sill with a bobby pin
and swings the window open. She climbs out.

EXT. WICKHAM ACADEMY GROUNDS—MOMENTS LATER

As Jacinta sneaks across the lawn, we can see
the tiny light of Mrs. Cale's lamp through the
glass of the front doors in the distance.

SHIPS IN THE NIGHT SHOOTING SCRIPT EP 1.8

EXT. JUDY'S PIZZA—LATE NIGHT

Jacinta has made it to town. She walks up to Judy's Pizza, which is a divey parlor with a neon sign. She opens the root beer colored front door.

INT. JUDY'S PIZZA—MOMENTS LATER

There's a small arcade inside, and Jacinta approaches. She stops in front of an old machine with a plastic chicken sitting above a bunch of bright eggs.

Pulling a quarter from her coat pocket, she puts it in the machine. The chicken spins around CLUCKING, then drops a half-red, half-blue egg.

Jacinta bends to retrieve her prize from the small door. She opens the egg, and inside is a cheap but simple chain necklace. A gold-tone robot charm hangs from it.

SHIPS IN THE NIGHT SHOOTING SCRIPT EP 1.8

Pleased, Jacinta puts the necklace on. Then
the root beer colored door opens behind her,
and she turns.

Warren Gettysburg, in his pajamas too, is
standing there, the wind blowing outside
behind him.

Jacinta smiles without smiling.

Acknowledgments

We'd like to thank both our families for standing behind us as we avoided normal jobs. Doug Stewart for believing in this book from the beginning. Leila Sales for making it so much better. Nicolle and Rob for a certain crazy-eyed Easter dinner years ago. Reda Trish Hernandez for letting us use her great photo. David Hernandez for not getting super annoyed with Andrea for never learning Photoshop. Pie'n Burger for having the counter where we first thought up this idea. Maria Felix for watching our daughter in the afternoons so we could write. And thank you to Winona, of course, because Winona is the best, forever.